BETHLEHEM PUBLIC LIBRARY
3 3150 002346

BETHLEHEM LIBRARY
P9-DYY-385

DATE			

WHAT GIRLS LEARN

WHAT GIRLS LEARN

A Novel

KARIN COOK

Pantheon Books New York

Grateful acknowledgment is made to the following for permission to reprint previously published material: Lastrada Entertainment Company, Ltd.: Excerpts from the lyrics of "Bad, Bad Leroy Brown" by Jim Croce. Copyright © 1985 by Denjac Music Co. Courtesy of The Lefrak-Moelis Companies, administered by Lastrada Entertainment Company, Ltd. • Edward B. Marks Music Company: Excerpts from the lyrics to "You Took the Words Right out of My Mouth (Hot Summer Night)" by Jim Steinman. Copyright © 1978 by Edward B. Marks Music Company. Used by permission. All rights reserved.

Library of Congress Cataloging-in-Publication Data

Cook, Karin, 1968–
What girls learn / Karin Cook.
p. cm.
ISBN 0-679-44828-4 (alk. paper)
I. Title.
PS3553.055385W48 1997
813'.54—dc20

Random House Web Address: http://www.randomhouse.com/

BOOK DESIGN BY M. KRISTEN BEARSE

Printed in the United States of America
First Edition
2 4 6 8 9 7 5 3 1

to

Dr. Walter T. Carpenter

for filling my life with books

and

my sister

Jennifer Barrett Cook

for sharing all of life's lessons

. . . treachery is the other side of dailiness.

—ALICE MUNRO

CONTENTS

PART I

PART II

PART III

PART IV

PART V

PART I

WHITE LIES

Mama raised us to be just. If not entirely honest, then at least well intended. Good intentions could justify almost anything, even white lies. White lies were merely polite untruths. Not something to aspire to, but to fall back on, a safety.

I grew up on white lies. My sister, Elizabeth, and I learned early that there was more than one way to bend the truth. There was the aspirin-crushed-in-grape-jelly kind of lie, where things were not always as they appeared. And the read-between-the-lines kind of lie, where what mattered most was left unsaid. But the worst kind of lie, the kind Elizabeth and I were forbidden to tell, was the bald-faced lie. Mama believed that telling an out-and-out lie was malicious and unnecessary. Unless, of course, it was to save someone's feelings.

Making the world appear better was Mama's speciality. Not the whole world, necessarily, but our world. Every time she moved us, it was always to some place better than the last. But the new place was never quite as she said it would be. The art gallery in downtown Atlanta turned out to be a makeshift basement studio with a darkroom that smelled of vinegar. And the mansion in Lawrenceville was really a garage apartment at the edge of an estate. We lived bunched up alongside other people's expanses, close enough to dream.

"Isn't it romantic," she'd say, whenever we showed signs of disappointment.

Within a day, she was always able to coax us toward appreciation. Each place had its own charm and adventure. A crack in the ceiling held mystery; the mark of a child's green crayon told a story. Mama had the kind of hope that could make you stand and watch one red balloon disappear into the sky, believing that it might come back on a bird's wing.

Some people are from a particular place, a somewhere that stays part of them no matter where they end up. You can see it immediately in the way they talk and dress, how they long for a certain time of year. No matter where we lived, Mama was always from Atlanta. But she must have known from the start that no one place would be part of me. She named me Tilden, after her favorite street, a quiet, tree-lined road that curved its way out of town. Elizabeth got a normal name. Perhaps because when she was born, a year later, Mama had already left our father and things were harder.

Moving as often as we did forced Elizabeth and me to present a united front—always allies against the unknown, we were instant enemies the minute our boxes were unpacked. We fought over drawer space and bunk beds, pillows and stray socks. Elizabeth wanted equal shelves in the bookcase, even though I was the one who loved to read and collected the most books. When finally Mama agreed to give me an additional shelf, Elizabeth demanded to know which one of us she loved more.

"I love you the same," Mama answered, "in different ways."

"How, different?"

"Well," she said, "you're different people so the way I love each of you has to be different. But the amount of love is the same."

Same but different. That phrase of Mama's extended to every aspect of our lives. As if we each existed only in contrast to the other. We both had Mama's smile, every store owner and teacher said it was so, but I was less trusting, more serious and reserved, where Elizabeth was lean and lanky and fearless. The knowledge of what we each lacked gave us ammunition. There were things we knew by instinct only to say in a fight.

"What if I murdered someone?" I asked.

"I would be disappointed in you," Mama said, "but I would still love you."

"As much as you love me now?"

"Yes."

"What if I murdered Elizabeth?"

Mama shook her head. "You know, girls," she said, "I would have given anything for a sister." She sat down next to me and gave my shoulder a little shake. "Tilden, a sister is forever." Her cheeks were surprisingly flushed. I felt ashamed.

I hated how lonely she was.

The year I turned twelve and Elizabeth eleven, Mama announced that we were moving North. I felt the gulf of a secret widen between us. She had gone to New York earlier that year for a wedding and met someone. She returned restless, talking endlessly about fulfilling her dreams. Nick this. Nick that. It had been love at first sight, she finally confessed. I didn't know how I was supposed to feel about her loving someone I had never even met.

Mama looked at me, her whole face open and promising. "Nick knows all about you. He's been waiting to meet you girls."

Neither Elizabeth nor I said a word. I could feel Elizabeth's body tensing up, her arms growing rigid with the thought of moving again. So some guy named Nick wanted to meet us? I crossed my arms and stared off into the distance.

The only thing I wanted in the world was for Mama to tell me the truth.

"This is permanent," Mama said, "you just wait and see."

Wait and see meant everything would be all right, justice would be done, ailments would be cured, and pain would go away. What wait and see did was keep us holding on, never saying good-bye, never believing that bad could happen and that when it did it could eventually be righted. Wait and see justified telling white lies, allowed us to cover ground, backpedal, and borrow time. It was that stale air of waiting before storms.

I should have known better than to believe her.

GEOGRAPHY

We were packed and ready on the front steps when Nick pulled up in one of TransAlt's limousines. He looked like a movie star, stepping out from behind tinted windows, with dark wavy hair and sunglasses. The neighborhood was early-morning still, the only sound an echo from the nearby highway. I checked to see if anyone else was watching, but the slight chill of a Southern winter had made activity scarce that Saturday. Nick was younger than I expected with a worried mouth that seemed tight and small. When he smiled at us, his lips parted and then sprang back quickly. He lifted his mirrored sunglasses onto his head, handsome still, but slightly more plain than he first appeared. He started talking before he even reached the front steps.

"I'm Nick," he said, "you can call me Nick."

I couldn't imagine calling an adult by his first name. Just the thought of it made my tongue feel thick. Nick knew our names without needing to be introduced. He squeezed Elizabeth's hand tight with both of his and held on for a long time. I gave him one of my dead fish handshakes, letting my fingers lie limp in his palm. I had already decided not to like him.

"These are for you," he said, reaching into his coat and handing us each a stiff white business card with an imprint of a shiny black limousine stretched across the bottom. *TransAlt*, it said, *Dependable Transportation Alternatives*. And in big block letters, *NICK OLSEN, PRESIDENT*.

I slipped the card into my back pocket and turned away from him, pretending to look for something in one of my boxes. Elizabeth skipped down the stairs toward the limousine, gushing and asking to see the inside. Springing off the porch after her, Nick held the door open and shadowed her head with his hand to keep her from hitting the roof as she crawled into the backseat.

"Let me give you the grand tour," he said, using his free arm to flag me in their direction.

I lurked outside, refusing to show interest. The limo was plush with carpet and lined with a miniature TV and bar. Nick demonstrated the automatic windows and channel controls, talking through each gadget as he operated it. When Mama walked onto the front steps, he stopped midsentence and turned to face her. For the first time I saw her not just as my mother, but as a woman belonging to the world.

Mama was beautiful, but didn't dwell on it. When other people did, she was quick to deflect attention back to her origins, revealing that she'd inherited her mother's fine features and her father's long, thin legs. I just think she liked to mention Grandma and Grandpa any chance she got. It was a way of keeping them with her long after they were gone. Mama had a glamour that set her apart from the other mothers I knew. Her cheekbones were high—the kind magazines taught girls to make by combining two shades of blush—and her nose sculpted. Her eyes were blue with flecks of brown and when she smiled they closed up at the sides in a wink. If you looked closely you could see that her lashes were blunt and stubby, which she tried to compensate for by filling in the corners of her lids with brown eyeliner pencil.

That morning, she had set her hair in curlers and pulled it back into a loose ponytail so that the ends fell in coils down her back. This was the style she reserved for fancy occasions and holidays. She was not dressed to match: her head looked more glamorous than the rest of her body, almost as if she had outgrown herself. Still, the familiarity of her clothes comforted me: a white cotton shirt belted over a long khaki skirt, white sneakers on her feet.

Mama's arms were full of the things that we had forgotten to pack—a painted wooden picture frame, a glittered pencil case, red sweatshirt, and one tattered sneaker. Nick moved to help her and I watched to see what would happen between them. But as he stepped nearer, she balked, turned away from him, and nervously looked over her shoulder in our direction. Nick bent next to her and closed the top flaps of the cardboard box, willing each side into place with his large, rough hands. When he finished, he reached out as if to touch Mama's face and ended up squeezing her ponytail instead.

"You ready, Frances?"

"Ready," she said, smiling at him and stepping back. She turned toward us. "Girls?"

Panic rose in me. Every time we'd moved before, it was just the three of us, setting out somewhere Mama had described as ideal. But this time, we were getting into a strange car with a strange man who wanted Mama's attention. As Nick began to load the boxes, heaving them high on his shoulders, I raced back into the house for a final look.

Standing in the living room, I was startled to see how empty the place seemed. I had been there when Mama sold the furniture, kitchen appliances, even her bedroom set. I'd watched as big men in cuffed T-shirts came and carried each piece away. Still, it seemed suddenly bare and lifeless. Except for the stencil Elizabeth had insisted on painting around the border of the kitchen and Mama's porcelain cabinet knobs, you would never have known we had been there. Everything else, we loaded into a box and gave to the Salvation Army. We were to pack light, Mama instructed, two boxes each and a share suitcase.

The week before the move, Mama didn't tell us much about where we were headed. Instead, she organized a cleaning session, where Elizabeth and I were encouraged to weed through our belongings and throw out everything that was not essential. It was a crisp, clear day. Mama woke up saying that she felt slim and clean, perky, as if she were ready to begin again. She had a saying for everything.

"A woman's relationship to clutter," she began, throwing away some of her hairpins, "says something about her character. A woman who allows things to accumulate, to stack up in the corners of her life, is in danger of being overrun by her past. A woman who can sort through and weed out, is free to move forward into the world unencumbered."

"What's essential?" Elizabeth asked.

Mama thought about this for a moment. "Only those things you need to survive."

We watched as she weeded through her bathroom cabinets, conflicted, would she or wouldn't she have a need for the eyelash curler, the plastic hair brush, the mandarin orange bath beads.

"First you smell it like this," she said, putting a bit of lotion on her wrist and holding it under her nose. She closed her eyes as she inhaled. "If it's off at all, chuck it right out."

She waved her hand under each of our noses and waited for us to respond. It all smelled the same to me. Chalky and medicinal with the faint flowered scent of her shelf paper. But Elizabeth could call it right away. She didn't seem to feel any responsibility to save.

"*Your* life," Mama said to Elizabeth, stroking her perfect yellow hair, "will never be cluttered."

• • •

The only thing left in our old bedroom was my empty bookshelf. I stood there, with my knees locked for a long time, waiting for someone to come and get me. I could hear the travel of voices, car doors, and footsteps. Finally, Mama came up behind me and crossed her arms around my shoulders.

"I'll get you a new one," she promised. "With new books and everything. Trust me. It'll be like starting over." I could feel the warmth of her body seep into my neck and back. "It's time to go," she said.

I stayed very still, hoping to hold her there. I was tired of starting over. Trying to fit our entire lives into one car made it seem more like we were skipping town than actually moving. Together, we watched out the window as Nick pulled rope across each corner of the bunk beds. Every so often, he stopped to wipe the sweat off his face with his sleeve. Watching the way he took charge made my legs start to tremble a bit. I had never wanted a father the way Elizabeth did and Mama knew it.

"It's going to be okay," she said, stepping away from me. "Now go wait with your sister."

When he saw me, Nick paused in the front doorway, re-tucked his shirt, rolled up his sleeves, and walked to the kitchen sink. He ran water over his hands and face and then through his hair while Mama stood by with a paper towel. I had never seen someone wash like that, use so much water, in the kitchen. I walked past them and made my way out to the limo.

"You don't like him, do you?" Elizabeth asked after I'd settled in the seat next to her. Boxes were stacked all around us, even on the floor between the two rows of facing seats. The inside of the limo smelled of new upholstery.

"He tries too hard."

We sat quietly and waited. I stared at Elizabeth's slender feet, balanced now upon the stuff from this last house. We took less and less with us each time we moved. There had always been boyfriends, but none that threatened to become permanent. Mama called them dreamers, men who came in and out of our lives with ideas about family but no way to make it work. Nick seemed different. He'd come a long way to get us. He had plans. It made me nervous, how willing Mama was to follow him.

"It's better than not trying," Elizabeth hazarded.

I hated that she was so easily convinced, so quickly won over. Even the idea of moving didn't seem to scare her. Elizabeth used every move as an opportunity to become someone else. She liked to imagine herself exotic, changing her hair by parting it on a different side or wearing more than the usual number of barrettes. She could reinvent herself, changing clothes and taking on so many new interests and habits that Mama called her a chameleon. First a gymnast and dancer, then a gum-chewing gossip and baby-sitter. The thing that amazed me about Elizabeth was that no matter how much she changed, she was always recognizable as herself.

I was always the same.

Mama and Nick emerged, flushed and giddy. I guessed that they had been kissing. Storing up for the trip. Nick planned to drive nonstop, almost a whole day, so we wouldn't have to unload or risk theft. Mama had filled our school thermoses with black coffee.

Some neighbors in bathrobes gathered on their lawns to watch us drive away. There was Mrs. Schafer in her usual lavender wrap, and her son, who must have been eight or nine and still never left her side. We had gotten to know so few people here, it didn't matter what they thought. Mama pulled down her windshield visor and pretended not to notice. I couldn't seem to get used to the fact that we could see out, but no one could see in. It made it easy to forget who we were. I tried to imagine that we were going somewhere fancy, that this was part of our everyday life. Then, I remembered the mattresses and bunk beds tied on top, and wanted to disappear.

I didn't cry. Not at first anyway. Not until Elizabeth began, the tip of her nose going red, her head drooped forward so the tears splashed on her legs. "All these places we'll never see again," she said to me softly. And then Mama, at the sight of Elizabeth, started in. Tears, like laughter, were contagious with us. Once one of us began crying, it never took very long before we all fell in, red-faced with swollen eyes, groping for hugs.

"Don't mind us," Mama said, embarrassed in front of Nick. "We do this a lot."

I waited for him to seem uncomfortable, but instead he rustled under his seat and unearthed a box of tissues. Then he offered everybody a Peppermint Tic Tac.

Getting to know Nick was slow.

Elizabeth ran out of chatter and games by Charlotte, North Carolina. I kept my head buried in an atlas and spoke only to call out certain facts: the miles on the odometer, a state motto, the name of a state bird or tree. "Did you know that North Carolina was the twelfth state?" I quizzed. "That their bird is the cardinal? And that Virginia and North Carolina both have the flowering dogwood as the state flower?" With each question, Mama barely turned her head to acknowledge me, her attention so focused on Nick.

Three or four times, Nick pulled over, stretched his arms high above his head, and walked along the shoulder of the highway. He stepped over the guard rail effortlessly, moving up the embankment and turning among the trees with his back to us.

"It's the coffee," Mama explained.

I watched him, a confident, but gentle-looking man, his step deliberate, his face calm. Nick and Mama had been corresponding with each other for a year after their first meeting. The phone calls had filled our normally quiet apartment late into the night. Mama even wrote her thoughts down on loose-leaf paper and mailed them off in plain envelopes with bright stamps. Letters came in return, too, sometimes three a week, which she wrapped in a ponytail holder and kept in her purse. This was the man of her dreams, she told us, the man she had been waiting for.

"How can you be sure?" I asked, seeing him fully in the distance for the first time.

"You just know," she said.

She had known right away, she told us, when she saw him on the dance floor at the wedding with the bride's mother, dipping and twirling, making her laugh and feel special. Mama liked his generosity and told him so. A real gentleman, she called him, the two of them talking until the sun came up, Mama hesitant to even catch her flight home. "If it hadn't been for you girls, I might've gotten in that car and gone North right then."

"Without us?" Elizabeth asked.

"Of course not," she said. "How could I go anywhere without you. You girls are my . . . everything."

By noon, we had eaten through both bags of snacks—squeezing the grapes out of their skins and scraping the peanut butter off each cracker. Nick pulled over at a rest stop to get gas and the fighting began. Elizabeth wanted McDonald's; I wanted Burger King. Mama stiffened. It was an old fight, one that usually got settled with pizza or some neutral sandwich shop. She gave us a sideways glance. I could tell that she didn't want Nick to see us bicker so soon.

"Heads or tails," Nick said, pulling a penny out of his pocket.

"Huh?"

"We'll flip for it. Heads we'll have Whoppers and chocolate shakes; tails, Chicken McNuggets and French fries."

His simplicity silenced us. As did his accuracy. Elizabeth and I exchanged a knowing glance. Nick understood something essential: Burger King made better shakes, McDonald's better fries. I was surprised by his knowledge and wondered if maybe I could trust him.

We watched as he rubbed the penny in his palm and took a few practice tosses. Leaving choice up to chance was disarming. We were accustomed to these decisions droning on and on, allowing time for each of us to create arguments, calling up past injustices with the skill and perseverance of a courtroom lawyer. This time there would be no logic. Only luck.

Even Mama looked uneasy.

Nick made room with his arms, spreading out in the seat, and blew into his cupped hand. Then, he tossed the penny into the air, catching it in his right hand and slapping it ceremoniously onto the back of his left. Elizabeth and I leaned into the frame of the window to witness the outcome.

"Frances," Nick said, "you do the honors."

Mama tipped Nick's hand, like a lid, and shouted, "Heads."

We all looked around, unsure of what it meant. In the excitement of the toss, no one could remember the ground rules. And just as Elizabeth and I geared up to have it out over which was which, Nick offered a suggestion.

"Why don't we have both?"

The car quieted. It wasn't that this had never occurred to us before. But, something about his fairness was so staggering that it felt like a new idea.

"Yeah," Elizabeth said. "It won't take long." She looked at Mama and then Nick, fixing herself between them. "We can take the limo to the drive-in windows."

• • •

Nick did not live on the beach as Elizabeth and I had been led to believe he might. It turned out that Long Island wasn't even a real island. I had imagined palm trees and shells, miles of sand and rolling ocean. Like Sea Island, only colder. I'd had trouble reconciling my image of an island with my fantasies of heavy northern snows, but I prepared for each, simultaneously. I figured Long Island was off the coast of New York, a sister to the more famous Ellis Island. I loved the words "melting pot." I'd seen pictures of the immigrants arriving off boats with trunks, their breath hot against the air. I was ready to explore these islands.

It was morning when Nick exited off the expressway to turn east along Route 25A. Soon there were horse farms, villages with quaint shops, and eventually, water. In between there were car dealerships and long stretches of traffic. Nick, who had been quiet during the drive, began to talk excitedly, pointing out what crop was grown in one field, shouting "horse," as we came upon some animals grazing, and promising the existence of an apple farm down a small road off to the left. Every unsightly spot, he excused as a development. Nick looked slightly wild, his eyes bulging and red from not sleeping, a faint shadow of stubble along his chin. His voice sounded raspy as he described places that he hoped Mama would like. There was a store for candles, one for monogram sweaters, even a store, he turned to look at us, that sold only fake mice dressed in costumes from around the world. He pointed in the direction of the train station. "In case you want to go to the city."

"He means New York City," Mama said.

We craned our necks in search of the train. Elizabeth had her hopes up, I could tell. While packing, Mama had promised us trips to visit the Statue of Liberty, the *Nutcracker* at Lincoln Center, and a store called Bloomingdale's that we'd seen a catalog for. I had my doubts. What if Nick was just showing us the highlights to try and win us over? I decided to hold out for the facts. When Nick said, "Only ten minutes to go," Mama sat up and began fixing her face in the mirror, licking her pinkie and wiping the smudged liner from the corners of her eyes.

"Wait till you girls see Nick's house," she said, reaching over and touching his hand. He grabbed her fingers and held on. She tried to pull away and when he wouldn't let her, she laughed and swatted at the air near him.

"You've seen it?" I asked.

"In pictures," she said quickly, catching my eye. She always knew when I was testing her. "It's beautiful. Two stories with windows everywhere and shutters. And the most charming yard. You just wait."

And it did seem beautiful when we pulled up, wooden shingles with forest green trim and a brick path curving toward the carved door with a brass knocker. A split rail fence set it apart from the square, white houses on either side. My stomach turned the way it always did before stepping into a new classroom.

One thing about Nick that surprised me was that he was good for a promise. Back on the road—somewhere around Philadelphia—he told us we would each have our own room. To me, this had the potential of being a lie, a way to get us there. But he made good; the entire upstairs of his two-story house belonged to us. Once inside, Nick encouraged us to explore on our own. He was tired from the trip, sank down in an easy chair and rubbed the heels of his palms in his eye sockets. "Why don't you go find your rooms?" he suggested.

We raced up the stairs, battling to be first to make the discoveries. I could hear Mama urging Nick to turn to bed, to get some sleep. But the sounds of us running loose above must have given him a second wind. He climbed the stairs with Mama and joined us in the hall. Our names were written on index cards and tacked up on two of the bedroom doors. The excitement of having our own rooms quickly shifted to wonder. How had Nick made these decisions? On what basis? Elizabeth wanted to know how come I got the room with an outdoor landing and staircase.

"Not many girls have this chance at privacy," Mama said, surveying our rooms. She had always talked about privacy as if it was a necessity like a rain slicker or good shoes. At the same time it had been very difficult for us to have it. "It's rare," said Mama, "like the Torrey pine tree and some blood types."

Maybe now I could finally know what it was like to sleep by myself, to see what privacy felt like.

It turns out my room had been Nick's original office from when he started TransAlt, the first transportation company in Brooklawn. The new office was located in the garage. It was smaller than his business card led me to believe. From the landing I could see the TransAlt cars parked in the lot at the back of the driveway. My bedroom walls were painted in the company colors—forest green with rust trim. I could tell that Nick had recently moved some furniture out. For me, I guessed. There were tracks in the wood and no rug to cover them. The back wall was corked and filled with yellowing neighborhood maps and train schedules. Nick moved closer to me as I stared at a timetable for the Long Island Rail Road.

"Thought you might want to see what's what," Nick said, "get situated, you know, find your way." He lifted a green push-pin from the cork and speared the map at the bottom of Connally Drive. "You're here," he said.

I leaned on the metal desk to get a closer look. It felt large and sturdy, like one for a teacher, with a lock on the top drawer and an extra key dangling on a ring. The cork on the wall gave off a musty smell that pricked the insides of my nostrils. There was nothing familiar anywhere in the room. I was used to this hollow newness. My stomach tightened as I imagined having to figure out where my things belonged. Usually, I'd be dividing the room in two, scoping out what side was mine. But not this time. I turned to Elizabeth, just to see her, to bring me back. She spun away from me and walked across the hall to her room.

After Nick went to take a nap, Elizabeth and I followed Mama as she walked from one room to the next, imagining her way into the space. She liked to do this, to search for possibility, every time we moved. But, this time she did so quietly—with a respect for what was already there, how Nick chose to live. The house hadn't looked large from the outside, but inside, it expanded. There were different rooms for different functions. The first floor had a den for watching TV, a dining room, a living room, and a big eat-in kitchen. Mama and Nick's room was at the back, off the living room.

There were no signs of neglect. Mama had moved us into places where men had lived alone, apartments where magazines took over chairs, lamp shades and curtains grew layers of dust, and mail went unsorted. Nick's place was comfortable, but still orderly. It didn't appear that he had straightened up just for us. Somehow, I could tell that he lived this way all the time: the calendar on his fridge was even turned to the right month.

We put our coats on before going back out to the limo for the boxes. The air had a cold bite to it, like nothing I had ever felt down South; the yard and trees were already battered from winter. Elizabeth eyed the neighboring houses. She was looking for signs of other kids; she was always scouting for new friends.

"Who lives there?" she asked, pointing to the house next door that had electric candles in the window left over from Christmas.

"I don't know," Mama said. "I think it may be an older woman. There aren't any other children on this block." She looked at me, "I asked Nick about this already."

We unpacked the car quickly, leaving the heavy stuff on top, and stacking the boxes along the slate path to the front door. It felt uncomfortable to be out in Nick's yard without him. There seemed to be a great deal of activity at TransAlt. Every once in a while, a car flew backwards down the driveway, the driver pausing and tipping his head as he passed us.

Just as Mama carried the last box from the car, a very blond woman stuck her head out the garage door and waved for us to come inside. Mama straightened herself in the window of the limo and called for us to follow her. When we walked in, the woman took off her earphones and extended her hand toward us. Her painted nails were so long that they curled inward toward her palms.

"I'm Lainey," she said, "the dispatcher. You gals are all we've heard about around here for months."

The way she said *gals*, with a twang, made me wonder for an instant whether she was making fun of us. But Mama didn't bat an eye, just nodded and smiled. Lainey sat at a table in the center of the room amidst the various machines of the dispatching unit. The walls of the garage were lined with metal cabinets. The only warmth came from electric heaters which hummed in every corner, their coils burning red.

"Looks like Nick's taken to sleeping in the middle of the day," Lainey teased.

Mama smiled. "It was a long drive," she said, her chin firm and high. I recognized this look. She was being polite. She seemed suddenly plain next to Lainey, who had big, frosted hair and greenish-blue eyeshadow.

The CB crackled, sputtering numbers and codes. Lainey held her hand up in a stop motion while she responded to the calls. The furniture was Salvation Army old, brown plaid with burn marks and exposed stuffing. The chairs were arranged intimately in a circle. When the radio quieted again, Mama placed one hand on each of our shoulders and edged us forward.

"These are my daughters," she started . . .

"Wait, let me guess," Lainey said. She pointed first to me and then Elizabeth. "Tilden and Elizabeth, right? Who's older?"

"I am."

"Barely," Elizabeth added.

"Like two sides of the same coin," Lainey said, looking between us and Mama.

Elizabeth flopped down on the couch and wrinkled her nose when a cloud of dust rose out of the cushions. She was in a smell-good stage, bathing twice a day in bubbles, and dousing herself with after-bath splash and powder. She looked clean against the couch. "She's the color of angels," Nick had said to Mama in the car while he thought we were both sleeping. It was true; as a child she'd always worn the frail, winged costumes of a princess or ballerina on Halloween. My costumes had been heavy, animals with tails and lots of fur—a lion, a dog, a cat—with whiskers springing out from my freckles. Looking at me in the rearview mirror, Nick had made a low noise that sounded almost like a warning. "But Tilden. Well, she looks . . . wise."

Great, I thought, I'm an owl.

The radio played quietly and constant in the background. A man in a nasal voice sounding excited, like a sportscaster, was predicting snow. Lainey saw me notice. "Nick tracks storms the way most men follow football," she exclaimed.

"Why?" Elizabeth asked.

"Weather is important to business," Mama started, then hesitated and looked to Lainey, embarrassed. It had been too bold of her to speak first, before this woman who clearly knew more about TransAlt. It implied knowledge beyond what she had. She shrugged a bit and waited for Lainey to answer.

"Weather is everything in this business," Lainey said, gathering up the slack. "Take a day like this: overcast and cold. Everybody wants to stock up, but nobody wants to walk or get caught in it. We've got three cars out just covering the grocery store."

"I guess we better finish getting unpacked before it starts snowing," Mama said, signaling for us to join her.

"Let me know if you need anything," Lainey said, following us out. "I can give you the rundown on the neighborhood if you want. All the best shops, the drugstore, anything you need." Lainey raced back to her desk, riffled through her bag, and came back at Mama with a business card. "Of course you can come to me for styling. I'm trained as a cosmetologist. See the number . . . " she said, "641-N-A-I-L, the first in Brooklawn to be name and number in one." She looked self-consciously around the garage. "I'm just doing this for the money until I get my license," she whispered, though there was no one but us in the room.

We stepped out to the driveway. Mama looked tired. She turned her head skyward and watched for signs of snow. Elizabeth inhaled the cool air deeply and pushed her breath out to make clouds. When we got around to the front of the house, Mama ran her hand lightly across her hair and turned to me, "Tilden, do you think I need a haircut?"

Nick had promised us that there would be snow at his house. Once again, he hadn't let us down. That evening, just after we'd finished unpacking the linens and setting up our beds, the sky fell. First in icy pings and then larger, quiet flakes. Nick dressed himself in thick layers and went out to salt the driveway. Elizabeth and I stood still on the landing of the outdoor stairs, with our arms out wide, so that the snow would stick to us. Every few minutes we moved over one step and watched our footprints disappear. When I couldn't wait any more, I scraped the banister clean, and packed a snowball.

"Don't," Elizabeth said, wincing and holding her hand in front of her face.

I waited until Nick's back was turned and transferred the snowball from palm to palm as it shrank under the heat of my bare hands. Twice, I cocked my arm back and pretended to throw as Elizabeth danced and ducked in front of me. When my hands got numb, I set the snowball on the railing and warmed my fingers against my mouth.

Elizabeth knelt down and wrote her name across the top step with one bare finger. After she finished, the *i* dotted with a heart, she looked up at me and said, "What if we don't fit in?" Her face was flushed, all pink and white with fear.

"That's stupid," I said, but didn't mean it. I was worried too. The amount of snow made me realize how far away we really were from anywhere we'd ever lived. Things were going to be different here, I could feel it. From an early age we both knew that there was some kind of shame in the South. Conflicts over flags and songs in school confused our notions of patriotism. Mama always said that Southern pride was best kept discreet.

"We don't even have the right clothes," Elizabeth complained. "And people talk so fast here . . ."

Just then Nick climbed the stairs, wiping each step clear of snow with his boots. "Have you girls ever built a snowman?" he asked.

Elizabeth shook her head no, even though I remembered a time when we had tried but couldn't get the snow to stick. We watched as Nick gathered snow into piles and packed the sides, rolling the balls to the edge of the steps and stacking one on top of another until the snowman took shape. Elizabeth pulled her hands into her sleeves and used them to pat the snow into place. I dug in my pockets, unearthing pennies to use for the eyes and a pen cap as a nose. When we finished, Nick tied his scarf around the snowman's neck. The snow hadn't been the best kind for packing and Frosty turned out small and lopsided, with edges instead of curves.

Mama finally came to retrieve us. "You're going to freeze to death out here," she said. She ushered the three of us inside as if we were goslings. "This cold! It can do *permanent damage*, you know." Nick looked at her and laughed. "I'm serious," she continued, "Haven't you heard of hypothermia?"

She filled the bathtub with hot water and instructed us each to soak for twenty minutes. Elizabeth went first and by the time she finished, I was already long in bed. Mama came in to my room with an armful of extra towels and lined my drafty windows. When she finished, she tucked me in, and blew warm breath on my icy fingers.

I couldn't fall asleep. I listened to the strange sounds settle around me. The click and rattle of the refrigerator, a slow drip somewhere in the bathroom, and the occasional sound of snow crunching against gravel each time a car went up or down the driveway. The headlights made me jittery, the way they angled across my room and illuminated the boxes that remained stacked against the wall. I decided that I needed to feel settled in order to sleep. I climbed out of bed and began to unpack my books, filling the small shelf at the side of the desk, and then stacking the rest in order along the floor. The atlas, I kept near my bed where I could reach it. I sorted my supplies—a ruler, erasers, pens, and scissors—into the top drawer of my desk and locked it, hiding the key in my pillowcase.

Outside my window, I watched the snow fall—blanketing the walk and drive, the cars and mailbox—making a clean slate of the world, the way wiping a chalkboard or shaking an Etch-A-Sketch erases what came before. For a few sleepless hours, I played a game from my bed: waiting for the headlights to flash across the room, I tried to name as many books from my shelf as possible before the light disappeared. I stared so hard at the spines in the darkest corner that the rest of the room fell away. I imagined Elizabeth curled on her side, breathing heavily into her arm, the wheezy rhythm my backdrop for night. I had never slept without her nearby. As I drifted off to sleep, I heard the unfamiliar cries of a train in the distance. I could have been anywhere.

POPULARITY

My lips were chapped, ringed red like a fruit punch stain that made my mouth seem wider than it was. It was so bad that even Elizabeth knew not to tease me. Mama gave me everything she had—Chap Stick, Vaseline, Carmex—and ordered me to keep my lips protected at all times. I coated my lips over and over until my mouth was slick, an oozy pucker standing out from my face. I hated what I saw in the mirror. I had never looked worse. Mama said the lack of humidity created flyaway hair, made it stand on end, charged with electricity. No matter what I did with the curling iron, the cowlicks made my bangs bend around my forehead like parentheses.

Mama took Elizabeth and me shopping to buy corduroys, turtlenecks, and thermal underwear. She was a firm believer in layers, even back home, where it sometimes got cold. "Once a chill gets through you, down in your bones, no heating system in the world can shake it out," she said the night before the first day of school. I dressed my chair in preparation: nylons and long johns spread out across the seat with the toes dangling just above my boots on the floor. In one boot, I put a pair of thin cotton socks, in the other boot, wool. My yellow turtleneck was pushed through a cranberry sweater, the neck flopping over the back, one sleeve on the arm rest. Around the chair back, my new down parka hung with matching gloves clipped onto the pockets.

I watched the chair as if it were a body sitting upright and tried to imagine myself inside those clothes, moving through the big front doors, down a crowded hall and into a room filled with sixth graders from New York. Nothing was worse than starting a new school midway through the year.

When Mama woke me up, I was tangled in my sheets. There was snow sitting four inches high on every slope and ledge. The drive-way had already been plowed and all around me I could hear the deliberate scrape of shovels against pavement. The trees were en-cased in ice, low branches bowing under the weight.

"Nick's been out in the garage since sunrise," Mama said looking out the window with bright eyes. "Tilden, the superintendent of the school district calls TransAlt first when deciding whether or not to have a snow day! Isn't that exciting?" I pulled the blanket up to my nose and stayed snuggled down in the bed until she threw the covers off me.

Elizabeth was disappointed in Mama's news. She wanted to hear the cancellations for herself over the radio. She waited in bed until WSKY announced that there would be delays in district two.

Downstairs, Mama was cooking hamburgers with sesame seeds and mashed potatoes. She thought it was important to have protein on eventful days. Her philosophy was that it was healthier to eat in reverse order—heavy to light. To help get us off to a good start, Mama usually served vegetables and meats with rice or potatoes in the morning. Our breath was strong at an hour when our friends smelled of sweet cereals and syrups. The smell of breakfast made me anxious and I moved slowly, dressing with dread. As I hesitated on the stairs, Elizabeth blew by me. She was wearing her pink turtleneck by itself. I didn't think it was supposed to be worn that way, but didn't say anything. I pulled the neck of mine up over my chin to hide my raw, chapped lips.

Mama had already made some minor adjustments to the kitchen, rearranging and making room. She'd found it cluttered, all those tarnished pans and mismatched cups. This is what it looks like, a man living alone his whole life, she told us. She moved some plants into the kitchen. One, a welcome gift from Nick's mother in Florida, was long and viny. It hung from the shelves above the windows and brushed above the appliances. Mama had to hook the froggy veins around a nail, like strands of hair behind an ear, when she used the toaster. Nick said not to expect much more from his mother. She wasn't the type to get involved.

"She's great with protocol," he said. "That's where I get my good manners."

We stuck fruit-shaped magnets on the fridge, hanging some work from our old school. Elizabeth's picture of a turtle, made with glue and yarn, was from art class in fourth grade. My scratchboard image of an American egret was bent from the move. Nothing we did made it seem more like home.

A snow plow drove by the house, banking the snow into walls and covering the road in sand. I watched out the window and counted the bird tracks on the lawn while Elizabeth twisted her hair to give it body. We had opposite sides of the same fear. I was terrified of standing out. She worried that she wouldn't. Neither of us said it outright. Elizabeth got demanding; she wanted hot chocolate in her thermos. I got quiet.

Mama set our plates down in front of us. The smell of meat at that hour made my stomach turn. I picked the sesame seeds off the burger and made as many trips to my mouth as there were seeds. Mama hated when I did that.

"You're using more energy than you're taking in," she said. "Maybe you're nervous?"

I wouldn't answer. Elizabeth excused herself from the table and out in the kitchen I heard Mama trying to talk her into wearing snowpants. Elizabeth said she would rather drop dead on the spot than put on a pair of snowpants. I understood how she felt. I could barely bend my limbs as it was.

Nick came in the back door and kicked his heels against the frame to unearth the clumps of snow from his boots. "Time to get going," he said.

"Are you going to take us to school in the limo?" Elizabeth asked.

"Not in this weather. We need something with better control."

"Aren't we lucky to be living here with the town expert?" Mama said to no one in particular.

I used the moment to scrape my plate extra loud.

In Atlanta we never went for a family drop-off at school. If we missed the bus and had to be driven, we usually made Mama leave us a block away. But Nick insisted on driving us door to door. Secretly, I was relieved. We had taken a tour of the new school the week before, but I was worried about finding my way. Doors had a way of changing on me, seeming distinct when following someone, and completely foreign the next time around. Elizabeth was worried about other things: the proximity of her classroom to the bathroom, would she have recess?

Mama had packed the outside pocket of our bookbags with Carnation breakfast bars. I put my hand in and felt the cool foil. It calmed me. Also, there was a piece of paper, folded in half, with Nick's telephone number on it. I went over the numbers in my head, trying to memorize it: my fourth phone number in six years. Elizabeth knew them all by heart. Every time we moved, Mama copied the new one in our schoolbooks and pushed it deep inside our pockets. In case of emergencies, she always said.

As we drove in the parking lot at Brooklawn Elementary, I panicked, unable to remember the location of the main office, and asked Mama if she would come with me.

"Left in the door and turn right," she said, "you'll be fine."

Just then a crossing guard with a neon vest came striding across the parking lot, blowing a whistle and waving a flag. There was some honking and the kids who were waiting on the platform outside turned their necks in our direction. Nick had pulled into the "buses only" zone.

"Keep going," Elizabeth demanded.

"Nonsense," Nick said and hopped out to open our door like a chauffeur.

We hurried out so quickly that I forgot to kiss Mama good-bye.

"They're going to love you," she said out the window. "You just wait and see."

Ms. Zimmerman, my new teacher, came all the way down to the main office to get me. On our walk to class, she explained that they were in the middle of current events. "Do you receive any kind of periodicals at home?" she asked.

I raised my chin out from under my turtleneck and answered that Nick received a daily paper and some monthly magazines that I'd seen stacked behind his chair. I explained that I hadn't been there long enough to know what they all were. "I also have a subscription to *National Geographic*," I said.

She looked at me with real interest. "You'll like this class." She patted my right shoulder. I could barely feel her hand through all my layers.

When we got to room 211, Ms. Zimmerman led me to the coat area and strode off across the room to find me a desk. I was startled to see that there was a whole section of the classroom just for coats.

I squeezed mine in between two identical parkas before realizing that I was in the boys' section.

Ms. Zimmerman pushed an empty desk up to a cluster of four girls. Each desk was set off from the other by a tall divider. She flagged me over and sat me at the end, closest to two big-eyed, curious girls. From the way they had decorated their dividers, I could tell right off that they were different. Girls with ideas.

Susie Rhombus had stapled black construction paper as a backing for a series of articles on nations outside the United States. She'd used red magic marker to color over the words she wanted to emphasize. All I could think about was my near-bleeding mouth. I held my hand over my lips, parting my fingers when I needed to speak. I was sure Susie had noticed. She pulled out a Cherry Chap Stick and smeared it over her mouth.

"Want some?" she asked.

"No thanks," I said, more quietly than I wanted to, "it's . . . too late."

Samantha Shaptaw had left her divider blank in some kind of protest.

"Her father is an environmental lawyer," Susie whispered as an explanation.

Samantha smiled at me in anticipation, but said nothing. The fibery board had a small hole which looked as if it had been made by a pencil. That way, I imagined, Samantha and Susie could look at each other or pass tiny scrolled notes through the hole.

Susie became my guide, pointing out the kids in the class—who was serious, funny, a teacher's pet; who had crushes on whom. She had once been new somewhere, I could tell. She knew how to get a lot of important details across quickly.

Jill Switt, a bouncy girl at the next table, craned her neck anytime Susie spoke to me. Jill's board was about fashion in different cultures. Ms. Zimmerman kept stopping midsentence to reprimand

Jill for something. She was not only chewing gum, but snapping bubbles. She would have been punished in an Atlanta school for bad manners. I remember Mama had said that New York had a broader definition of good behavior.

Christy Diamo's board terrified me. She had stapled pictures of Jesus on the cross to a red background.

"Isn't it weird?" hissed Susie. "She's totally into Christ and the Crucifixion."

It wasn't long before I was asked to explain my religion.

"Episcopalian," I said with more confidence than I felt.

"What's that?" Susie asked.

I didn't know exactly. Mama only took us to church on Easter. So Susie asked Christy, who I could tell liked to be asked, but didn't like to show it.

"It's a cross between Protestant and Catholic," she said primly.

I started to add "nonpracticing," which is what Mama had always said when someone came by the door dressed in a suit and tie and carrying a pamphlet, but I decided against it.

The bulk of my cluster—that's what they called them in this school, I realized—maybe even half the class, were Catholic. Susie, Christy, and Jill attended church together. They were planning to be confirmed the following spring.

During speed reading Susie told me that Samantha was Jewish. She said it nonchalantly, without whispering. "Her grandmother came here from Russia."

I'd never met someone Jewish before, not that I knew of anyway. But I pretended it was old hat. "She's Jewish?" I asked, trying to be just as casual as Susie had been. But my question must have come out wrong because she looked surprised and narrowed her eyes at me. I could feel my face flush and I began sweating under my layers. I should have kept quiet.

When Ms. Zimmerman asked the class what they knew about

Georgia all anyone could talk about was that Jimmy Carter had farmed peanuts. And that his daughter, Amy, was caught picking her nose and was pictured that way on the front page of the newspaper. I had heard Mama talk about what Northerners thought of the South. She said it went back to slavery and the Civil War, old stereotypes about ignorance and prejudice. But she believed that Jimmy Carter being in the White House had changed everything. "He has shown the world that a Southern man can lead with fairness and intelligence," she told me. But by now I had read enough history to know that the Civil War had more to do with hate and selfishness than ignorance. But nobody would talk to me about how stereotypes still existed, especially not Mama.

Ms. Zimmerman called the class to order and announced Dictionary Time. She handed out one dictionary per table and told us each to look up a word that had been on our minds. We were to say the word, read the definition, and tell why we had chosen that particular word. I decided to look up stereotype. When she got to me, I said the word, read all three of the definitions out loud and told the class that I never knew that the word came from a mold or cast used for type.

I think Ms. Zimmerman was worried that I had already had a bad experience, because she cut Dictionary Time short to give a little speech about appreciating our differences. "Sometimes it takes a while to get to know what is underneath the surface," she said. "Everyone is special, everyone has some qualities that make her or him unique." She seemed prepared to leave it at that and then out of nowhere announced that she had an idea; it had just come to her, she said. For our homework, she wanted us each to write a conceited poem.

"Like bragging?" Jill Switt asked.

"Not really," Ms. Zimmerman said. "Conceited is an exaggerated opinion of one's self. Now I know that no one in this class is a bragger, but I want you to pretend, play up everything about yourself that's good. The more conceited the poem, the higher the grade you'll get."

This struck me as odd. In Atlanta we made grades, not got them. The way Ms. Zimmerman said it sounded as if she handed out grades like gifts. The room erupted in a low murmur of nervous laughter and accusations. Who was the biggest bragger? Who would get the best grade?

On my way to lunch Ms. Zimmerman stopped me and asked if everything was going all right. I told her that it was. But deep down I was feeling worried about lunch. Mama had made me bologna with lemon pepper on an onion roll. My bag was light brown with a waxy finish. Everyone else seemed to be buying the cafeteria food.

As it turned out, before I even had time to open my lunch, Jill Switt took me table to table to introduce me. "Talk Southern," she demanded. I tried to tell her that I didn't really have an accent, not compared to most of the friends I'd had in Atlanta.

"You'll make more friends if you exaggerate," she whispered to me in front of a whole table of our classmates.

"What do you want me to say?" I asked, half hiding my mouth behind my hand.

"Anything," she said. "Just talk."

"I really don't know what to say."

"Introduce yourself," Jill coached, leaning toward me and moving my hand away from my face.

I said my name, my lips burning and cracking. No one seemed impressed.

"Say something your mother says," Jill suggested. She acted as if she had as much at stake as I did.

I thought hard, trying to come up with something that would sound the way she wanted it to. I had already noticed little things. Northerners stood on line instead of in, said take instead of carry, referred to Cokes as sodas. And there was the most recent difference I'd noticed between getting and making grades. I could see that Jill was frustrated; she took deep, huffy breaths, crossed and recrossed her arms.

"Your grandmother?" she coaxed, "she must say something Southern."

The only thing I could remember was that when Grandma Burbank was alive she called a bowel movement a duke. Every time Elizabeth and I came and went she'd ask, "Did ya take a duke?" I didn't think I could say that out loud.

Then, something lunch-related came to mind. I remembered a fight that Mama had had with Grandma when I was in the fourth grade. Grandma was angry that Mama had let me buy my lunch instead of take it. She said that cafeteria food wasn't worth a hill of beans. I remembered this because it happened not long before Grandma and Grandpa died in the car accident and Mama was angry at herself because that fight was the last real conversation she'd had with her mother. After that, Mama always made our lunches.

"Cafeteria food isn't worth a hill of beans," I said at last.

Jill smiled, almost gloating. The other kids at the table seemed impressed. "Wicked accent," one boy said. "Cool," said another. "Decent."

"School lunches aren't that bad," Susie Rhombus added, betrayed. It turned out that her mother was a lunch lady, pink-smocked with a hairnet and plastic gloves. She was the one to serve the popular cinnamon rolls. Still, Susie never acknowledged her.

During recess, Samantha Shaptaw came up behind me. "You shouldn't let Jill do that to you," she said.

"Do what?"

"Treat you like a puppet."

• • •

Elizabeth's first homework assignment was to make a family tree. When I told her that I had to write a conceited poem, she was jealous.

"You're so lucky," she said. "I hate all this family crap."

I would have offered to switch with her, but knew better than to enter into a bargain around schoolwork. Elizabeth liked to wait until the last minute, always scrambling in a panic and getting Mama to do it for her.

Nick seemed to think that helping with homework was the best way for him to get involved. He offered to work with me because he thought Mama might be more useful to Elizabeth creating the family tree.

"I don't really need help," I told Mama.

"Can't you pretend, just this once," she said wrinkling her forehead, her eyes pleading.

So I pretended to need help with rhyming, allowing Nick to find matching words for all of my end words. If I had been doing it on my own, I would have gone down each letter of the alphabet in my head, imagining new words with the same sounds. But it was different with Nick. He had a pocket rhyming dictionary from which he read off lists and lists of similar sounding words, until he struck upon one of interest. This meant that I had to construct a thought from the chosen word rather than finding the right word to complete my thought. It felt backwards.

I ended up writing about myself as a friend.

All the letters I would send, to every need I would attend, when down and out, my hand I would lend, my time I would spend, trying never to offend, in every way, my heart I would extend, to be the very best kind of friend.

It wasn't really conceited, but I figured it was safe. Other girls would write about being beautiful and smart and rich, winning gymnastic meets, being in the ballet, even the Olympics. The boys would be star athletes, big and strong and muscular. They'd win Nobel prizes, cure diseases, and discover planets. It would be more acceptable for them to admit their strengths.

Nick drove me to the stationery store to get a plastic report cover. I picked out a green spine to hold it in place. He bought another one in red and showed me how to lay my poem in the Xerox machine to get an extra copy. He wanted to hang it on the refrigerator.

Elizabeth's family tree would take longer to finish, there were missing branches and dates. Above our names, Mama penciled in the date of her divorce from our father, two years after I was born. Elizabeth had been only a year old.

"Do I have to write this in, Mama?" Elizabeth asked.

"Always remember that you . . . both you girls, were conceived in love. Your father and I became incompatible over time, but you were the two most wanted children in the world. Don't you forget that."

Elizabeth didn't look convinced. She narrowed her eyes at Mama. I could tell that she was worried about appearances. She told us about some girl in her class who'd boasted that she had French royalty in her genealogy. Another had family who had survived the Holocaust.

I glanced at our tree for something noteworthy. It spooked me to see Grandma and Grandpa's dates, the same years both in birth and death, like Siamese twins. There were not many living relatives on either side. Mama analyzed the dates, explaining that there had been illnesses and accidents all around. Diphtheria it seemed was common. Or pneumonia. There were female relatives who had died in childbirth.

"People didn't used to live as long as they do now," she said, her finger gliding past as many *d*'s as *b*'s, "that was before penicillin and other things."

I was interested in the branch of brothers, six in all, who died within months of each other in the same year.

"That was during the Civil War," Mama said.

Elizabeth and I watched Mama, her pencil suspended above the page. Finally, she turned the pencil upside down and rubbed at the date of the divorce with the pink eraser. Then, she drew an extra branch, grafted like a scion for Nick and his ancestors. While she worked, she referred often to a list of names that she'd scratched on the back of an envelope. Elizabeth tensed up, her shoulders high around her ears. She didn't have to say anything. Mama was making it seem as if Nick was our father.

When she finished, she ran her hand across the page, her fingers spreading wide over all the names. She stopped and pointed to Nick's grandfather. "He was some kind of civic leader," she said, "a congressman or something. You should ask Nick to tell you about him."

Elizabeth thrived on making friends—loud, opinionated girls with colored fur lining on their hoods. They took her flexi-sledding and built ice forts. Soon she could skate backward on Breyer's Pond. Within a month, Elizabeth was talking back and walking tough. She shed her bookbag and held her notebooks under her arm. They were training her to be the tallest girl on the bus.

I found myself eavesdropping on Elizabeth's phone conversations, reading through the slips of papers tucked into her books to look for notes from her new friends, watching for pointers. She'd been accepted so easily, trading clothes and throwing back handsprings in gym. She had one of those memories made for dance steps, titles of songs and where movie stars were born. It was the kind of memory that made it possible to try out for drill team and school plays. The kind that made you popular.

I chose Samantha Shaptaw to be my friend and waited for her to choose me. She wrote about being a genius in her conceited poem, using only two- and three-syllable words.

I am a genius. I can perform arithmetic without an abacus. Study philosophy and religion even a teacher can't discuss. So productive, many people assume I exhibit the appendages of an octopus . . .

She came in second. The first-place winner was a boy who promised to be president. We each had to read our poem out loud and then display it at the back of the room. After I read mine, Samantha passed me a note, giving me another word that rhymed with friend. It said, Do you want to know who I would *recommend as a friend?*

The first time Samantha came over she was wearing jeans with patches and a fringe jacket. She twisted a bandanna around her head and let her hair, which she kept up in a ponytail for school, hang down below her shoulders. I could tell that she was impressed with my bookshelf. She slid each book out from its slot and put it back in place. She walked around my room, eyes everywhere, picking up the individual pieces of my desk set, turning them in her hand, and putting them down. I showed her where I kept the keys to the top drawer. I hadn't noticed until then that my pillow case didn't match my sheets.

"Were you popular in your old school?" she asked.

I shrugged. I hadn't stayed in one school long enough to say for sure.

"Do you have a best friend?"

"Not really," I said and then thought about Tess Callahan from Atlanta.

Tess was an only child who, lonely and lingering, was always watching me and Elizabeth, following us around to catch a glimpse of sisterhood, eyes wide with envy. And sometimes judgment. I could tell when she thought I was being ungrateful or selfish. She was often disappointed by our bickering and her looks of disapproval were enough to send Elizabeth and me home to fight in private. The day before we moved, she told me that she liked to pretend that I was her sister, too. We wrapped an old dish in a dust rag and broke it over a pointed rock. We pulled a rugged piece across the tops of our hands until they bled, and tied ourselves together with a rope made of onion grass. We stayed like that—promising to write, not to change, not to tell—for ten minutes. "Sisters," she whispered as we untied the grass and put wet leaves over the cuts.

"Actually, yes," I said, not wanting to appear needy. "I do have a best friend."

Samantha sat down next to me on the bed and crossed her legs Buddha-style, with her feet resting on top of her knees. Her eyes were bright, a greenish blue. She probably used an aqua Magic Marker for the eyes on her self-portrait in art. "You can't have a best friend long distance," she said.

"We're blood sisters," I revealed, hoping to impress her with my loyalty.

"But you have a sister already."

"Yeah, but I didn't choose her."

Samantha got up and looked out my window. The snow had melted, leaving the trees and yard dull. The lot outside TransAlt was tarred with bits of glass that were shining in the afternoon light. From Elizabeth's room came the sounds of Rod Stewart's new record.

"What's it like?" Samantha asked.

"What?"

"You know—your sister. Your real sister, I mean."

I hesitated, thinking again of Tess. Girls without sisters always thought it was better than it really was. Samantha had brothers who tortured her with pranks. They hung her stuffed animals from trees and unlatched the rabbit cage. In school, they ignored her.

"Mainly we fight," I said.

Samantha grew quiet. At the other end of the hall, I could hear the familiar sound of Elizabeth's steps as she practiced dancing in front of her mirror. Samantha reached out to touch the faint scar on the back of my hand.

"You're lucky," she said, finally.

CURRENT EVENTS

When it came time for my next homework assignment, I made sure not to tell anyone at home. Ms. Zimmerman asked that we clip a week's worth of articles about a topic of our choosing and write an essay that discussed our views of that topic. Every night, I sneaked the newspaper up to my room and returned it to the stack before morning, hoping that Nick wouldn't notice the neat holes I'd made. I knew he meant well, but accepting his help was like cheating. He would have taken my project on in earnest, combing through the papers, marking articles with sprawling asterisks in red pen. I had always done everything on my own; that wasn't going to change now. My last Georgia report card called me "an independent worker."

But it wasn't long before I was discovered. I had clipped articles about wildlife and endangered species and in the process cut through a story about the president that Nick had wanted to reread. At breakfast one morning, he held the paper up between us and looked at me with raised eyebrows through a big rectangular space.

"Tilden, what have you been working on?" he asked. From that angle, his nose was the same size as Jimmy Carter's whole head.

"Nothing, really."

"Then I guess you don't need my help."

I shook my head.

"Well," he said, shifting his weight and clearing his throat, "if you're doing some current events, feel free to look through that stack of magazines. There might be some recent *Time* magazine articles, stuff a newspaper doesn't explore in depth."

I could tell that he was hurt, but didn't know what to do. Mama gave me a sideways look when she delivered my toast. Even Elizabeth treated me as if I had done something wrong. It was the quietest breakfast ever.

When we had finished eating, Nick pushed back his stool and stood behind me. "You've given me an idea," he said. He tore out a local article about the school board and stuck it on the refrigerator. "There's no reason we can't have a little current events here at home."

From that day on, Nick couldn't seem to keep from clipping pieces of the paper. He took this new enthusiasm to work with him, implementing an incentive strategy at TransAlt. He thought the drivers could do with some reading. That way they would be able to make conversation with the passengers. Nothing lofty, he just wanted them to keep up with the news. Those people who didn't have time to read the paper might appreciate a little update. The drivers could come in early, if they wanted, bring their coffee. Nick would make sure to have lots of material on hand. He ordered extra papers.

There was some initial grumbling and confusion. The drivers didn't think this ought to be part of the job. After all, some of them had been dropouts, had avoided homework. Others read the paper on their own and didn't see the point in discussing it. But Nick stayed firm. Mama said he had never gotten the education he wanted; he went to work early, building a business. He told her it was his civic responsibility.

"It'll probably help your tips," he suggested to the drivers.

Something clicked. They began lingering by their doors, batting around some last point on an issue of local importance. Zoning. The dump. They had a lot to say about where traffic lights should be installed. Road conditions and speed limits. A couple of guys even got together and drafted a letter to the editor of the local paper. Lainey DeWitt typed it up and sent it off.

> We at TransAlt are concerned about what we feel to be laziness on the part of some homeowners who leave their garbage unsecured along the roadside. This makes for dangerous driving, especially along the bottom curve of Zigfried Street near Frock Avenue. Trash cans and lids are blown into the street, causing nervous drivers to swerve into the other lane. Trash torn loose by raccoons and other animals clogs the drains and causes flooding during rain storms. Please, for the sake of a safe community, use consideration when disposing of your trash.

The day that letter appeared, you would have thought they'd won the lottery with all the yelping and high fives. They had been published. Nick bought up every paper in the deli. The drivers sent copies to relatives in other states. Mama hung it on the fridge. There was great excitement and pride all around the garage.

But they hadn't counted on the responses. It had seemed so simple. A matter of common sense and community concern. But for weeks they heard back. The families along Zigfried and Frock felt singled out. Why had TransAlt picked on them? Why didn't they mention the sanitation workers who are always in such a hurry? They often forget to tie down the lids. They often leave loose trash behind. The sanitation company was furious. It always came back to the workingman. They were always the scapegoat. The Mothers Against Drunk Driving wrote that surely there were other things more hazardous to driving in Brooklawn. Why hadn't TransAlt said something about drunk driving? Why didn't they help sponsor a SADD chapter at the local high school? Had they ever considered running a late-night escort service in conjunction with the bars? The bars wanted everyone to know that they abided by New York State Law, they were aware of their legal responsibilities and did not have a problem refusing to serve any patron who appeared too drunk to drive. They thought the community should know that TransAlt had always cooperated when called upon to take an intoxicated patron home.

Lainey stayed longer shifts just to field the phone calls. Was TransAlt becoming more involved in politics? Did they want to donate a car for the Driver's Ed program? What was TransAlt going to do about the broken railroad crossing? Lainey had been nervous under fire; they had been so insistent, so upset. She wanted Nick to know that she had made some promises.

"I had to do something," she said.

Lainey arranged for some of the boys from the motor vehicle program at the high school to work on the TransAlt cars when they weren't being used. Just to practice. She shrugged. "I'm sure nobody will follow up."

By the end of March there was a host of boys in the yard. Each with his own set of tools. They took things apart, leaving batteries and carburetors in a pile outside the garage while they went for deli runs. Straw papers littered the driveway. Old cars lay like carcasses against the back fence. Elizabeth and I watched, first from the landing outside my room and then as we got braver, from ground level. These guys were serious, older boys; they seemed closer to the rest of their lives than the boys we knew at Brooklawn Elementary. With

Nick's permission, we stood nearby and gave them tools—fishing through the hard metals for the right grip or head, the thrill of our fingers brushing against their calloused hands, grease under their nails—my first twinges of attraction tied up in that smell of gasoline and tires.

Those late-winter afternoons, Mama would find us lingering outdoors past dusk, putting off chores and homework to watch the boys in action. Our conversations with them were minimal, mainly "hand me this" and "pass me that." Elizabeth was the first to break into more. Jamie Sanders was her favorite; at fourteen, he was still in junior high. He had been left back once and had friends at the high school. He had shiny black hair and eyes so intent, people often looked away from his gaze. Nobody was supposed to know that he drove without a permit, but I'd seen him do it, parking at the bottom of Connally Drive and walking up the hill to TransAlt. He kept to himself and didn't say much. Elizabeth would talk extra loudly when he was around. I liked that he didn't pay any attention.

One Monday evening, we stayed out late at the garage, eavesdropping on the guys talking about their weekends. Gradually, but steadily, the conversation took an uncomfortable shape: it was no longer engines or hubcaps, movies or concerts, but second and third base. Elizabeth stood red-faced and quiet off to the side. A few yards away, Jamie Sanders was revving an engine, walking back and forth from the front seat to check under the hood. He walked right by me with each pass. His baseball hat was turned backward, a small piece of black hair sticking up through the clasp.

"Why don't you make yourself useful," he said finally, and I jumped to help. "Come here and hit the accelerator when I tell you to."

I climbed into the car and waited, with my foot just above the pedal, for him to give the sign.

"Okay," he shouted and I pressed down steady. The engine raced, straining harder and harder. I could see Jamie working through the crack in the raised hood until he lifted up his hand and motioned for me to stop. We went on like this for twenty minutes—his gesture, my response, like a conversation. Finally, he closed the hood, pitching it gently upward to undo the catch and letting it come down hard. The slam echoed in the silence between us. He wiped his hands on a rag, twisting it into a rope and letting it go against my leg.

"Gotcha," he said, when it connected with a snap. It was the first time I had seen him smile.

"Nick says you're really good," I offered cautiously, and then grew shy. "I mean, he thinks you're amazing with engines."

"Yeah?" Jamie looked up, switched his hat from backward to frontward. "It's nothing."

We stood there in an awkward silence, the fumey smell of gasoline and oil all around us, until I heard Mama calling me for dinner.

"Gotta go," I said and raced by Elizabeth toward the house.

Nick was in the kitchen, helping Mama pull TV dinners out of the oven. I stood behind them, breathing heavily and waiting to see what was under the aluminum covers.

"Where's Elizabeth?" Mama asked.

"She's too busy flirting to eat."

Mama went quickly to the back steps and screamed for Elizabeth. She even went so far as to count to ten.

"I'm coming," Elizabeth shouted. She came into the house, frantic, cheeks blotchy. "God, Mama. I was only in the driveway." She slammed the fridge closed and poured her juice. "You made it sound like I was halfway to town."

"Don't you have any homework to do?" Mama asked, when Elizabeth joined us at the table.

"No."

"Well, I want Tilden to help you with that report that's due next week."

"I don't want her help," Elizabeth said.

We ate the rest of the meal in silence. When Nick had finished his last bite, he balled up his napkin and pushed back his stool.

"I'll help you," he said. "What's it on?"

Elizabeth flashed me a nasty look.

"Energy," Mama said. She excused herself to do the dishes and dragged me with her.

Over the stacking of dishes and clanging of pots, I could hear Nick talking about waterwheels and windmills, nuclear and solar. He walked through the kitchen toward the den in search of some article he'd read recently. Elizabeth was sulking behind him.

"I hate you," she said as she walked by me.

Mama looked up when she heard this. She always said that hate was a dangerous word and we were not to use it lightly. Hate had been known to cause the dissolution of families, sometimes even whole countries.

"Take that back," Mama called after her. "I mean it."

Her words seemed to make no impact. Elizabeth marched after Nick without apologizing. Mama turned on the water to rinse each plate before putting it in the dishwasher. I stepped alongside her, offering to do the loading. After we'd settled into a rhythm Mama asked, "What's with you two?"

I shrugged, hoping that my silence would make her keep asking. I wished she really wanted to know how I felt.

"I've never known you to be so cold to each other. Ever since we got here . . ." She paused and looked startled by her own thought, "Is it about being here? Did something happen at school?"

I forced myself not to answer. What if it was about being here? What if after the past four months I decided that I didn't like it, that

I wanted to go back home or at least have things as they had been before.

Mama looked worried, stared deep into my eyes, then gave up and became irritated. "If you're not going to talk to me, there's nothing I can do. All I can say is that we live with a wonderful man in a beautiful house in a neighborhood with a good school . . ." She trailed off. "You have a nice new friend. What's not to like, Tilden?"

I held my tongue. Nick, I wanted to say. Nick. Nick. Nick. But I knew that there would be no taking it back. Anyway, it wasn't really his fault; he was okay on his own. What I disliked was how distracted Mama had become, as if there wasn't room in her for all of us.

PART II

DIRECTIONS

On the first warm day of April, Mama called me out from under the droop of the weeping willow at the edge of the yard. "Come keep me company," she said. She had on big sunglasses and a loose, cotton skirt that caught the breeze like curtains and billowed beneath her winter coat. Her hair was twisted up and clipped at the back of her head.

Nick had given Mama a car as soon as the weather broke, a station wagon that he bought used and had the guys from the motor vehicle program fix up. Jamie Sanders had taken it on as his special project. Parked as it was, in the lot, the station wagon stood out among Nick's fleet of darker, more formal cars. Mama waited for me by the driver's side and scraped at an old sticker on the windshield with a key.

I parted the branches and stepped into the light, holding on to the end of one branch, and taking it with me as I walked, like a ribbon on a maypole. When it pulled taut, I let the pointed leaves slip through my hand.

Elizabeth emerged from the back door eating a piece of fruit. Her hair whipped around her face in the wind until she caught it in a clump and wrapped an elastic holder around the ponytail. When she saw me heading toward the car, she broke into a run, clomping down the stairs and practically twisting her ankle in her clogs, those long limbs flailing out from under her.

"I call it," I said and slapped the roof first. As I ducked into the front seat, Elizabeth threw a wet paper towel at my head.

"Stop it." Mama put one arm out in each direction, her hands tilted upward. "One argument and you both stay here." She kept her head raised between us as a warning, her chin high and waiting.

Elizabeth gave in. She slumped down low in the back, extended her skinny legs across the seat and kicked her clogs onto the floor. Her feet were blistered and raw from not wearing any socks.

"You can navigate from there," Mama said as she reached back and locked Elizabeth's door and then her own. She adjusted the rearview mirror and gave herself a quick look, lowering her sunglasses and digging through her purse for the makeup bag. She sucked in her cheeks, making a fish face, and highlighted her cheekbones with a touch of cream blush. When she finished, she held her rouged finger out to me.

"Want a dab?" she asked.

I leaned my face toward her and closed my eyes, breathing in that chalky smell while she rubbed a small circle on each cheek and then dotted my nose. Mama wore makeup when she went out in the world, smoothing on blusher and gloss, making her eyes big and bright. She snapped the clasp of the makeup bag and set her heavy purse beside her like a small child. Then, she put the car in reverse and swung back toward the garage where Nick was washing a town car. He had a squeegee in his hand which dripped milky-colored water down the leg of his pants as he walked toward us.

"Where are you going?" he asked.

"Just some errands," Mama said, blinking up at him, "want to come?"

"No thank you," he said and leaned in to kiss Mama on the forehead. He smelled like Windex. I turned my head away; I hated when they kissed in front of me. He blew an air kiss at me and stopped to squint at Elizabeth in the backseat. She let out a deep sigh and turned away.

"What's with her?" he mouthed.

"Nothing," Mama said.

"She's being a brat," I announced.

Nick sponged off the little triangle of a window closest to Elizabeth's head and wiped it clean with the squeegee. She didn't look up, just kept picking at the Band-Aids on her feet.

Mama swung around in her seat to face Elizabeth. "Chirp up," she said, "I mean it."

Nick tiptoed backwards away from the car. "Have fun," he said and gazing at Mama in that lovey-dovey way I hated, waved with his fingers, each dipping and rising, as if he were doing scales on a piano.

It was Sunday. Throughout the neighborhood landscapers were surveying winter's damage, raking piles of rotting leaves and branches into large black bags. Nick didn't have as much to do. Half of our backyard was tarred, the driveway swelling behind the house into a miniature parking lot.

Mama drove slowly, watching Nick in her mirrors as we rolled down the driveway. When she turned left off Cranbrook, instead of right toward town, I knew we were in trouble. It was the long way to the Walt Whitman Mall, the route she reserved for quality time. I put my feet on the dashboard and brought my chin to rest on my knees.

"Girls, we have to talk."

I pulled down the makeup mirror and eyed Elizabeth, waiting for her to look up.

"I don't know about you," Mama said, "but I'm still finding it hard to be new." She turned onto a narrow back road. Elizabeth sat up and watched out the window, her eyes taking inventory of each sign and landmark. "Being new can make you susceptible," Mama continued, "more likely to fall victim to peer pressure."

Again, with those sayings. Why did she have to always teach us something? There was static on the radio and as I moved to find a station, Mama pushed my hand away and turned it off.

"I know you girls are very responsible, but still I worry that you might get in trouble. Not on purpose or anything, but by accident. Things are different here. Faster. So you've got to be even more careful."

"I wouldn't worry about it, Mama," I said, looking over my shoulder to check the blind spot as she merged lanes.

"I just can't help but think of my good friend Lila Davenport . . . have I told you about her?"

"About a hundred times," I said. I could feel myself fading out, glazing over. Mama could never just come out with what she was thinking.

"Well . . . Lila could never manage to stay out of trouble. It started small, of course—breaking rules in school, always late with her homework, then . . ."

"We've heard this story," Elizabeth said, cutting her eyes at me.

"My point is simply that something that might seem like nothing can get out of control." She blinked hard, raising her eyes over the rim of her sunglasses, looking first in my direction and then at Elizabeth in the rearview mirror.

I pressed the ball of my foot against the silver button on the glove compartment, opening and closing it, until Mama reached over and squeezed my ankle.

"Tilden, I want you to hear me."

"Green," I said, as the light going the other way was turning yellow. I wouldn't look at her. I knew how she hated that. Mama stepped on the gas and shot into the intersection too early.

"Wrong way," Elizabeth warned.

"Damn it, girls," Mama said. "Let me do the driving."

Elizabeth and I exchanged shocked glances. Mama rarely cursed, and almost never at us.

Elizabeth knew how to get to the mall. She was sure we'd gone right, back at some giant birch. She mentioned her concern in a small voice and, when Mama didn't argue, she continued to rattle off each turn, like a waitress repeating an order. I could see her memory working behind her eyes.

My mind was filled with things no one would ever ask about, not on tests or at sleep-overs. I remembered scraps mostly, like a book of swatches in a fabric store, thumbed over quickly and cast against bare walls. A chip, the shape of Africa, on the handle of Mama's favorite mug. A missing z on the neon pizza sign. A picture of my real father leaning against a tool shed, his thumb raised high in the air, on the day I was born.

As Elizabeth barked directions and cited landmarks, Mama gave in. I didn't say a word, just tipped my head back and let the nameless streets and trees whirl around me. We drove in silence farther away from the beach, past the train station and the high school. No one ever said it, but I knew it mattered which of those places you lived closest to. The people who actually took the train always lived the farthest from it and were usually closest to the beach. The train tracks ran behind the library and sliced Brooklawn in three places: once at Rampart Street, once at Main, and once at Connally Drive. We lived all the way at the end of Connally, yet I could still hear the churning of the diesel trains coming from and going to the city.

When we drove past a hitchhiker at the edge of town, Elizabeth sat up straight in the backseat and swiveled around to look. "Mama! He's cute," she said. "Pick him up."

Mama glared at Elizabeth in the mirror and started in again. "Under no circumstances are you to get into a car with someone you don't know," she said, "especially high school boys or men." She hesitated and took off her sunglasses. "And while we're on the subject of boys, there are some other things you should keep in mind . . ."

I could tell that she hadn't planned on this part of the discussion. But here we were again on the brink of another lecture, too late to turn back. "Certain things are just not acceptable . . ."

Elizabeth let out a sigh, pushed her feet through my headrest, and touched her bare feet to my neck. "We know all that," she said.

"You don't know anything yet," Mama said. "You remember that." It was meant as a warning, but she waited for a response as if it were a question. "When I was growing up girls who got pregnant had to be sent away," she turned to Elizabeth. "Lila Davenport left school one day and just never came back."

"God, Mama, why are you looking at me?" Elizabeth shot back.

We both knew what was coming. Lila Davenport had gotten alcohol poisoning as early as the sixth grade and gave herself asthma from smoking in junior high. Mama thought maybe she'd even been one of those early bulimics. Elizabeth and I had long stopped believing in Lila Davenport. And now here she was, pregnant and disappeared.

"Did Lila have VD too?" I asked.

Elizabeth began to giggle. Slowly at first, hiding her mouth with her hand, until she could no longer contain herself.

"That's not funny," Mama said, "VD can make you infertile."

"Doesn't sound like Lila was infertile," Elizabeth said.

Mama caught a glance of her in the rearview mirror, her lips tightening into a scowl. "I'm serious," she said.

"What ever happened to Lila?" Elizabeth asked, making her voice extra sweet.

"Who knows?" Mama said. "I'm sure she turned to the street."

I burst out laughing. "The street" had been one of the horrible ends that Elizabeth and I'd imagined over the years, lying awake in our bunk beds, reading *People* magazine with a flashlight.

"You girls have no idea," Mama said. "This world is a very dangerous place."

We looked into each other's faces, sharing that secret language we had, all eyebrows and squinched noses—each expression an entire conversation—until at the exact same instant, we became hysterical, tears streaming down our faces. Finally, we made Mama pull off the side of the road so that we could pee.

Leaping out of the car the second it stopped, still shrieking with laughter, Elizabeth and I balanced our backs against each other and crouched between the doors on the passenger side. I spread my feet wide and bunched my corduroys tight between my knees. We strained silently, each waiting for the other to finish. Elizabeth tilted her bare foot away from my small stream. When we got back in the car, Mama looked at me, seeming to have more to say, but didn't. Her face collapsed with fatigue. She dropped her purse into my lap instead.

"Find me a Tylenol, will you please?" she said and pulled back into the traffic.

Elizabeth and I had birthdays two weeks apart in early June. Irish twins, Mama called us, even though we weren't really either thing. When we got to the mall, Mama announced that she wanted us each to pick out one outfit as a birthday present. Elizabeth was immediately suspicious. Usually Mama surprised us with presents rather than letting us choose.

"We're here," Mama said, "you might as well get what you want."

"But it's not for two months," I said.

Mama crossed her arms. "You don't have to wear it right away if you don't want to," she said. "I just thought it would be fun." She shook her head and walked off toward Macy's.

Elizabeth and I raised our eyebrows at each other and followed her inside. From the time we were babies, Mama dressed us alike, but always in different colors. My clothes were fiery, reds and orange; Elizabeth had cool blues. She would say how important it was to give a child a say, and then she'd let us choose among accessories for barrettes or bows or the pattern on our underpants. But that warm Sunday, the Junior Department at Macy's represented our first experience with true selection.

The mannequins were dressed in pastel and Elizabeth went wild, pulling matching tops and bottoms off racks and bending the clothes over her arm. It took her an hour to narrow it down and settle on one outfit. I knew what I wanted without even having to look. A pair of white overalls and a red-and-white striped sailor's top that I'd seen in *Seventeen* magazine.

Mama seemed distracted at the register; she filled her check out incorrectly the first time, spelling a different amount than what she wrote in numbers. "Damn," she said, "damn, damn, damn." She wrote VOID across the front of the check, ripped it out, and started over with a fresh one.

"What's wrong, Mama?" I asked.

She didn't look up, just continued scribbling in her checkbook to calculate the balance. She used her fingers to subtract; it was how she taught me to do math and I resented her for it. I had to count with my hands behind my back or under my desk. Seeing Mama subtract this way, out in the open, embarrassed me.

At the car, Elizabeth opted for the backseat so that she could spread out. She pulled her new clothes out of the bag and gnawed the tags off with her teeth. Then she lay each piece against the corresponding part of her body. Mama turned on the radio and let me tune it to station WPLJ. We were silent for the rest of the ride. When we pulled up to the house, Elizabeth bolted out of the car before Mama had even cut off the engine.

"Thanks," she called back, her new clothes clutched in her arms as she ran up the steps.

Mama removed the keys from the ignition and took a deep breath. As I undid my seat belt and reached for the door, she touched my arm. "Wait," she said.

I stopped and looked at her. She pushed her sunglasses to the top of her head and wiped a stray piece of hair out of her face.

"I have something to tell you," she said. "I have a doctor's appointment tomorrow." She wasn't looking at me. "It's just a checkup, but I want you to help Nick when you get home from school."

"Why?" I asked. "What's wrong?"

I watched as she gathered up her things. "Please don't say anything to your sister," she said, clutching her purse to her chest, and climbing out of the car.

I was so pleased to be included in a secret that for a moment I forgot that she hadn't actually told me anything. Instead she left me, the way she always left me, wordless and wondering what was really going on. Learning, as I had so many times, that silence was just another way to tell a lie.

EUPHEMISM

The next day signaled spring in a way we could all feel—early, bright light and birds, a kind of recklessness during recess. The boys swung wildly from the metal bars of the swings, smacked handballs hard against the cement wall. Even the lunchroom monitors stepped outside, squinting at the sun and bending to look closely at the new bulbs growing on the playground. This was the day that Mr. McKinney, the school principal, decided to call a special meeting of the sixth-grade girls to talk about the Period Movie.

Mr. McKinney could bring a room to silence by his very presence. Once he started talking, nothing could make him stop: not the assistant principal, not even a fire drill. This day, he stood before us in the huge auditorium, stone-faced and serious, only to introduce the school nurse, Ms. Penny. We had all seen her before, in her cardigans and thick white shoes, real nurse clothes that meant she took her job seriously. There was a rumor that Ms. Penny had once smelled the inside of Susie Rhombus's mouth to make sure that she had actually vomited. But no one had ever seen her out of the world of her office. She looked small leaning against the stage. Mr. McKinney had someone bring her a chair.

Fortunately, Ms. Penny did not talk for long. She announced that we were required to see "And Then One Year," an important movie about something we would all experience very soon: a process called menstruation. Our mothers were required to go with us. Ms. Penny directed our teachers to hand out permission slips and booklets about menstruation and asked that we keep them in the backs of our desks.

Mr. McKinney cleared his throat. He held up a copy of the booklet, *Growing Up and Liking It*. "No one else need see these," he said. "It is very important to be discreet."

When we filed out of the auditorium with our booklets, Mr. McKinney shepherded us down the hall, away from the curious onlookers. You could see it on our faces for the rest of the day, every girl who had been in the room shared the look of having been caught at something. The way people appear just after kissing or coming out of the principal's office. Faces flushed and heads hung low, like scolded dogs.

On the bus, after school, I watched as some boys played keep-away with Elizabeth's new windbreaker—tossing it around in a circle and passing it just over her head. She didn't grab for it the way they wanted her to. If she had, her pink shirt would have lifted to reveal a band of pale skin. She crossed her arms and waited, scowling furiously in fake protest.

When the bus stopped, Elizabeth made her way down the aisle toward the driver, as if she didn't care whether the boys returned her jacket or not. Shouting, "Hey, Elizabeth, wait!" and "C'mon," they let it fall from the back window like a parachute. They were just playing around, they said, couldn't she take a joke? Elizabeth dusted the jacket off and tied the sleeves around her waist.

After four months, coming up the stairs and through the front door still felt like walking into someone else's house. There were signs of us everywhere: pictures hanging on the mirror in the foyer; random pieces of clothing slung over the backs of chairs; and stacks of our papers waiting to be carried upstairs. But all this could easily be cleared out and the house could go back to looking and smelling as if Nick lived there alone.

When I walked in, Nick was standing in the kitchen, the counter behind him lined with grocery bags. Elizabeth grabbed a box of Entenmann's crumb doughnuts and went to the TV room. I hid the permission slip for the Period Movie in my five-subject notebook and set it on the stairs.

"Give me a hand?" Nick asked. He was wearing a button-down shirt with the sleeves cuffed above his wrists. He unpacked, one item at a time, and folded the empty bags along their original creases. The sound of his thumb against the paper made my teeth hurt. The counter looked like the forbidden aisle in the grocery store: frozen waffles and pop tarts, ice cream sandwiches and cheese snacks. Nothing felt familiar. I realized I had never been alone with Nick.

"Catch," he said and tossed me a loaf of white bread to put on top of the refrigerator.

"Where's Mama?" I asked.

"At the doctor's," he said.

"Still?"

Nick nodded.

I made space in the freezer, fitting the metal ice trays one on top of the other. My finger got stuck to the frost and burned red when I pulled it away. I stacked the frozen foods by size on the shelf and had to slam the freezer door twice to get it to stay. When everything was put away, Nick said he had something to tell me.

"I think now is a good time," he said and gestured to the TV room.

Elizabeth was watching *The Brady Bunch*. It was a rerun, the one where Jan rubs lemons on her face to get rid of her freckles.

"You should try that," Elizabeth said.

"It doesn't work."

"Shut that off for a minute, would you, Tilden?" Nick said and tapped Elizabeth on the leg to get her to make room on the couch. I turned down the volume and left the picture. Elizabeth nodded her approval, egging me on to disobey.

"No." Nick said, snapping off the television and settling back on the couch. He pitched his elbows forward on his knees and clasped his hands together. "Here's the story," he began. "Everything is fine, so I don't want you to get upset or worry, but your Mama had to have a few tests today."

Elizabeth took her feet off the coffee table and sat up straight. "Where is she?"

"At the doctor's . . ." he said, "the hospital, actually."

The hollow TV screen glared back at me. Who was this man, really? What was he trying to say?

"When is she coming back?" I asked.

"Soon," he said, "real soon."

Elizabeth glared at Nick, her brows bunched tightly. "Tonight?"

"I don't think so," Nick said, "but we can call her later."

"What kind of tests?" I asked.

"I'm not sure," he said. "We'll know more tomorrow." He closed his eyes and rubbed the lids with his thumbs.

"Can we call her now?" Elizabeth asked.

Nick hesitated. I could tell he didn't want to say no. "Let's try," he said, as if she were on some remote island and difficult to reach.

We gathered around the phone in the kitchen while Nick squinted at the number and dialed. After a few long moments his face relaxed.

"Did I wake you?" he asked in a gentle voice. "The girls would like to speak to you." He cupped his hand over the mouthpiece. "She sounds sleepy," he said and finally handed me the receiver. He walked away and stood in front of the refrigerator, the doors opened in a cold hug.

I tilted the earpiece toward Elizabeth and she leaned in so close that I could feel her breath on my neck.

"Hello," Mama said, "how are you?" Her voice sounded faint and far away.

"Fine," we answered at the same time and then said nothing.

"Is everything okay?" Mama asked.

"What's wrong with you?" I asked. "What are the tests for?"

"I had a little lump," Mama said, "but the doctor scooped it right out."

"Where?" Elizabeth asked.

"On my chest," she said. "Don't worry, you can come and visit. Tomorrow even, if you want."

"How long are you going to be there?" I asked.

"Just a few days."

I stared at the corkboard next to the phone. Brightly colored pins pushed at odd angles to each other. Mama had put exclamation points on everything. Report cards. Our chore list. Her handwriting was small and restrained with sharp, bony letters that stopped long before the end of the page.

While I gazed out into space, Elizabeth took the phone out of my hand and began jotting things down on the back of an envelope, making lists and promises. "Anything else?" she kept asking, "anything at all?" She leaned over the counter and cleared the mail away with her forearm. Her face looked pale and worried, like a little girl, lost.

"What about nail polish?" she asked. "Slippers? Toothpaste? Do you need lotion?" *Nothing with perfume*, she wrote down and underlined it. "Are you really okay?" she asked in a high and strained voice.

Nick didn't move from the refrigerator. He stood, rearranging the bottles in the door. On the top shelf there were six peanut-butter-and-cucumber sandwiches, wrapped in Baggies. Stacked up, they reminded me of new shirts, the kind I'd seen in the closets of my friends' fathers. On the second shelf, there were five boxes of Carnation breakfast bars. He stared at the ground and kicked his toe against the grating.

"I love you, Mama," Elizabeth said and handed me the phone.

"Make sure your sister doesn't buy the whole drugstore," Mama said charging me with the weight of responsibility. "Tell her I'm fine."

"Are you?"

"Sure."

"Promise?"

"Don't worry," Mama said. "I'll see you tomorrow."

"Everything's under control," Nick said, when he got back on the phone. "You get some rest." He returned the receiver to its cradle and rested his hand there for a moment without saying anything. Elizabeth rewrote the list for the drugstore, gripping the pen tightly and striving for neatness.

Nick cleared his throat. "Let's take a ride," he said and we filed out after him, relieved to have a plan. In the driveway, he opted for Mama's car and slid her seat back as far as it would go. Elizabeth and I squeezed in beside him and pulled the seat belt across our laps. It felt good to leave the house. Nick let out a deep sigh. He was more at ease in a car, any car. He turned on the radio, twisting the dial until he found the Oldies station.

"What happened?" I asked once we were under way.

"It was a routine procedure," Nick said. He seemed angry. His wide face red, his neck clenched. I felt afraid to ask anything more.

We were quiet for a few minutes while "Runaround Sue" played on the radio.

"What's a lump?" Elizabeth asked at last.

Nick gripped the steering wheel tightly. "It's like a growth," he said, "only on the inside."

"Does it hurt?"

"I don't think so," he said, blinking thoughtfully, "I hope not."

The trees whizzed by interrupted by telephone poles and large birds crouching on high wires. For some reason I found myself picturing the sketches in the menstruation book, a girl inside a girl inside a girl, each growing taller, her chest and hips swelling. The drawing showed the different sizes of breasts, like lumps, pushing out from under her arms in broken lines, like a paper doll.

At McNeary's Pharmacy, Elizabeth and I went straight for the sampler baskets. We worked side by side like factory workers, twisting caps and smelling for perfumes.

"What's wrong with perfume?" I asked.

Elizabeth looked up from her bottle and shrugged. "Maybe she's allergic."

I picked up a pink bottle of calamine lotion and read the label. I'd developed a rash on my arms and thighs which Mama called winter bumps, even though they lasted all year long.

"You don't need *lotion*. You should loofah," Elizabeth said, looking at me as if I never bathed.

Behind us loomed the sanitary napkins. The boxes were enormous. I did everything I could not to look at them. But one, with blue lettering, caught my eye. It had a white bird in flight painted on the corner.

"Can I help you?" the druggist asked. He had been watching us. He looked serious in his lab coat and glasses, like a doctor. I wanted to ask him about lumps and growths, but his eyes narrowed at my armful of miniature bottles, as if I were planning to steal them.

"We need something without perfumes," Elizabeth announced. "For our mother."

He pointed to a glass case of hypoallergenic cosmetics and bath products and stood over us calling out prices. I closed my eyes, willing him to go away.

"Never mind," I said, "thanks anyway." I moved to the hair accessory aisle.

At the register, Nick sifted through a fist full of Hallmark cards—all get well soon and missing you, with balloons and happy elephants and bandages in bright colors. He held each one up for us to see. "I couldn't decide," he said, "so I bought all of these. You can each give her some."

For the first time, I saw that he looked scared too. But I didn't know what to say. Wasn't he supposed to be making us feel better?

Elizabeth chose a nail kit with pastel emery boards, a clipper, and frosted polish—all in its own case. I presented a row of miniature bottles, samples of shampoo and conditioner. Nick paid for everything with a new twenty-dollar bill which the druggist snapped between his fingers before putting in the drawer.

On the way home, Nick went through the drive-in window at Burger King and let us order Whoppers, onion rings, and shakes to go. A treat, he called it, even though we already had a week's worth of groceries at home. I could see him wrestling inside himself, something I couldn't quite understand. His eyes were a bit red around the lids, watery and twitchy, and wouldn't stay on either Elizabeth's or my face very long.

When we were deep into our food, he turned the radio up. A twangy man's voice sang, *Bad, bad Leroy Brown. Baddest man in the whole damn town.* Nick held his fist up like a microphone and began to sing along, a wide smile on his face, eyes dancing crazily. Elizabeth and I rolled our eyes at each other, embarrassed. *Badder than old King Kong. Meaner than a junkyard dog.* We drove down along the water, past the clam stand and the town dock. The pussy willows were bursting; white silky hair pushing out of the brown velvet capsules like a torn couch. Elizabeth made a plate of her paper bag and spilled some onion rings in a neat pile on her lap. She guarded them with her elbows. I wanted to wait until we got home to eat mine. Nick reached over and plucked a ring off Elizabeth's lap. *Leroy looked like a jigsaw puzzle,* he sang, *with a couple of pieces gone.*

Nick let us stay up late to watch *The Love Boat.* The captain's daughter, Vicki, usually wore a halter top, but when Julie McCoy helped dress her in a long, strapless gown, the captain didn't approve. It took Elizabeth the entire show to wrap Mama's present with loose-leaf paper and tape.

After Nick turned the TV off, I went upstairs to my room, took my dictionary down from the bookshelf and climbed into bed. I looked up the word lump, searching each letter for hidden meanings and wrote the official definition in my notebook. Suddenly I heard footsteps and panicked. Elizabeth nudged my door open, like a cat, and creaked across the bare floor to the edge of the bed, her pale green nightie twisted around her. She wedged herself next to me and read aloud over my shoulder as I wrote.

"*Lump, a solid mass of special shape . . .*" she paused. "What's *esp.?*" she asked.

"It doesn't matter," I said.

She continued, her voice soft and halting, "*. . . one small enough to be taken in the hand; hunk.*"

I took a deep breath, impatient.

She stopped. "Don't make fun of me."

"I'm not," I said. "Keep reading."

"*Three. A swelling or . . .* what's that word? *p r o t u b e r a n c e.*"

"A bulge," I said. Her eyes opened wide, impressed. I didn't tell her I had already looked it up.

"*. . . as one caused by a blow or formed by a tumor or cyst.* What's that last word?"

I shrugged.

"Look up *tumor*," Elizabeth said.

And I did:

> **tu mor** (too͞'mər) n. 1. a swelling on some part of the body; esp., a mass of new tissue growth independent of its surrounding structures, having no physiological function; neoplasm; tumors are classified as benign or malignant

Silently, I copied the words, one at a time. *Benign*, *malignant*, both with their g's followed by n's—one hidden and silent, the other lodged harshly in the center. I knew somehow these were the key words.

"What does it mean?" Elizabeth asked.

"I don't know." I stared at my bookshelf, squinting until I lost focus. Above my desk, the TransAlt maps curled and flattened in the draft from the window, the little streets rising and falling, like they were breathing.

"Look up *surgery*," Elizabeth said.

"You look it up."

I shoved the dictionary at her and pushed my head under the pillow. Quiet and cushioned from the world outside, the new words pulsed against my skull: *growth, bulge, tumor.* Elizabeth pushed the dictionary aside and let it fall to the floor with a thud. I didn't turn over. Before long, I felt her curl up next to me.

"Can I sleep with you?" she asked softly.

Mama loved when we slept together. It usually meant that we

were getting along. It also meant that she could prolong the bedtime ritual, tuck us in with stories about when we were babies, the way we seemed to look out for each other in the world even as infants, how she could see our personalities forming almost from the beginning. Her voice would grow more and more faint. Then, when one or the other of us yawned and grew sleepy, she'd wrap her arms around our shoulders, and pull us into a giant three-way hug. She never left us right away; she'd linger in the doorjamb, watching as we squirmed into place, witnessing our ease with each other's bodies as the covers took shape, admiring that she'd made two such perfect little girls.

The next morning, Elizabeth and I begged Nick to let us stay home from school.

"I don't feel well,"

"Me either."

"I might even throw up." I said.

"You can't go see your mother if you're sick," Nick said.

Elizabeth pleaded in tears. "Please don't make us go to school."

"Okay, okay, girls," he said, "just, you know, get dressed—we'll go visit."

At the hospital, Nick parked in the lot marked "Doctors and hospital staff only."

"The little rules don't apply to me," he said when Elizabeth confronted him. He liked to see how much he could get away with, using freight elevators to avoid lobbies and cutting lines in the deli. But he would never speed or run a red light. He had respect for the rules of the road.

"Visiting hours aren't until ten," he said, "but let's see what we can do." He smoothed his shirt down into his khaki pants.

"Are we dressed all right?" Elizabeth asked. It frightened her that we'd been allowed to come to the hospital without any attention to our clothes. She'd fussed all morning over what to wear, trying on sundresses over turtlenecks.

Nick stopped and looked us up and down, spinning Elizabeth around as if she were on a runway. He watched her closely, narrowing his eyes until the lines around them deepened. His eyes met mine; he seemed momentarily to be asking for help. But before I could respond, he gathered himself. "I think we look great," he said at last, extending an elbow to each of us. He walked us to the side door and left us with instructions to stay put while he went around to the main entrance.

Elizabeth was furious. "Now where is he going?" She kicked at some roots under a shrub until the dirt flung up on her new Capezio dance shoes. She licked her thumb and rubbed the white leather. "I don't see why he gets to go in first," she said.

"Just shut up," I said. My palms were clammy. The smell of the tar in the parking lot made me nauseated. I was nervous, worried that I wouldn't know what to do in a hospital, or what to say to Mama.

The door released and Nick swept us in under his arm. "Three flights up," he said and began the climb two steps at a time. Elizabeth let the bottom of her bag strike each step until I came up from behind and grabbed one handle. When we got to the top of the stairs, Nick turned to wait for us. "Try to be cheerful," he said, "you know, for your mama—she might need a little cheering up."

The hallway of the hospital was bright but empty. There were metal carts of food, wet vegetables that smelled like bad breath, waiting outside a few of the rooms. Nurses darted in and out of open doors with pockets full of plastic and gauze. As we walked down a long corridor counting off room numbers and checking for Mama, I caught sight of one gaunt patient tented by a white sheet, her bare leg draped over the side of the bed.

When we arrived in the doorway of room 14 West, Mama was sitting up, waiting. She had on a blue-and-white-striped robe that I had never seen before. She adjusted the front and retied the belt as we entered. Her chest looked padded underneath the printed gown. She pulled a sheet up high on her waist. Her hair was arranged in a tangled ponytail that hung off to one side. Smiling as Nick had told her to, Elizabeth went straight to the bed and cozied up next to her. I felt a large hand on my back—Nick's pushing me forward. I was forced and awkward, as if in the presence of strangers.

"I'm feeling so much better," Mama announced, looking at Nick. She had a plastic bracelet on her arm. I stayed back, afraid of her dazed eyes and messy hair. She had applied too much blush. I sat in the beige, rubber-cushioned chair at the foot of the bed.

"Tell me some news from the outside world," Mama said.

"Well," Nick started, "you're sorely missed. The neighbors, the drivers, everyone's asking for you. Right, girls?"

"What did you tell them?" she asked.

"That you were here, having a minor procedure."

Mama nodded at him and then turned to us. "It's not a secret," she said, taking a sip of water from a straw. "I just don't know if it's anyone's business."

"I see my mother has already sent you some flowers," Nick said, plucking the card out from among a basket full of pink and white carnations. "You can always count on her to be there with a bouquet."

"I thought it was sweet," Mama said.

Elizabeth slid off the bed and went to retrieve our gifts and cards from the shopping bag. I could see how Nick stiffened each time she climbed on and off the mattress, but Elizabeth didn't notice.

"Lizzie, can you open it for me?" Mama asked. "I'm not supposed to move so much." She gestured toward her right arm. It was propped up on pillows with her hand above her elbow. The corner of a plastic sac hung out from under the sheet at the side of the bed. Hemovac, it said in black letters on the tab. It was dark with blood.

Elizabeth held one card open while Mama looked at the inside. The Magic Marker words. Hugs and kisses. Our careful, looping signatures. Mama patted the bed twice, motioning for me to join them. I moved toward Elizabeth.

"Come, get on the other side," Mama said, her bottom lip quivering. "But watch the IV stand."

I walked around the hanging plastic bags, sat down on the edge of the bed and lifted the tubing away from my legs. I was afraid to hug her. I had images of myself yanking the tube out of her arm, causing her to bleed, the fluid spilling onto the floor. I watched the sugary water drip down the tube, toward the needle and disappear behind the tape into her skin. She held each of our hands in her left one and rubbed her thumb across our knuckles.

"What I need you both to do," she said, in a mock whispering voice, "is cooperate with Nick. Men need more help than they let on. Just do everything he tells you, go to school, and look after him."

"When are you coming home?" Elizabeth asked.

"By the end of the week," Mama said.

I leaned in close. "Where's the tumor?" I asked.

Mama seemed startled, sat forward and shot a look at Nick. He stared back blankly.

"Who told you anything about a tumor?" she asked.

"I looked in the dictionary."

She softened. "The tumor's gone, honey. The doctor took it out."

"Where was it?"

"Here," she said, pointing to her right breast. "Right here." She patted her robe gently. "I'm fine now."

• • •

In the parking lot, Elizabeth attached herself to Nick, walking with her hand in his and questioning him nonstop. I dragged behind. So Mama had told Nick all about the tumor. She'd told him more than me, as if her tumor had been a secret between them. When it was just Elizabeth, Mama, and me, I was the one she told her secrets to. Elizabeth's thick ponytail swung side to side as she walked.

"Nick, is Mama in pain?" she asked.

Nick put his hand on the back of her neck. "No," he said, "these doctors are taking very good care of her."

"Maybe she should have more visitors?" Elizabeth suggested when we got to the car.

"No. Not at all," he said. "She's fine with just us looking after her."

"How do you know?" I said. "You haven't exactly known us forever." I could hear my teeth gnashing, my jaw clenched, in the long seconds of silence I'd made. I slammed the car door behind me and curled up in the backseat.

By the way Nick stomped around to the driver's side, I half expected him to explode at me. But he was silent and stayed silent all the way home. When we pulled into the driveway he turned around, his arm hugging the headrest, and looked right at me.

"We're all upset," he said, his brows arched high. "I think it is best if we try not to take it out on one another."

At 4:00, Samantha Shaptaw called to find out why I hadn't been at school. I stretched the phone cord through the pantry and sat in the stairwell.

"Mama had to have a tumor removed," I whispered.

"Oh," she said, drawing in breath between her teeth in a kind of hiss. "How bad is that?"

"I don't know," I said. "Ask your mom."

"What about your permission slip for that movie?" Samantha asked.

After hanging up the phone, I went upstairs and sat at my desk. I unfolded the letter about "And Then One Year" from Mr. McKinney, careful to keep it looking fresh. The prerequisite for getting your period involved your parents going to a screening of the period movie. *You are encouraged to attend the second viewing with your daughter. If you are unable to attend, please send a legal guardian.* A dotted line separated the notice about the movie from the permission slip. I cut along the tear-line and flattened out the creases. Then, after rummaging around in my cardboard box of important papers, I found an old spelling test Mama had signed. Carefully, I traced over her signature, practicing the slant of the F in Frances and the looped B in Burbank. I copied her name onto the permission slip, first in pencil, then in pen. Finally, I erased the faint shadow of pencil and brushed the eraser shavings onto the floor.

Downstairs, Nick was heating up dinner. He seemed distant, cloaked in a quiet brooding that I hadn't seen before. I felt bad for what I'd said, so I decided to help. I poured some frozen Tater Tots into the toaster oven and turned the dial to the right until the oven glowed red inside. Nick opened a can of peas and heated them on the stove. Elizabeth was busy digging in the kitchen drawer looking for batteries. I could see that she and Nick had forged some kind of bond in my absence.

"Will these work?" she asked and held up a new pack of double A's.

"They have to be bigger," Nick said, "check in the flashlight."

When she came back into the kitchen, there was a tape recorder tucked under her arm; the buttons were as big as piano keys. She looked over at me and smirked, tossing her hair confidently. "So

Mama doesn't miss anything," she said, resting the machine on the table.

I set the table for three, folding the paper towels in triangles the way Mama would have. I could never remember which direction the silverware went, something about the knife protecting the spoon, or the other way around.

As soon as we were seated, Elizabeth pressed the red record button and said, "Talk."

"Mmm," Nick said as he chewed his meatloaf.

"Yum," I said.

Elizabeth hit STOP. "Have a *real* conversation."

"I don't want to."

"You're ruining it." She slumped on her stool and pouted. "I'm starting to hate you."

"Real nice," I said, holding my gaze, hoping to make her feel guilty.

"Come on," Nick said with his mouth full, "the last thing we need right now is a fight."

The wooden table had a wobble and Elizabeth and I waged a silent battle with our elbows, each willing the table to rest on her side.

"Can we start over?" Elizabeth asked, holding the reverse button on the recorder until it began screeching.

She held it out to me. "Talk about school."

"I didn't go today," I said.

"Yesterday."

"Nothing happened."

"That's a lie," Elizabeth said.

I glared at her, horrified that she would threaten to reveal my secret about the period movie in front of Nick.

"How about we just talk about this nice dinner we're having,"

Nick said. "I'll start . . ." He straightened into his six-foot frame and combed his hair with his fingers as if he were about to be filmed. His long-sleeved shirt was unbuttoned, his white T-shirt showing. He ran his tongue over his teeth and smiled his warm smile. Elizabeth pressed RECORD and held the silver and black box up to his face.

"Act natural," she mouthed.

"Well, Frances," he started, "we're having some meatloaf tonight. Lainey DeWitt made so much, you'll even get to try this batch." Nick talked easily, citing the specifics of his day, as if Mama were right there with us, her face cupped in her hands, smiling wide at him.

Even though she was only going to be gone four days, my mind had taken to playing tricks on me. In the middle of a sentence, while walking down the stairs or brushing my teeth, suddenly the question would overtake me. What did she look like? Just for a second or two, I would forget. Sometimes, a particular feature would disappear—her nose, her hands—and I would have to focus deep within me to bring it back. The house felt large without her. There were new sounds and shadows at every turn. I narrowed my eyes at the empty place setting, the bulb from the overhead lamp shining hot on the seat of her chair. On a normal day, she might have been perched there, drawing each of us out, as insistent as the conductor of the band, reminding us to chime in with the news of our day. We still needed coaxing to talk in front of Nick. Everything here was still new.

"And Tilden has volunteered to clean up," Nick concluded and winked at me.

"Cut." Elizabeth hit STOP. She set the recorder on her lap and jabbed me with her elbow. I pinched her thigh under the table. When Nick wasn't looking, Elizabeth punched me hard in the arm. But I didn't make a sound.

• • •

On Wednesday, Ms. Zimmerman stopped me on my way to lunch and asked how I was feeling. She removed her dark-rimmed glasses, revealing a red indentation on the bridge of her nose. "Now, Tilden," she said, quietly in a no-nonsense voice, "you may not realize this, but this kind of thing has an effect on the whole family. Have you felt the effects? Any pain?"

I shook my head and tried to listen. All the while, I was watching over her shoulder for a sign of my classmates. I wanted someone to interrupt, to make her stop talking.

"Sometimes it hurts those of us on the outside even more because we feel helpless. Sometimes we blame ourselves. Was it something I did? But it's not." Ms. Zimmerman forced a smile. "It's nothing anyone can control. That's what's so hard about it." There was a strange, faraway look on her face.

At lunch, the girls at my table suggested just the opposite. They all watched *Charlie's Angels* on TV, had even adopted the hairstyles. They were looking for causes, for clues. Somehow, somewhere along the way, someone was culpable. If they could pin it down, they could prevent a procedure from happening in their families.

Jill Switt wanted to know if we had been drinking the water. Her reddish brown hair was brushed back in a Farrah Fawcett feather. "Do you have asbestos in your cellar?" she asked.

Susie Rhombus's jet black hair was half-feathered, half-rolled back like Jaclyn Smith's. She asked how much red meat we ate a week. She'd heard that hot dogs were particularly bad.

"And catsup," someone added.

"And coffee," Libbie Gorin chimed in from the next table. "Anything with caffeine."

Jill continued. "Did your mother smoke? Did anyone around her smoke?"

Susie shifted in her seat. Her father and her two older brothers all smoked.

"Cigarette smoke is definitely the worst," Christy Diamo added, tossing her stick straight hair—a longer version of the Kate Jackson wedge.

Jill wanted to know if I had been breast fed.

"Oh give me a break, Jill, that has nothing to do with cancer," Samantha said.

It was the first I'd heard the word *cancer*. A slow panic grew inside me, like gallons of toxic tap water sloshing up and choking me. Grandma had once smoked. I had been breast fed. We probably did have asbestos in our cellar. If not now, then at one of those places down South. We'd been remiss. Other families drank bottled water. Ate cauliflower and broccoli. My eyes welled up.

The table got quiet. We picked carefully through our lunches. I willed myself not to cry by counting the butter pats on the ceiling. But the sight of Elizabeth in the lunch line brought my attention back. She waved from across the cafeteria. It was a low wave from the hip. Usually we weren't nice to each other in public, and at school, we acknowledged each other only to point out what the other one was wearing that did not belong to her. But now, our eyes locked for an extra-long second before she clasped her fingers tight around the tray and headed for the milk cart.

In the girls' room, I locked myself safely inside the stall, sat down on the toilet with my clothes on and waited. The smell from the green linoleum floors was of wet chlorine and muddy shoes. I heard the outer door open and slam. One navy Ked appeared under the bathroom stall, a smilie face on the toe. Samantha. She slid a large book wrapped in a plastic shopping bag under the door.

"It's my mom's," she said. "Don't let anyone see it."

I pulled the book out of the bag and set it on my lap. *Our Bodies,*

Ourselves, it was called. The cover was white with a large black-and-white photograph of older and younger women standing together, holding signs. Inside, was a collage of women with severe parts in their hair: women running, studying, hugging, jumping rope, crossing the finish line, doing backbends and self-defense. Slowly, I turned to the table of contents and realized that I didn't know what I was looking for. I flipped through the pages looking at the diagrams and sketches of naked women, some with their legs spread wide enough to see their insides. There were photos of real women, unlike the paper dolls in the menstruation pamphlet. On one page was a picture of a bloody woman, dead on the floor of a motel room. On another, a woman with only one breast and a tattoo as a scar. All around me walls were turning, the lights buzzed. I put my head on my knees.

"Are you okay?" Samantha asked.

"Uh huh."

"My mom says you could come with us to the movie on Saturday," she said. "If you want."

On Thursday after school, Nick left Elizabeth and me alone at the hospital with Mama while he went on some errands. Elizabeth brought Mama some keepsakes from her bedroom at home. She stacked fashion magazines on the windowsill and hung a sachet of potpourri from the IV stand. She filed and painted each nail on Mama's hands and feet. I was jealous of her usefulness, and of her ease with Mama's body. In her soft denim dress and bandanna on her head, Elizabeth suddenly seemed more like Mama than Mama herself.

I stared at Mama's chest, but couldn't see anything through the layers of bandages and hospital gowns. I had stayed up late the night before trying to read *Our Bodies, Ourselves.* There was a section on women's breasts I kept turning to. But mostly the words washed over and confused me. I made a list of questions and fell asleep with the book open next to me.

"Mama," I started, "is there a hole where they . . . "

"Not really," Mama said. She tapped the place next to her and told us to sit down. "Girls, they removed my whole breast," she said, "they had to—so the disease wouldn't spread."

"They did?" Elizabeth asked, staring suspiciously at Mama's chest.

I waited for Mama to look at me.

"Do you have cancer?" I asked.

She nodded. "I *had* cancer. And I'm going to have a little chemotherapy as a follow-up," she said, "just to be sure they got it all."

"You had cancer?" Elizabeth asked.

"Don't worry," Mama said, "I'm fine now."

Elizabeth released Mama's hair from the ponytail holder and worked at the tangles with a brush. Her normally blond hair looked darker against the blue hospital gown as it fell around her shoulders. To keep it from tangling, she let Elizabeth and me practice our braiding. We each took a side, competing for speed and style, and held up our finished ropes like reins. Mama's hair felt fine and cool as I let it slip between my fingers. I pulled tight across for a box knot and wrapped Band-Aids around the ends. We weren't really looking at each other. Every time I caught Elizabeth's eye, she'd turn away.

The door of the room swung open, startling the three of us. "You look like Bo Derek, Mrs. B., " the doctor said, clutching his clipboard.

Mama blushed. He was younger and even more handsome than

the doctor on *The Love Boat*. He had red, curly hair and blue eyes. His name was Dr. O'Connor. He wore a tie under his white coat. I didn't know whether or not to like him. He leaned against the heater, crossing one foot over the other.

"There are some exercises I need to show you," he said. "They'll help you recover. Do you want me to go over them now or . . . " He looked at Elizabeth and me uneasily, then back to Mama.

Mama nudged Elizabeth and me off the bed, motioning us to sit in the chair by the window. We squeezed into it together and watched as the doctor demonstrated the exercises.

"Okay. First do this . . . " He took a deep breath in through his nose and let it out through his mouth. "Deep-sea diving," he called it. "This will help maintain full lung expansion." He tapped his chest and looked around for smiles. "Also," he continued, "you'll need to strengthen that right arm." He opened and closed his fist in a pulsing motion. He waited for Mama to try it.

She touched her thumb to the tips of her fingers, as if working a hand puppet.

"Very good." He smiled and nodded. "I have an idea," he said and turned to face us. "Do you girls have any Play-Doh at home?"

Elizabeth nodded her head, even though we didn't; she hadn't played with it since the second grade. She was always pretending in order to get approval or attention. This time Mama didn't even seem to notice.

"Take a good amount and make it into a ball," Dr. O'Connor said. "Then, squeeze it gently." He cupped his hands together around air. When he was finished with the demonstration, he wrote something on the chart and clipped the pen back in his pocket. "These first two weeks are crucial to recovering your mobility," he said and tapped Mama's foot through the blankets. He turned back on his way out the door. "We'll have you doing laps in no time."

Mama tried to take a deep breath and let it out. "Want to practice with me?" she asked.

We spilled back onto the bed, breathing quickly and flapping our hands like so many frantic birds.

Friday, when we got to her room, Mama was gone. The sheets had been changed and the blankets were folded on the end of the bed; the steel pans and trays looked clean and especially cold. I froze, terrified. Something had gone wrong. Nick touched his hands to our shoulders and walked quickly toward the nurses' station. Elizabeth stood against the windowsill eyeing the stack of cards near the air vent. The afternoon sun reflected off an adjacent room and made the windows appear hazy. Long, long, long minutes. Then, before either of us could say a word, Mama came in the door behind me.

"Surprise," she said.

It hadn't occurred to me that her absence could be a good sign. She had on sneakers and cotton stretch pants under her robe. Someone had pulled her hair back in a tight bun. Her face was all excitement and anticipation.

"I'm ready to go home," she said, beaming.

Nick looked calmer when he returned, the head nurse alongside him with a wheelchair. Mama took her place in the chair while Elizabeth and I stuffed the edges around her lap with her belongings.

"What about the magazines?" Elizabeth asked. "And the flowers?"

"Let someone else enjoy them," Mama said.

We left everything but the potpourri, which Mama looped around the nurse's wrist almost playfully as she wheeled her into the elevator.

PRIVACY

Despite Mr. McKinney's attempts at discretion, a week after the permission slips were distributed, everyone in school knew about "And Then One Year." The secrets that the sixth-grade girls had been keeping, smug and grown up, were suddenly wielded against us. The lower grade girls were relentless. They spit out the names of each private part as if it were a dirty word. With every gesture, they flaunted their smooth, clean bodies and made obscene gestures at us in the halls.

Elizabeth quickly emerged as a leader. She stole my copy of *Growing Up and Liking It* and read it aloud to a mixed group at lunch. Everywhere she went, gusts of laughter rose up around her. Terms like vulva and fallopian tube became passwords for all the new clubs.

"She's just jealous," Samantha said, twisting her bandanna tighter around her head. So jealous became my defense; it didn't really hide the humiliation, but could be used against younger girls and boys of all ages.

On the bus, Elizabeth joined forces with the same boys who had been tormenting her the week before. "Oily, pimple face," they shouted at me and Samantha. "B.O." They pinched their noses. "P.U."

When we got to our stop, I stuck my legs across the aisle to prevent Elizabeth from getting off the bus.

"Give it back," I demanded.

Elizabeth kicked my shins and pushed by me. The bus driver glared at us in the large mirror and waited before opening the door. We stood, pressed together in the little staircase, until the driver cranked the metal arm.

"I'm going to kill you," I said.

Elizabeth took off running, the boys on the bus cheering her on from a distance. I chased her up the driveway to the garage where a group of TransAlt drivers were gathered over an engine. She ran behind the car and shouted, "Tilden has hairy pits."

I turned my back and pretended to walk away. When I heard her come up behind me, I dropped my books and lunged at her feet, bringing her down to the pavement on the driveway. She fell hard, scraping one arm from elbow to wrist, and lay there for a moment, stunned.

Nick rushed out from the garage, kneeled by Elizabeth's side, and wiggled her arm gently to see if it was broken.

I stood over them, watching. "I'm sorry," I said. My pants were scuffed from where I'd hit the ground, but not torn.

"Go away," she said.

I picked up Elizabeth's books first, then mine, and stood off to the side. Elizabeth sat with her legs crossed and held her bloody arm away from her clothes while Nick picked a piece of gravel out of her hand. Lainey DeWitt brought out the first aid kit. She held the hydrogen peroxide in one hand, her long, painted nails curling around the width of the bottle, and poured it over Elizabeth's entire arm. The wound bubbled, turning white then yellow, as Nick blew on it. He helped Elizabeth to her feet and wiped her tears with his grease-stained thumb.

All of the commotion in the driveway brought Mama to the back door in her bathrobe. She'd been sleeping; her hair was matted against one side of her face.

"What happened?" she asked, squinting at the afternoon light.

"She tripped me," Elizabeth said.

"Now, now," Nick said, "I'm sure it was an accident."

"No, it wasn't."

"Is that true, Tilden?" Mama asked.

"Sort of . . ." I said. "I didn't mean it. She stole something of mine." I was frightened by the way Mama looked, but too scared I'd be punished to dwell on it.

"Go upstairs," Mama said, "I'll talk to you later."

I lingered in the hall on the way to my room and listened to Elizabeth's accusations over the running water. Nick said something about making a sling out of one of my shirts and made her laugh. The TV drowned out the rest of Mama and Elizabeth's conversation. I turned to my homework and waited.

Two hours later, Mama knocked lightly at my door and popped her head inside. "Aren't you coming down for dinner?"

I looked up, searching her face for some sign of forgiveness. "Is Elizabeth okay?" I asked and stacked my books at my feet.

Mama nodded, watching me.

"I didn't mean to . . ."

"I know."

She walked across the floor, to the edge of my bed, and placed the menstruation booklet on top of my stack. Her movements were slow and deliberate. She was out of breath from climbing the stairs.

"Why didn't you tell me?" she asked.

I shrugged, looking everywhere but at her.

"Do you want me to call Mrs. Shaptaw about the movie?"

"I don't really want to go."

"Of course you do," Mama said. She tugged me toward her, bringing my head to rest against her left shoulder. When I hugged her, gently, I could hear the bandages and tape crinkle beneath her robe.

"Keep notes in this little book. We can talk about it afterward." She handed me a pocket-sized calendar, one I could use to keep track of my period someday. There were extra blank pages at the back. "Elizabeth's turn will come," she said, "you just wait and see."

On Friday, Samantha asked me if I wanted to spend the whole weekend at her house. She said her mother would take us to Friendly's for ice cream after the movie, the way she usually did after band concerts.

"How come?" I asked.

"I don't know," she said and looked away. I watched her, hoping for her to look back. Something was weird. It wasn't like her not to know everything.

While I was packing an overnight bag, Elizabeth came in my room and sprawled out on my bed. She had a square of gauze taped over her cut. I kept waiting for her to say something, but instead she sat there braiding the fringe on my pillows and kicking her feet against the bed frame. I wasn't going to be the one to talk first. I swung the bag over my shoulder and headed for the door.

"Have fun," she said, looking up at me at last. "You can tell me about it later if you want."

As parents went, Ivy Shaptaw was a bit younger than most. And wilder. Ivy was spindly as a spider, with long skinny limbs and curly black hair like electrician's wire. She had a way about her, always turning normal conversations into something funny, half secrets that would send Mr. Shaptaw from the room, his fist to his mouth, coughing. That's when we knew it was dirty. She'd follow him out of the room, saying the thing over and over, until he bent around a corner, out of sight. When the guys at the lot talked like that, Mama called it innuendo.

But it wasn't just her parents who indulged. Samantha's brothers had made a peep show out of the Land-O-Lakes package and hung it on the fridge. The knees of the Indian woman were sliced off and pasted behind the package of butter she held up in front of her. The sides of that little box at her chest were cut free by a razor and bent up to show her knees, turned into breasts, with inked nipples. I couldn't imagine the Land-O-Lakes lady looking like that in anyone else's kitchen.

In the bathroom there was a deodorant bottle, that when opened the right way, would release a huge pink penis, almost leaping off its spring. You had to push hard on the tip to stuff it back in its jar. The Shaptaws had pictures of naked bodies, women mostly, out in the open. But one postcard, taped to the front of an old-fashioned scale in the corner of their downstairs bathroom showed fruit. From a distance, it was just a nice orange cantaloupe sliced open, but up close, its interior was dangerous: wet and red, the seeds making folds in an oval slit. Leaning hard against the opening was a banana, half out of its peel, the tip slightly curved. *Wish you were here*, it said on the other side.

Before dinner, Samantha and I rummaged through the Shaptaw's bookshelves, looking for sex in magazines and '60s records. We found an old porn novel behind some medical reference books. It was about a young servant girl who gets licked by a dog named Gustav while the husband of the house watches, his wife asleep in the next room. We read parts out loud, laughing. Then we decided to write our own story. *Erotica,* Samantha called it. We weren't sure exactly what it meant, but it had to involve animals, we thought because of Lance Engler. Jill Switt had told us that Lance had fingered his cat and we were both disgusted and intrigued. When a group of us confronted him in the lunchroom he said there wasn't anything nasty about it.

"I am an erotic being," he announced.

I think that was when Samantha decided to like him, but she didn't tell me then.

Piled high, the artichokes looked like a pagan crown when Ivy brought them from the kitchen on a tray with seven finger cups full of melted butter, shining like coins. In the middle of the table was an empty bowl for the throwaways. I had no idea how these green sculptures were to be eaten, so I watched closely as the Shaptaws each peeled away the first level of leaves. Samantha dunked her first leaf in the butter and stripped it clean, leaving her teeth prints on the leftover leaf, and some leftover leaf in her teeth.

The Shaptaws always played strange games at the dinner table. That night was no exception. Stephen, the oldest Shaptaw son, started us off on some palindromes.

Come shall I stroke your whatever darling whatever your stroke I shall come.

Mr. Shaptaw coughed into his napkin. We moved inward on our artichokes, fingers damp and slippery with butter, as we took turns thinking up words and sentences that were the same frontward as backward.

"Artie Choke too small to choke Artie," Samantha said. She had a buttery sheen on her chin.

"Does it count?" I asked, "with two different *to*'s?"

The leaves got thin and light, and Stephen and Seth pretended to be green lizards, the leaves adhering to their tongues. In his attempt to outdo his older brother, Seth got too close and touched his tongue to my ear.

"Seth licked Tilden," Stephen said boldly. "Seth has a crush on Tilden."

"Yeah right," he said in a way that hurt my feelings.

"Here she is," said Ivy, holding up a pale and slimy center and gazing into her husband's gray-green eyes.

Stephen spooned around the coating of hair that was gathered at the top of the heart. "Don't eat the pubes," he said and flung a clump of hair onto Sam's plate.

"Enough," Mr. Shaptaw said, his cheeks flushed.

That night, Samantha and I put a chair against her bedroom door and hid in the closet. She explained how the saleswoman at Macy's had taken her measurements and calculated her band and cup size with a special formula.

"Do mine," I said and held my arms out from my body. Samantha wrapped the tape measure around my chest, making sure to keep it level, and held her thumb at the line. She did the math in her head, adding the number six to the number on the tape and subtracting one.

"We're the same size," she declared.

This seemed impossible to me from the looks of things, but I didn't question her. Earlier that month, Samantha had won a contest for naming over thirty uses of math in our lives. I imagined going to the mall with her, the saleswoman mistaking us for sisters, ringing up our equipment together, and putting it in a bag with one staple through the receipt.

Outside, Samantha's brothers were wedging a boomerang under her bedroom door, making it difficult for us to get out. She settled quietly into this fact, pulling me down to a sitting position in the bottom of her closet, her neatly hung pants and shirts brushing our backs. We became saliva sisters that night, touching our spongy tongues together for over a minute.

The school looked different on Saturday. It seemed bigger.

"They never had anything like this for us," Ivy said as she flipped through the information in the handouts. I remembered what Samantha had told me about her mother faking her period throughout high school. As an adult, Ivy would announce hers, darting through the house in a towel searching frantically for a pad. With Mama it was different. She kept everything neatly tucked away, a secret. The only hint was a red-rimmed tube of cardboard in the trash, or the little string I could sometimes see through her nylons.

I wished that mothers hadn't been required to go. They were so silly, so sentimental greeting each other at the back of the auditorium. The first words out of each mother's mouth were "Can you believe it's almost that time!" But the daughters didn't leave their sides; they nodded at each other and looked away. I stood behind the Shaptaws until Ivy reached back and looped her arm through mine.

When it was time to begin, Ms. Penny called the group to order. Ivy sat down between us despite Samantha's protests.

"The film you are about to see will explain the physical and emotional changes that a girl goes through during puberty." Ms. Penny paused. "Are there any questions?"

No one spoke. She flipped the light switch. The projector whirled and clicked at the back of the room.

"There will be time for more discussion at the end," she said, as the opening credits began to roll in squat black letters on the white screen.

The film was boring and relatively straightforward, but still I took down the important points. I had read all about menstruation in *Our Bodies, Ourselves* anyway, so this seemed really hokey to me at first. I knew Mama would have written down every word, drawing time lines and stick figures. I felt Ivy watching me. I wanted it to seem as if I knew more than I did. The film said that when it finally did happen, it would reoccur every twenty-eight days. And that everyone's body was different, therefore menstruation could begin anywhere between the ages of ten and eighteen.

"Duh," I wrote in my datebook and passed it to Samantha.

"Double Duh," she wrote back.

I still didn't know about the starting and stopping. What exactly brought it on? When did it end? After the film was over I passed Samantha a note asking her to find out how we could tell when it was coming. Ivy intercepted and volunteered to ask. She stood up for her delivery, a long rambling question that mentioned a few of her own experiences. She was speaking quickly and gesturing alternately toward her breasts and her uterus. Samantha slunk low in her chair.

Ms. Penny, cited the warning signs—"secondary sex characteristics," she called them—the enlargement of breasts, rounding of hips, pimples, and the beginning of pubic hair and body odor. Ms. Penny suggested that we all order a Starter Kit from Personal Products in New Jersey to have nearby just in case. I wrote Starter Kit? in my notebook.

In the end, I suppose the mother rule was a good one because as we were filing out of the auditorium, Christy Diamo, who was known to have the largest breasts in our class, fainted. As she folded to the ground, I thought about the elk that I'd seen in *National Geographic*, the way they fall as they die, on their knees as if in prayer.

Christy went chalk white and sweaty before her mother was able to shuffle her out to the girls' room. What happened after that, none of us knew. Was this the initiation, what it meant to bleed once a month, to carry water weight and toiletries?

In the car, I read the pamphlet about the Starter Kit—maxis, minis, belts, and panty liners. Ivy offered to stop at the drugstore so that we could each get a box of sanitary napkins. I wanted to wait for the official kit.

Ivy ran her hand over my head and brought an open palm to my cheek. "Whatever you want, sweetie," she said.

"I want to go home."

"What about Friendly's?" Samantha asked.

"You didn't want to stay at Sam's?" Mama asked, sliding me one of her pillows as I climbed in bed next to her.

Nick brought apple cider in wineglasses on a silver tray. "Room service," he announced and closed the door firmly behind him.

"Well?" she asked. "How was it?"

I presented her with my notes. She put on her reading glasses, the kind with magnifying lenses that made her eyes look large and shiny, like a horse's. She read with her pencil, leaving a light trace of coal next to my words.

Watching her, I thought about her body and wondered if I would ever see it again. Just last month, she'd let me sit on the wicker hamper while she took her bath. The tub was long, with ceramic feet, like paws. She covered her pubic hair with a navy washcloth, which sometimes floated above and away. Her breasts, large with mahogany nipples, looked lighter under water. Suddenly, I felt like crying, but I squeezed my hands into a fist to stop myself.

"Did Mrs. Shaptaw answer your questions?" she asked.

"Sort of," I said.

"What else would you like to know?"

About you . . . I wanted to ask. Did you wait until you were married? Did it hurt? And, Are you okay? Will you still get your period?

"Can I take baths when I . . . get it?" I decided to ask.

"Of course," she said, suddenly distracted by her own need for one. She ran her hands across her slick scalp, stopping to massage her forehead. "Can you help me wash my hair?" she asked.

Mama balanced herself precariously on the edge of the tub and wrapped the shower curtain around her neck and shoulders. Her hands looked pale and fragile as she gripped the tub tightly on either side of her. After I got the water to the just-right temperature, Mama eased forward and let her hair fall into the wake of the spout. Her face was red when she sat up. She swayed a bit and steadied herself against me. She brought her fist to her face and pressed it against her forehead.

"That Herbal Essence is strong stuff," she joked.

I lathered the shampoo between my hands first before putting it in her hair and working the bubbles into a foamy helmet. When it came time to rinse, Mama pointed to a plastic cup on the sink. I poured the water over her until it ran clear down her neck, the strands squeaking against my fingers. When I finished, I towel-dried her hair and wrapped it into a terry cloth crown at the top of her head.

CHORES

After two weeks, Mama stopped wearing her bathrobe around the house and put on a new three-piece sweatsuit that she'd gotten from our next door neighbor, Mrs. Teuffel, as a get-well-soon present. It had large, symmetrical pockets on the shirt and a matching, zip-up jacket with a hood. She looked beautiful that morning when she walked into the kitchen, a gust of peach, her shoelaces flapping with each step. Nick got down on one knee and tied the laces in double knot.

"We're off to see the Mosquitoes," she said. That's what she called the blood doctors—the ones in charge of the chemotherapy. I pictured them thin and pale with long gangly arms and receding hairlines.

"How long are you going to be gone?" I asked.

She smiled. "Just long enough for the two of you to clean up this house."

Mama drew a haphazard line down the center of a sheet of paper and wrote our names at the top. She knew how to balance our responsibilities to help keep the peace. We were both in charge of starting the laundry and washing the stairs. I had been asked to vacuum and Elizabeth was to load the dishwasher.

Elizabeth scowled at the list. "This will take forever."

"Please don't talk back," Mama said. "Just do what I ask."

Neither of us said another word. We stood around the kitchen, staggered apart from each other like chess pieces. Mama walked to the fridge, took out a bottle of milk, and poured three large glasses.

"I don't like milk," Elizabeth said under her breath.

Mama took long careful sips, picking her glass up and putting it down each time. She pushed at her sweatsuit bottoms with her toe, her pale shin peeking out between the squeeze of the elastic grip and her socks. Her hair was clipped up, the ends tucked under and pinned—the way she'd always done it to clean the house or when she was in a hurry.

Nick pulled the car around to the back door, got out and leaned against the hood. His mouth was drawn into a worried line. He made a Y with his thumb and pointer and rubbed his forehead. Mama drank down the rest of her milk and set the glass gently in the sink. While she dug in her pocketbook for her frosted lipstick, Elizabeth and I tilted our glasses in unison and slowly, silently poured the milk down the drain. By the time Mama got to the door, Nick had jogged up the stairs to meet her. He seemed formal in his navy blue blazer, as if on a job, guiding her by the elbow and opening doors.

Out the window, Mama looked smaller than I had ever seen her. She walked across the yard, watching each step, and sat carefully, her left hand holding onto the door and then the dash as she lowered herself into the car. There was some fumbling in the front seat before Nick started the engine. I could tell that they were arguing over the seat belt. He pulled the belt out wide and then wrapped it around her stiff and defiant body. As they drove away, Nick gave a quick, happy honk and Mama waved, small, with her fingers from a bent elbow. Halfway down the driveway, I saw her slip the shoulder strap under her arm.

"I call it," Elizabeth said and raced for the beanbag chair in the TV room. She startled me and I ran after her, my heart racing. Usually we battled it out. One got the chair, the other got the controls. This was only fair, Mama assured us. A compromise. Though she never understood why we couldn't just share.

Elizabeth turned on the television while I struggled to get the long and unwieldy vacuum cleaner out of the hall closet. For more drama, I let the carpet attachment bang hard against the wall as I dragged it out. Elizabeth ignored me and turned up the volume. With the tubing around my neck, and the extra pieces under my arm, I thumped the vacuum down next to her. I looked around for an outlet, walking back and forth in front of the television. Finally, Elizabeth pulled the beanbag chair right up to the TV and stared into the screen.

"You're breaking the rule," I said. "You're going to go blind."

Mama had a four-foot rule for the TV which she enforced with stories about migraines and blindness.

"Like I care," she said.

I turned on the vacuum and made parallel passes across the carpet, under the couch and the coffee table, purposely sucking up thumb tacks and pennies. Elizabeth turned up the volume and pressed her ear to the TV. I thrust the attachment up against her chair. She didn't respond. When I rolled the vacuum into the hall, she pulled the plug.

"Put it back," I shouted.

"Can't hear you," she called over the TV.

"Plug in the vacuum cleaner," I insisted, leaning against the wall and waiting.

She lowered the volume. "What did you say?"

"Elizabeth, please put the plug back in."

"Okay," she said. "At the next commercial."

I gave up and stormed to Mama and Nick's room at the back of the house. Mama's room had never been off-limits to us before, and that didn't change when we moved in with Nick. But after Mama's procedure, I knew without ever being told that I was not to go in unless I needed to. There were things in there now—paper bags and pill bottles with labels from the Pharmacy, gooey salves and bandages—things I knew she wouldn't want me to see. Also, she wouldn't want me to walk in on her. I lived simultaneously with the fear and hope of seeing Mama's scar. I thought that if I could just see it once, then maybe everything would go on normally. And at the same time I was terrified.

I went straight to the bathroom and stopped short. In Atlanta, I always knew what I would find in there. But Mama had become more of a mystery since she'd started sharing a bathroom with Nick. He had strange toiletries, brown soap and dark bottles with emblems on the labels. The whole room smelled like mouthwash. Nick's socks were slung, dirty-toe out, over the side of the shower stall. Around the adjustable shower head was a pair of underpants that looked like a slingshot. My eyes darted around the room searching for familiarity.

I opened the storage cabinet behind the door. Mama had lined the shelves with scented paper. Lily of the valley. A plastic bag full of cotton balls leapt out at me. Her hot pink hair dryer was propped up next to a bin of vitamin samples. I was surprised by how jumbled things looked; when we first moved in, Mama had arranged everything in little plastic organizers. She didn't own much jewelry, but she kept her pendants and clip-on earrings in a Tupperware cup. I swirled my finger around in the cool metals and stones. It sounded as if I were stepping on broken glass.

Before I knew it, I was pulling out a bra and putting it around my waist, hooking the clasp where I could see it, twisting it around, over my clothes and putting my arms through the straps. I slipped a pair of socks into each side and studied my profile in the mirror. I looked like an overstuffed chair. I had waited too long to ask Mama for my first bra, had to stand by and watch as Samantha began wearing hers, a pink rose stitched at the center.

"You don't have boobs." Elizabeth was leaning against the doorway, watching me coldly.

"I know."

She snapped the bra strap hard against my back. "What are you doing with Mama's private stuff?"

I crawled quickly out of the bra, avoiding myself in the mirrors. One pair of socks rolled under the tub. While I bent to get it, my face pulsing against the cold tiles of the floor, Elizabeth returned the bra, folding it back under itself, and putting it in the correct spot. Then, she turned and left without a word. I realized with a start, that she had been there before me. How much more did she know?

When I resurfaced from Mama and Nick's room, I heard Elizabeth downstairs in the basement starting the laundry. Washing the clothes was our favorite chore, one which gave us a chance to explore the storage areas and dark corners of the basement where Nick kept things he didn't want us to see. I sat on the bottom step and watched as Elizabeth sorted the clothes, tossing whites and darks into separate piles on either side of her. The clothesline was covered with TransAlt work shirts, making the laundry room look like the garage on payday—a sea of orderly green tops.

Elizabeth scooped up the whites in her arms, dropping a tube sock and undershirt, and stuffed the load into the washing machine. I picked up the stray clothes and threw them into the rising water. Elizabeth closed the lid and looked at me. Without saying a word, we hurried to the far room where, on a bottom shelf, next to the paint cans and under a coiled garden hose, Nick kept a box of old

Playboy magazines. Elizabeth unearthed the box and pulled out a stack. She handed me one and we crouched next to each other, flipping through the pages.

Carla Alexander was my favorite centerfold. She wanted to be a veterinarian. She liked photography, horses, and coffee. She was Miss August—straddling a pitch fork and wearing a pair of leather chaps with nothing underneath. Her handwriting was large with rounded vowels and consonants that dipped outside the lines. Her nipples stuck out like hard candies. Even when I twisted and pulled them, my nipples never looked like that.

Elizabeth stood up and pretended to be Miss May, unzipping her jeans and opening all but one button on her shirt. She posed, arching her back against the cinder block wall, and wrapped the garden hose around her waist. The open end of the nozzle gaped near her zipper. She had the belly button of a grown woman, half inny, half outy, like a pout.

"Do you think Nick really reads these magazines?" she asked.

"Probably not anymore," I said, but couldn't be sure. I wondered if Mama knew about them. My skin chilled, sending goosebumps up my arms. There was so much we didn't know about Nick. Elizabeth and I looked at each other without blinking for a long minute, saying nothing.

We took extra care to put the magazines neatly away and moved to the second-floor staircase to finish the rest of the chores. Elizabeth crouched at the top, wringing a sponge over a bubbling bucket and streaking the black tread on the steps with soap. She gestured toward the plastic bowl filled with clear, hot water.

"You rinse."

We worked like that, in silence, moving down the stairs, for almost an hour. I kept refilling my bowl with new water, sometimes letting it spill and cascade down on her. Not enough to seem purposeful. When we finished, Elizabeth's jeans were soaked. My sleeves were heavy up to my armpits. We left sock prints across the kitchen floor.

At the cellar door, we stripped down to our panties and left our clothes in a wet heap. The clean steps squeaked under our bare feet as we ascended the stairs and ran naked down the hall to our bathroom. Exhilarated from having done what we were supposed to do, we climbed in the tub together. While Elizabeth worked the faucet, I poured in the shampoo and waited bent in half for it to bubble up over my thighs. As the steam fogged the mirrors, and the water rose around us, puckering our fingertips and the pads of our toes, we forgot about what was happening to Mama, forgot about our fears of Nick and who he was, even forgot our fights. We stayed this way a long time, waiting for Mama to climb the stairs and find us, wrinkled and pink, rinsing our heads under the faucet. We were too big really for a share bath, our knees knocking against each other, careful in the placement of our feet.

PART III

BLASPHEMY

Our neighbor, Mrs. Teuffel, wanted us to pray. She didn't say anything outright, but the glass tray of lasagna and aluminum-wrapped zucchini bread she brought over from next door one afternoon had a prayer on the note card. Nick laughed, dismissing the Almighty with a wave of his hand. But Elizabeth saved the card, slicing it free from the tape with her longest nail and bending it into her back pocket.

That night, before bed, I caught Elizabeth kneeling on her mattress with her eyes closed and head bent. She was whispering the prayer over and over again by memory.

Hail Mary, full of grace, the Lord is with thee.
Blessed art thou amongst women and
  blessed is the fruit of thy womb, Jesus.
Holy Mary, mother of God, pray for us sinners
  now and at the hour of our death.

I leaned against the doorjamb and watched as Elizabeth lifted her arm high in the air. She was holding a fistful of pale pink beads that reminded me of the 25¢ plastic jewelry in those machines in the grocery store. I listened to the rhythm of her words and waited for a break.

"What are you doing?" I asked.

Elizabeth ignored me, continuing on with her prayer, over and over, until she was left holding the beads upside down. Then, she looked at me seriously. "Mrs. Teuffel gave me this rosary," she said. "Did you know that the Virgin Mary's cousin, the one to first say this prayer, was named Elizabeth?"

"So? Lots of people are named Elizabeth."

"You don't know anything," she said, dipping her head and beginning again. "Hail Mary, full of grace . . ."

"I know you don't really know how to pray."

She stopped and glared at me. "Then how come Mrs. Teuffel's going to take me to church with her?"

"Stop acting so weird," I said. "Mama's going to know."

"How is she going to know?" Elizabeth held my eye a long time and then started over. "Hail Mary, full of grace, the Lord is with thee . . ."

We had only been to church a handful of times when we lived in Atlanta, and each time with our grandmother. Mama liked the idea of church more than the practice. Something about making a commitment to attend every week and risking disapproval when she didn't show up kept her away altogether. But now, I remembered that Elizabeth had always risen to the calling, weaving special colorful ribbons in her hair and polishing her shiny black shoes. She could sit taller and straighter than any other girl in a pew. This, she believed, brought her closer to God.

One of my last memories of our grandmother was that she bought us each a pair of white gloves with lace trim to wear to church on Easter. They fit perfectly and made my hands feel springy and clean. Elizabeth wore them every Sunday around the house. Mama suggested that we wear them on the day that Grandma and

Grandpa were buried even though she wouldn't let us go to the church.

Mama didn't talk much about their deaths. Maybe something about their dying together so suddenly helped Mama feel as if it were meant to be—the two of them in heaven, keeping each other company. "It's the way they would have wanted it," she said in a distant voice.

The Mosquitoes administered Mama's chemotherapy in a twenty-eight-day cycle. She had to go to the doctor's office twice a month, on the first and eighth days, but could rest the last two weeks of the month. I kept track of her cycle in the datebook she'd given me. The first week she was hit hard with nausea. She took to the TV room, which was transformed by the comforts she kept near her—a bucket, a box of tissues, a pitcher of water, and her favorite drinking glass. Nick even bought a set of plastic sheets to put under the blankets on the couch. She kept a bunch of projects nearby, hoping she'd feel well enough to catch up on some things she'd let slide. On the coffee table was a box of note cards, her address book, the checkbook she'd been meaning to balance, the photos that needed to be organized. But mostly she watched cooking shows, copying down recipes on the backs of envelopes and absently slipping them between the plastic sugar and flour canisters in the kitchen.

She was too sick to do all that tasting and preparing. Instead, she relied on habit—foods that required one big fix and then could be eaten day after day.

"Why can't we be normal and eat pancakes?" Elizabeth wanted to know.

On the morning of my thirteenth birthday, I woke up to the smell of steak and eggs wafting up the stairs from the kitchen. It was a Saturday and outside the bits of glass in the driveway shone in the morning sun. I pulled the Macy's bag out from the back of my closet, where I'd kept it since that day we'd gone shopping, slipped into my new clothes, and stood in front of the mirror. I didn't look thirteen. Even Elizabeth, who would be twelve two weeks later, had bigger boobs than I did. I tightened the straps on my overalls, hoping that the bib would help hide my flat chest. I styled my hair under with a round brush and flipped my bangs back with a curling iron. I had expected to wake up with a new body. A grown-up, teenage body with curves and hair. I looked exactly the same as I always had: skinny and disappointed.

Downstairs, Mama was engulfed in a cloud of kitchen smoke. She was holding a spatula in one hand and a fork in the other. When she hugged me, the implements clanked behind my head. "It isn't the same as a party," she said, "but it's the best I can do."

"That's okay," I said.

"So you don't mind a two-for-one with Elizabeth?"

I did, but didn't say so.

Nick came in from the yard with his arms behind his back. "Come sit down," he said and walked backwards toward the dining room table. Elizabeth and I each chose a side and he presented us with rosebuds, clipped prematurely from Mrs. Teuffel's rose bush. "A rose is a rose is a rose," he said and kissed the tops of our heads.

Elizabeth stuck the stem carefully behind her ear and sat up proudly, straightening her spine toward God. Mrs. Teuffel had offered Elizabeth piano lessons and I imagined the two of them on that hard bench, with their backs and shoulders lifted, wrists raised and fingers curled—every muscle poised to make music. Elizabeth had an ear, it turned out. She practiced twice a week next door on Mrs. Teuffel's upright piano and each time came home nearly singing the word of God.

"I can't believe this family," she said as we hovered over our birthday breakfast. "We don't even say grace."

"What do you care?" I asked.

"We're the only family I know who doesn't go to church on Sundays," she answered.

"The Shaptaws don't go to church," I said.

"They're heathens," Elizabeth said.

"They're Jewish," I said.

"Same thing."

Mama sat up and pointed her finger at Elizabeth. "I won't have that talk in this house," she said.

"Do you think we're going to hell?" I asked.

"Unless we repent for our sins," Elizabeth answered.

Mama swung around on her stool to face Elizabeth. "Where did you get that?" she asked. "Nick, do you hear this? To think, I've done my best to keep those rigid beliefs away from my children and here they are sitting at breakfast with us."

"Don't pay any attention to Mrs. Teuffel," Nick said. "She's harmless."

"When her beliefs end up at my table, it's high time I start paying attention," Mama said.

"They aren't her beliefs," Elizabeth said, "they're mine."

Mama took a deep breath. "There are many kinds of spirituality," she started, "what if we use the time before meals to explore what gives us peace in our lives?"

"Out loud?" Elizabeth asked.

"No, privately," Mama said. "Spirituality is a very private thing."

"Instead of grace?" Elizabeth asked.

"You can say grace if you like," Mama said. "Just don't be thanking God for a meal that *I* cooked."

I wanted to laugh, but the table got quiet. Elizabeth bowed her head. Nick cut his steak in quarters, exposing the undercooked center, and arranged them in clusters.

"Amen," Elizabeth said.

Nick picked up his head and clapped his hands together. "Cheer up," he said. "This is supposed to be a birthday celebration."

What did he know about our birthdays? In Atlanta, Mama had always decorated the door to our room with balloons, the same number as the years. When we got home from school, the balloons were tied on the mailbox or front fence and she'd let us release them into the sky. A gift to the gods, in celebration of the day we each arrived.

"Why isn't anyone eating?" Mama asked.

"It's too pink," I offered.

"Not really," Nick said, spearing a piece of steak and biting into it.

"Tilden thinks we eat too much red meat," Elizabeth said.

Mama set her fork on the plate and looked at me. "What?"

"I just thought that maybe that could be why you're sick."

"And tap water," Elizabeth said, "tell her we shouldn't drink the water."

Nick eyed the food on the table.

"I want to know who told you that," Mama said.

"Everyone."

"Well, it's not true," she said. She held a forkful of steak up to her lips. "I am not sick."

Elizabeth and I didn't look at each other. Nick buttered a piece of toast and chewed noisily. After we finished eating, Nick cleared the dishes and went to the kitchen.

"You stay," Mama said and left us sitting at the table.

In the kitchen, I heard her strike a match to light the candles. "Happy Birthday," she sang, slowing the words down to match her steps. Elizabeth tapped out the notes with her fingers on the placemat. Nick walked behind Mama, carrying two plates with doughnuts, each full of candles. In the holes of the doughnuts, Mama had arranged some rose buds in a film canister. The flames on the candles flickered under Nick's breath as he sang.

Late that night Elizabeth came into my room and told me that she was planning to sneak off to church the next morning. Normally, I wouldn't have helped her. I had seen her go through stage after stage. But this was different. She had convinced me: a direct line to God was the best chance Mama had.

Mrs. Teuffel had told Elizabeth to wear her Sunday best and to bring an offering for the collection. I remembered those big bins I'd seen in the church parking lot and figured that Mrs. Teuffel meant clothing. Elizabeth had thrown out all but her most essential belongings in the last weeding.

"I don't have anything," she said.

"You have to sacrifice something," I said. "Isn't that the whole point?"

Finally, Elizabeth settled on a red shirt that had a tiger instead of an alligator on the front and some leg warmers. She stuffed them in a plastic bag and set it under her bed.

The next morning, I helped Elizabeth dress for church. She put on a yellow sundress and sandals with socks. I cleaned up an old makeup bag and pinned a ribbon on as a strap.

"Shouldn't you put your hair in a bun?" I asked.

"Don't make fun of me," she said, her face scrunched up and wounded.

"I'm not." I waited until she was almost down the stairs, then whispered frantically after her, "Make sure you say something for me."

I tried to distract Mama in the kitchen while Elizabeth went out the front door. But Mama saw her trying to climb the split-rail fence, her dress hiked up around her waist, the plastic bag clenched in her teeth.

"Where is she going?" Mama asked.

I shrugged. "Piano lessons?"

"On Sunday morning?" Mama challenged.

"I guess so," I said.

Mama walked over to the screen door and followed Elizabeth with her eyes, watching as she slipped onto Mrs. Teuffel's front porch and disappeared into the house.

"Come here for a minute, Tilden," Mama said. "Let me ask you a question." She leaned against the screen door and rested her forehead on the mesh. "Is Elizabeth praying because she thinks I'm very sick?"

"Maybe."

She didn't speak for a few moments. At TransAlt, the first of the weekend drivers were beginning to arrive. Nick was talking to them, one hand deep in his pocket, the other tight around a cup of coffee.

"Mama, do you believe in God?" I asked.

"In a way," she said and smoothed her hand absently over my face, "sometimes."

HOME REMEDIES

After the first round of chemo, Dr. O'Connor gave Mama some new exercises to do, movements that involved holding onto household appliances and groceries. Mama held the diagrams up for us to see and with a strange, twisted smile on her face, she complained that the worksheet read like the *Ladies' Home Journal.*

"What if you don't have a giant wooden salad spoon or a feather duster to hold above your head?" She pretended to dust the juicer, lightly and then the kitchen shelf. "What if I wanted to use a flashlight or my favorite pair of pliers?"

"They just don't want you to have to go out of your way," Nick said.

"And why not?" Mama braced herself for a fight. "How far do they think I have to go?"

Nick took a deep breath and settled himself. "It's just until you're healed."

"Bull," Mama said, disgusted. "I bet if men were having their you know what's taken off whole gyms would spring up. There would be rehabilitation programs tied into construction companies. First you'd stir paint. Then hammer over your head. And work right up to chopping wood. That way things would still get accomplished. I bet they'd even let you drive."

Nick didn't argue. He blinked slowly, flashing his dark, kind eyes, then retrieved the toolbox from the garage and set it in the kitchen. He stepped closer to Mama and put his hand on her shoulder. "I'm not *them*," he said. "I'm not the enemy."

Mama softened. "I know," she said, relaxing under his hand. "I'm sorry."

Despite her protests, I caught Mama doing her exercises religiously. She tried not to draw attention to herself, slipping her workout into everyday life. The staples were arranged by weight on the middle shelf: cereal, macaroni, soup cans, box of brown sugar, flour. The sacks of flour and rice rested at the end of the shelf like a goal post.

Nick encouraged us to look on the bright side—even on the bad days, when Mama did nothing but throw up. "This is the worst part," he'd say. "But it means the medicine is working."

On the good days, Mama took longer to dress, concerning herself with makeup and scarves. "Readying herself," Nick called it. Those mornings she'd emerge with a certain sense of purpose, ready to greet the world—a bustle of enthusiasm and promise that took her only as far as the mailbox at the end of the driveway. There, she'd wave at Mrs. Teuffel from a distance before retreating back to the house, suddenly frail against the outdoors.

Mrs. Teuffel and Lainey DeWitt were concerned that Mama might need some company. They extended invitations, shouting to her across the driveway. Did she want to have tea? Go shopping? By the third week of the chemotherapy cycle, Mama was feeling better and invited them for lunch on a Saturday.

The day before the luncheon, Mama prepared recipes from that cooking show on TV. She sent Nick to the store twice and asked Elizabeth and me to dice celery and onions while she practiced her food sculptures, a paring knife in one hand, some hard, scrubbed vegetable in the other. She decorated the center of each tray with a carved radish crown.

It didn't matter, she said, if there were leftovers. We could always take the sandwiches to school: tuna with apples, egg salad with olives, and cashew butter with honey. Some cut in thin rectangles, some in triangles, with carrots curling from underneath, like tongues.

"I hope they eat a lot," Elizabeth whispered.

Elizabeth, Samantha, and I were lying on the lawn in our bathing suits when Mrs. Teuffel and Lainey arrived. They stopped at the edge of our blanket to say hello. Lainey was wearing all white. I could see her bra strap through her shirt.

"Getting warmed up for the beach?" she asked. Her permed hair was teased out wide. She was wearing pink lipstick, larger than her lips.

"Don't get too much," Mrs. Teuffel said. She stood in our sun. "Elizabeth, you especially, with that baby-fair skin of yours. Take it from me." Mrs. Teuffel's leathery skin was covered by a long, flowered dress and matching visor. Her charm bracelet tinkled with the silhouettes of her grandchildren. "Watch it. The sun is at its peak right now."

They walked toward the house, weaving their way through the yellowjackets in the grass and sharing the weight of a large shopping bag. At the staircase, Lainey clutched the bag to her chest while Mrs. Teuffel put both hands on the railing to climb the steps. The apple trees were in full bloom, each white flower blushing pink in five perfect petals.

Elizabeth sat up and tested her tan, poking her arms and legs and lowering the band of her bikini bottoms. She squeezed the juice from a cut lemon over her scalp and mashed the leftover pulp along the ends of her hair. Then, she covered herself in baby oil and turned on her side, glistening.

Samantha watched her carefully and then popped the lid on her sunblock. "You're gonna fry," she said. She rubbed the sunblock on herself, leaving streaks in the hard to reach places.

I wanted to lean over and smooth out the lotion. Without saying a word, Samantha tilted the bottle toward me and turned on her stomach. I covered my palm with a cool dollop and began, making sure to keep a layer of lotion between her skin and mine. I started with her feet and moved up her legs, covering the swell of her calves and the dip at the back of her knees. I stopped an inch from the bottom of her suit.

"That's gross," Elizabeth said.

"What?"

"Touching her there."

"I didn't," I said.

"Grow up," Samantha said. "At least I'm not going to get skin can——" She stopped midsentence. The three of us sat silently, blinking in the sun. In the distance, Nick was shouting instructions to someone over a revving engine. Elizabeth turned over on her other side.

"It's not the same," I said, but wiped the leftover sunblock on my chest anyway.

At one o'clock, I sat up, hungry, with sunspots in front of my eyes, and headed for the kitchen.

"Bring me something," Elizabeth said.

"Me too," Samantha called.

Inside, the floor felt cool against my bare feet. I wrapped a stack of sandwiches in a paper towel. I heard Mama's voice in the dining room. She was saying something about the tumor, about lymph nodes and chemotherapy. Why didn't she ever tell me the things that mattered? I lingered in the corner near the refrigerator, holding myself still. I could see all three of them hunched over catalogs and newsletters, spread out among them on the table.

"My sister had this one," Mrs. Teuffel said, tapping a picture with her finger. "You'd never know there was anything the matter."

Mama studied the page and raised one eyebrow. "I don't think so," she said.

"Why not?" Lainey said.

"I'm just not going to buy into the commercialization of cancer," Mama said, holding the catalog up in front of Mrs. Teuffel and Lainey. She sounded defensive, rehearsed. She cleared her throat and shrugged, "I'd just rather use one of those natural sea sponges I read about in some magazine."

Lainey and Mrs. Teuffel exchanged glances.

"Have you looked into a group?" Mrs. Teuffel said.

"A group?"

"For support," Mrs. Teuffel suggested. "No one can go through this alone."

"I'm not alone," Mama said. She arranged the magazines and pamphlets in front of her, pushing the stack back at them. "I have Nick. The girls."

I leaned my face against the smooth wall, happy to hear her say our names, relieved that she didn't feel alone. There was a long silence. Mrs. Teuffel chased a stray radish around her plate with her fork. Lainey folded open a catalog and set it in front of Mama.

"Frances, have you thought about a wig?" she asked gently.

"I guess I'll have to," Mama responded, "just in case."

I stepped away from the wall, straining to be sure I had heard correctly. My knees felt stiff from standing so still. My heart pounded loudly in my ears. Mama with a wig? It didn't make sense.

"Natural wigs are the best," Mrs. Teuffel offered, leaning over to look, "like this one from China. Really good wigs are made with Chinese hair."

Mama gasped. "Eight hundred dollars . . ."

"If you figure it in over a lifetime," Mrs. Teuffel said, "that is not a lot of money."

"That's right," Lainey said. "Think how much most women pay for a good haircut. If you paid thirty dollars, six times a year, you'd have it paid off in almost four years."

"Then what?"

"You'll have it forever."

"I'm not going to wear a wig for the rest of my life," Mama said.

"Of course not," Lainey said, soothingly, "but you could keep it styled and ready for emergencies."

Mama's face furrowed. She seemed to have a different idea about what constituted an emergency. She started to speak and then stopped, looked as if she was searching around for something else to do or say. My legs were numb, my left foot asleep. I cleared my throat and waited for Mama to notice me lurking in the hall.

"Hey, sweetie," she called, "what are you doing inside?"

"I'm hungry. Can I have a sandwich?"

"Of course," Mama said, pushing her chair out from the table and joining me in the kitchen. "Take some fruit, too."

She loaded my arms up with food and pressed me toward the door. I tried to get her to look at me, but her eyes were darting from the dining room to the countertop. I stepped onto the landing, the sun bright in my eyes, my skin stinging in the heat. Back at the blanket, Samantha was telling Elizabeth about how Jill Switt tanned her boyfriend's name onto her bikini line using vinyl stick-on letters.

"Cool," Elizabeth said.

"Not really," Samantha cautioned, "they broke up."

The bottoms of my feet were still cold from the kitchen floor. When I looked back at the house, I could see Mama's shape against the glare in the window; she was washing dishes, her head turned toward her guests, the flash of her blond hair bobbing in conversation. Maybe I'd made it up. Everything I'd heard, the whole conversation seemed of another life.

"Hey Tilden, toss me an apple," Nick called from the center of the lawn. He dropped the sprinkler by the maple tree and went out for a pass. I threw a small red apple at him, harder than I meant to, and hit him in the shoulder. He caught it in the crook of his arm and pretended to limp, clutching his upper body, as he walked over to the sprocket at the side of the house.

Samantha laughed and pulled apart an orange, passing around the slivers in even clumps of three. "He's kinda nice, isn't he?" she said, licking her arm from elbow to wrist to catch the juice.

With a sputter, then a hiss, the sprinkler rose up out of the lawn. Elizabeth and Samantha took off chasing the spray back and forth and leaping over the lowest part. Between sprints, Samantha adjusted her bathing suit, pulling it downward and snapping it under her bottom. Finally, Elizabeth stood still and let the spray hit her stomach, coming and going in both directions. They were laughing uncontrollably, their voices melding in the hot noon air. I covered my burned legs with a towel and sat as still as I could, imagining Mama in a long, black wig made of real Chinese hair.

That afternoon, when everyone had gone, I walked in on Mama doing her exercises in the pantry. She was bent over, her right arm rotating in a wide circle, a box of dried plums in her hand.

"Just a little circumduction," she said casually. "How was your day?"

"Okay," I said.

She put down the box, picked up a can of Campbell's, and started over. I watched as she rotated her arm in the other direction. I studied her hair carefully—shiny with streaks of brown. It was looped under and clipped low at the back of her head with a wooden barrette. I stared at the pinkness of her part, trying to imagine her bare scalp.

"Are you going to lose your hair?" I blurted out finally.

"I might," she said. "But it's only temporary." Once again, she wouldn't look at me. She stopped and put the can on the shelf. "The Mosquitoes say we have enough hair cells to make many different heads of hair."

She took a deep breath, her eyes cast downward along the floorboard. She seemed a million miles away.

"Will you have to wear a wig?" I asked.

"Not yet, Tilden." Her voice was suddenly shaky. "But Mrs. Teuffel's going to take me to get one to match my real hair just in case."

I kicked the toe of my sneaker against the base of the wall, gently rocking the food on the shelves.

"Don't worry," Mama said, forcing a smile and catching my eye at last. "It'll be kind of like having a makeover."

BEAUTY

I hadn't had a haircut with a name since Dorothy Hamill. And there I was, the night before my sixth-grade graduation, about to get an Artichoke. From Elizabeth. I'd gotten the idea to go short from a news story I read about a group of guys in the Midwest who shaved their heads in a show of support for a teammate with leukemia. Given notice, Mama would never have allowed that kind of cut—had planned, herself, to keep her hair as long as she possibly could. She liked hers best when it was twisted up the back. If she'd used more bobby pins, it could have been a Lobster Tail.

Elizabeth didn't believe me when I first told her about the side effects of what the Mosquitoes were doing. I had to read out loud to her from the section under cancer and chemotherapy in *Our Bodies, Ourselves* as proof. Then, our pinkies linked in a promise, the way we'd have them when we were little, we made a pact to each cut the other's hair after dinner. We voted over a selection of photos and diagrams from *Seventeen* and *Young Miss* and settled on the Artichoke because the top could be styled to spike or curl. The caption under the drawing said, *For soft days and hard nights . . . the artichoke is the most versatile style around.* I agreed to go first.

Elizabeth propped the diagram up on an empty chair and set out her tools. With her eyes narrowed in concentration, she combed my wet hair over my face, down past my chin and cut around the top of my head, just above the eyebrows. Slick brown pieces fell onto my legs and covered the floor around me like twigs. She hummed as she worked to the tune of "Piano Man." Before long my hair was falling away from me in loose hunks. I could feel Elizabeth making mistakes, the sound of the scissors clanking fiercely, the blades cold against my head. It didn't look anything like the artichoke I'd had at the Shaptaws. Not even upside down. Not even when I fluffed my hair with my fingers to make the top pieces stand up straight.

Afterward, she bent to the floor. "You want it?" she asked, gathering the longest pieces at one end and holding them out to me. "You could save it and make a braid."

I knew Elizabeth would back out even before she started to justify herself. It had gotten late, the scissors were wet and beginning to jam. I locked myself in the bathroom and refused to come out. I wet down my cowlick and singed my bangs with a curling iron trying to get them to feather. In the mirror my head looked small, my eyes huge and hollow. Nothing like this ever happened to Elizabeth.

After awhile, Mama knocked on the door. "Tilden, honey, come on out," she said. "Let's have a look."

"Never," I said.

"What about graduation?" Mama asked.

"I'm not going." I dunked my head under the running water and started over with the blow dryer.

"How short is it?" I heard Mama ask Elizabeth.

"Promise you won't be mad," she said.

"I won't."

"Promise."

"I promise," Mama said.

"It's pretty short," Elizabeth said, "like a boy's."

"Tilden, what will make you feel better?" Mama called.

I told her that the only thing that would make me open the door was if she forced Elizabeth to get an Artichoke too.

"Will you come out if I get one?" Mama asked.

When I unlocked the door, Mama was waiting in the hall. "It looks pretty," she said, reaching out to comb what was left of my bangs over to one side with her fingernails. She sat me down on the lid of the toilet and moved my hair back and forth under her hands. She pulled at some pieces near my neck. "We'll just get Lainey to clean up these edges."

Then, she called Elizabeth into the bathroom. "I want to tell you girls something," Mama said, positioning herself between us and sitting on the edge of the tub. Elizabeth sat as far away as possible, on the counter near the sink, and kicked her heels against the cabinets.

"You're perfect the way you are," Mama continued, "don't ever change anything."

Mama said that focusing on beauty would distract us from what really mattered. It had always been her belief that beauty came in cycles. And that all women were beautiful in one of three ways: striking, classic, and inner. She said that to be strikingly beautiful meant that people would stop you on the street, do things for you that they might not otherwise do. "It is a beauty that elicits unusual responses," she said. "On the surface striking might seem like the best kind of beauty, but really, it prevents understanding."

Elizabeth gnawed at a hangnail, pulling it with her teeth until it bled.

"Don't you wish for striking beauty," Mama said, when she caught me staring at Elizabeth's blond mane. She looked me right in the eye. "It will prevent people from seeing you."

Classic beauty, on the other hand, was useful in that it told a great deal about a woman's life. It meant that her lineage was reflected in her face and that over time, after she'd worn it through experience, it became her own. I remembered that Grandma had said that. Mama had come from a long line of classic beauties. Women who received their rewards later in life.

Elizabeth gazed at herself in the mirror, then over at me, looking for the resemblance. At twelve, she had already developed a reputation as a beauty. The TransAlt guys acted surprised each time she passed, as if the wind had been knocked out of them. Her blue eyes were set in close to her nose and when she smiled, her full cotton-candy pink lips stretched to expose one tilted front tooth. When we pressed our cheeks close, it was easy to see that together we shared Mama's face. Apart, left to my own face, I felt separate, more a glint of Mama than actually part of her. I remembered overhearing Grandma say that Elizabeth had our father's features. I stared at her, trying to tease out the parts of her face that were different from mine, looking for clues about him. Imagining him, all light and laughter, with stronger bones and thicker lobes.

Mama took her hair down from the twist at the back of her head and bent it up to see what an Artichoke might look like on her. She smiled at her reflection and then at me. "I'm going to ask Lainey to cut my hair, too. That way we'll both have new looks when you start up at the junior high."

Elizabeth looked impatient. "Can I go now?" she asked, her fingers drumming at her sides.

"Sure," Mama said, dismissing her. Then, she turned to me and squeezed my arm. "Tilden, it isn't about hair, you know. The only beauty to strive for is inner beauty," she said. "That's what matters over the long haul."

• • •

Lainey came by at the end of her TransAlt shift. It was 9:00 o'clock, almost past our bedtime, and Elizabeth and I sat silently watching as Lainey quartered Mama's ponytail with rubber bands and began sawing the hair just above the top band with the scissors. Little pieces sprang free. Mama pulled and measured each strand against her chin. I watched her face for disappointment. But she smiled the way she always did in the world, making it hard to know what she thought. At the end, Lainey was left holding a solid rope of Mama's hair, like a tail. She dropped it in a plastic bag and set it aside. She glanced at the photo of the Artichoke in the magazine and went on to give Mama some layers, talking through each step. When she held up the mirror, Mama dipped her chin to each side.

"You have a wonderful line," Lainey said. "You could even go shorter."

Mama blew her hair out with the dryer, fuller at the top and longer at her neck.

"She looks like Mrs. Brady from TV," Elizabeth whispered to me.

"No, she doesn't," I said. "It's shorter." To me, she looked the way the model in the magazine had looked, just the way I'd wanted my hair to look—perfect layers with a wave in back. Nothing ever came out right on me.

Lainey trimmed the jagged edges of my hair and painted my fingernails while Elizabeth sulked in the corner. It was almost eleven o'clock when Lainey left and Nick came upstairs to investigate. He appeared apologetic as if he was intruding. I watched his expression, waiting to find surprise in his face. Instead, he smiled big at Mama and kissed her hard on the neck.

"I feel like I'm living with two Twiggys," he said over her shoulder.

I gave him a blank stare.

"That's a compliment," he said.

As we were cleaning up, sweeping stray hair into a prickly pile, Elizabeth picked Mama's rope of hair out of the bag and held it up to her nose, inhaling the smell of it deeply.

"Put that back," Mama said. Her tone was a shock: harsh and punishing, it made Elizabeth cry. Mama moved to comfort her. "I just don't want it floating around," she added softly.

The next morning, I overslept and by the time I arrived at Brooklawn Elementary, the entire sixth grade was lined up in the hall, ready to march. Samantha leaned out of her place in line, showing off her sandals with wedge heels. Her hair was braided down her back with sprigs of baby's breath at the top and bottom.

"You look *so* different," she called to me.

The graduation march came over the loudspeaker in the gym and just as we had rehearsed, the whole line swayed forward to the beat. As we walked slowly across the waxed gym floor, I felt a sadness rise in me. This hadn't even been my school for very long and already it was time to leave. There were schools in Atlanta I had been at longer and had no certificates from. I didn't understand what the big deal was about the sixth grade. I looked at the bleachers to see if I could find Mama, but only the top of her head was visible over the crowd. Nick stood at the side taking pictures of kids who weren't even my friends. The slow, hollow sound of the music made my throat tighten. When Mr. McKinney called my name, I felt hot and flushed. Ms. Zimmerman squeezed my hand for a long time before giving me my scrolled certificate. Her touch almost made me cry.

That afternoon, Elizabeth and I made up, silently, while Mama and Nick were out getting a cake. Mama's room was still, the light making window panes on the carpet. I found Elizabeth up to her elbows in the large mahogany dresser by the bed. We moved wordlessly through Mama's things—holding up scarves, leg warmers, wooden beads—and draping each other in her favorites. At her closet, we pushed through the hangers, coming by her fancy clothes: a denim dress, maroon suit, and beige Angora sweater. Elizabeth smiled. These were the clothes Mama wore when she had something official to do involving the school or any occasion when pictures might be taken. We slid pieces of these clothes on over our own and moved around the room like grown women.

It was Elizabeth who found the wig, hidden at the back of the closet, tucked away behind Mama's shoe boxes and shrouded in tissue paper. She put her hand out as if to touch a shy dog and brought it into the light. Neither of us said a word. Similar in style to my own hair, round with stiff dirty blond hair, the wig looked more like an overgrown cabbage than an artichoke. Elizabeth folded her thick, blond hair up and tucked in the stray pieces with her free hand. From an angle, in the mirror, she looked almost exactly like me. For a moment, I was filled with pride. Myself, but better. It wasn't the right feeling, I knew. Looking at her, I imagined for the first time what it would really feel like to be beautiful. Elizabeth turned from side to side in front of the mirror, making pouty, sexy faces, watching herself from all angles.

No matter what Elizabeth did, I would always look more like Mama.

HEAT

Elizabeth exploded into summer—her limbs long and brown, her hair light from the sun. She'd moved easily from the bulk of cotton to silky shorts and tank tops. She smelled of watermelon lip gloss and carried a spritzer bottle in her see-through plastic sack. The first week out of school, Elizabeth landed a job at the Y and became the youngest girl ever to walk the preschool campers from the locker room to the pool for their swimming lessons. She held it over me, packing and repacking her goggles, her pink neon zinc. The head lifeguard had given her one of his old sweatshirts with the hood cut out. She modeled it for Mama and me in the TV room.

"This means I'm practically guaranteed a spot on the swim team," she bragged.

"Big deal," I said.

"I'd like to try swimming," Mama said, raising herself up on the couch and bringing her knees into her chest. She was wearing a soft cotton skirt which fell around her like a nightgown. She was near the end of the second cycle of chemotherapy and ran a constant low-grade fever. The backs of her hands were still bruised from the barrage of injections. She borrowed Nick's shirts and wore the sleeves long.

Elizabeth narrowed her eyes, "Really?"

"I'm supposed to," Mama said, "if I feel like it. Dr. O'Connor said so."

Elizabeth glanced at me across the room, hopeful. She believed that Dr. O'Connor was the good doctor, the one set on healing. Neither of us trusted what the Mosquitoes were doing. The medications that were supposed to be helping Mama made her feel worse. Her face tightened when she stood up or reached for the telephone. Her skin turned yellow at the sight of raw hamburger meat or egg yolks.

"Besides," Mama said, "I'm feeling much better today."

Elizabeth and I gave each other a knowing look. Mama usually said that she was feeling better than she had the day before, without ever saying outright that she'd been feeling poorly.

The next day, Mama came into my room wearing a matching shirt and skirt outfit with sandals. I could see right away that her tiredness had lifted; she'd used a hair dryer and had on mascara.

"Come shopping with me," she said, "I want to get a new swimsuit."

"Where's Elizabeth?"

"Nick dropped her at the Y already," she said. "Let's hurry so we can surprise her."

It was disorienting to hear Mama talk of surprises after weeks of sitting still. I was afraid her enthusiasm would vanish so I rushed around the house, gathering my bathing suit and a towel, and stuffed them into my knapsack—scrambling to get ready the way I did in order not to miss the bus.

Mama overpacked, filling her own small duffel with a robe, towel, and extra set of clothes. She stored her sea sponge breast in her swim cap and jangled the car keys at me. I dashed to the station wagon, threw our bags in the back, and waited, breathless, for Mama to start the car. Once we were settled, she paused and stared blankly at the dashboard in a way that made me worry.

"Does Nick know we're going?" I asked.

"Of course," she said, turning the key in the ignition. She stopped to look at me. "I am my own person," she said, "I don't have to tell him everything."

I crossed my arms and wedged myself against the door. "I know."

There was a small silence and then Mama said, "I feel a little too self-conscious for high fashion today."

She opted for Margaret's maternity store in town, said that they would be more sensitive to physical concerns and might even have a suit with a specially padded top. But when we arrived, the saleswoman seemed bewildered and eyed us suspiciously. I lingered a few feet behind Mama who didn't seem to notice; she just kept sorting through the racks and fondling each suit. For some reason, everything she said embarrassed me.

"This ought to distract attention." She held up a red, white, and blue suit with a giant star on the top.

I recited the summer suit advice from *Seventeen* magazine, "Horizontals broaden, verticals lengthen, patterns accentuate, and solids conceal."

Mama looked at her selection. "Oops," she said, tucking three brightly patterned suits under her arm. She picked out a solid suit and brought them all into the dressing room.

I waited outside, watching her feet under the door, the labored pulling on and off of swimsuits. When she settled on one, she opened the door a crack and let me peek.

"It looks nice," I said, automatically.

The solid navy suit gaped around her middle like elephant skin and fell into a short skirt. She'd stuffed one of the other suits into the right side of her chest. She caught me staring and stepped back behind the door. When she resurfaced, I could tell that she had been crying. Her eyes were glassy and red and she wouldn't look at me.

At the register, Mama explained that she would be wearing the suit home, under her clothes and lifted her shirt slightly to show the saleswoman the item number and the price.

"You wouldn't have a pair of scissors?" she asked at the end of the transaction.

The woman grumbled, dug through a drawer and held up a pair with heavy-duty blades that was attached to the register by a ribbon. She pointed the handle in Mama's direction. Mama leaned her upper body over the counter and tried twice to reach her right side with her right hand. By the time she looked up at me, I had already positioned myself to help. The saleswoman pretended to be busy, shuffling through receipts and separating them into piles. As Mama pulled the tags out from the seam under her arm, the suit lifted away from her skin and revealed a razor thin line down her chest and under her arm. I snipped quickly and stepped away. It looked as if someone had drawn on her with indelible red marker.

When we got to the Y, Elizabeth was sitting in the lobby drinking orange soda with a flexi straw. She put the can down slowly on the floor when she saw us come in. Mama went right to the front desk to sign up for the pool. Even in the lobby, the air smelled of chlorine.

"What are you *doing* here?" Elizabeth hissed.

"It's a free country," I said.

"Surprise," Mama said, joining us. "Come take a swim with us."

"I can't," Elizabeth said. "I'm *working*." She looked around anxiously. "Besides, there's only ten minutes left of free swim."

It occurred to me that she was as nervous as I was. Mama had seemed so fragile since the surgery. What if she inhaled too much water? What if her new suit didn't fit correctly? What if someone saw her scar?

"Ten minutes?" Mama said. "We better hurry."

In the locker room, there were other women Mama's age walking shameless and naked from the showers to their clothes, stopping at the scale on their way. Their flesh moved with them. One woman's breasts and stomach swayed with the weight of each of her steps. Her skin looked gray, spider veins exploding across her thigh like a road map, her breasts pendulous. The word udder came to mind. I peeked at Mama to see if her body showed that much strain, but she still had her clothes on. I sat on the bench and pulled my suit on in that quick way I'd learned from having to change in gym—crouched low, a flash of skin and limbs until everything was in its proper place. Mama went into the bathroom stall and came out in a bathrobe with her swim cap on.

"You don't really need that," I said. "It's only for long hair."

She looked confused at first and then touched her head gently. "You're probably right," she said, "but I better wear it anyway. You never know."

Elizabeth ducked into the lifeguard office, pretending to look busy and important, when she saw us emerge from the locker room. At the pool, Mama folded her robe in half and placed it on a chair against the wall.

"Grab me a kickboard, honey," she said and walked quickly down the steps into the water at the shallow end.

When the water reached her waist she dipped down with her knees bent so that only her head floated above the water. Each time someone passed, she turned her face away from the splash, her face squinched up like a tentative child. I walked in with my arms bent, controlling each moment of my skin against the water until I reached Mama with the kickboard. She pulled it to her chest and flicked a wet finger at me. "It's warm once you're in."

She leaned her weight forward on the board and pushed off, kicking her way across the shallow end. I'd forgotten what a strong swimmer she was. In Atlanta, she'd take us to the lake, pulling us on inflatable rafts, her hair floating around her shoulders like sea grass as she swam with her arms stretched over her head. When we reached the raft at the center of the lake, she'd let us warm our bodies on the wooden slats of the dock. I liked to pretend that we were on our own island, the edge of the beach miles away, the only sound, an ebbing of water against the red Styrofoam floaters beneath us.

I sank down under the water and sat on the bottom with my eyes open. All around me, legs and arms thrashed in slow motion, dipping in and out of sight. Each time I went up for air and came down, the muffle of voices comforted me. After one short lap, Mama stopped to catch her breath. She pulled the Lycra away from her skin, bloating her suit with air bubbles and moving the elastic high under her arm. She pushed off and kicked her legs gently, not using her arms at all.

At the end of free swim, the lifeguard blew the whistle four times. Elizabeth appeared at the edge of the pool with an armful of towels for the campers. Mama stayed in the shallow end and bobbed slightly, squatting on the steps until the last of the child stragglers had reclaimed their nose clips from Elizabeth. Then, with her back to the crowd, she began the climb, her hands holding fast to the railing, her step unsure. Just before she came entirely out of the water, I caught her check the top of her suit and give her sponge a quick squeeze. I'm not sure which embarrassed me more: that someone might think she was touching herself or that there was nothing there to touch. I waited with a towel, my arms stretched out wide until Mama stepped up to me and folded the towel around her like a cape.

"That was fun," she said when we were safely in the locker room. She put her clothes on over her swimsuit and mashed her wet feet into the sandals. After she was dressed, she wedged two fingers under the swim cap and lifted it off carefully. Her hair was matted to her scalp in a way that made her look as if she'd just awoke. The longer pieces at the back of her neck were wet.

Elizabeth joined us in the lobby and held the front door open, impatiently, as Mama waved good-bye to people she didn't know. Elizabeth was mortified, all hunched over in hiding with exasperated sighs. She marched ahead of us to the car in the parking lot. I watched Mama from behind, a broad wetness seeping into the back of her skirt.

"Why did you do that?" Elizabeth asked when we got to the car. She looked as if she was about to cry.

"Do what?" Mama asked.

"Show up like that."

"I wanted to go for a swim," she said, her lips slightly blue. "Besides, I didn't think it would bother you." Elizabeth wedged herself into a corner, crossed her arms, and stared out over the parking lot. Mama got in and slammed the car door. "I'm sorry if I embarrassed you," she said.

She didn't look at either of us before pulling out of the lot. Her words hung in the air between us, like shame. I held my arm over my face and breathed in the chlorine from my skin for the entire ride home. My mouth tasted like metal. When we pulled in the driveway, Mama cut the engine and got out, leaving us alone in the car. Elizabeth's eyes remained wide and stubborn.

"You're such a jerk," I said. "She wanted to surprise you."

Suddenly, Elizabeth's face collapsed. She cried in gusts of halting breath, her cheeks wet and shiny. "I didn't mean it," she sobbed. "I don't know why I said that."

"Me either," I said and walked away.

• • •

The house was dark and quiet as I made my way down the hall. I tapped lightly on the bedroom door; Mama was sitting on the edge of the bed in her robe, the swimsuit in a heap on the floor next to her. I picked it up and shook it right-side out.

"It's ugly, isn't it?" she asked.

"Not really."

"Yes it is," she said, her eyes full of disgust.

"Well, maybe just the skirt . . . it's kind of old-ladyish."

"I should have looked harder."

"Not with that grumpy saleslady." I glanced down over my nose, imitating the judgmental look the woman had given us.

"Yeah," Mama said. "What does she know? I could've been pregnant."

I laughed.

"Better yet," Mama continued, "*you* should have tried on something."

"That would have shown her," I said.

We were giggling like this, back and forth, when Elizabeth appeared in the hall, looking timid and distraught.

"Come here," Mama said and Elizabeth began crying all over again. She buried her head in Mama's lap, weeping. "Don't cry," Mama stroked Elizabeth's head. "Tilden and I have just voted this the world's ugliest swimsuit. We need your vote to make it unanimous."

"Count me in," Nick said. He walked over to where I stood with the bathing suit, wrapped his arms around it and pretended to slow dance, box-stepping around the area rug in the bedroom while we watched in silence. He looked handsome, the way I imagined he must have looked that first time Mama saw him, with his dark hair shining in the afternoon light.

"You haven't asked *me* to dance in a long time," Mama said.

Nick stopped midstep and flung the suit off to the side. He

stepped up to Mama dramatically with one arm outstretched. "May I?"

Mama waved him away. "I was just kidding." She blushed and dipped her head toward her chest. Nick didn't move.

"Come on, Mama," Elizabeth said. "Please."

Mama took a deep breath, lowered one leg and then the other to the floor. She tightened the belt on her bathrobe and stepped into Nick's arms. He cupped one large hand around hers and pulled her close to him with his other hand pressed against the small of her back.

I leaned over to the clock radio to find a station.

"Something slow," Mama called to me. She watched her feet, taking two steps to each of Nick's until she found the rhythm.

Elizabeth folded a pillow in her lap and counted to herself—one, two, three, one, two, three—trying to will Mama's steps to match Nick's. After Mama had the hang of it, she rested her head against Nick's neck and moved to the beat of "This Magic Moment."

They swayed slowly even after the song had ended, Nick's mouth pressed to the top of Mama's head, his eyes closed. And for the first time since it all began, I believed that she would get better.

That night, Nick ordered pizza for dinner—half cheese, half mushroom and onion. The mood around the table was light. We threw out ideas for the future, the wants and needs we'd been keeping to ourselves. Nick suggested hiring a neighborhood landscaper to spruce up the yard. Mama talked about getting new curtains in the dining room.

"Maybe we can get a new rug for the TV room too," she said.

"And cable?" I asked.

"I think we watch enough TV around here," Nick said.

"Can I get a perm?" Elizabeth asked.

Nick froze above his plate and looked over to check Mama's face. She put down her pizza and took a long sip of her milk.

"What did I say wrong?" Elizabeth asked.

"Nothing," Mama said. "It's just that all those chemicals are bad for your hair."

I kicked Elizabeth under the table. She glared back at me. "I was just asking," she said.

After a little while, I asked to have a slumber party.

Mama didn't say anything at first.

"Kind of like a late birthday party," I added, "but with no cake or presents."

"I don't know," Mama said. "How many friends would you invite?"

I counted off a handful of girls, naming each of my fingers and held them up. "Six including me," I said.

"That's too many," Mama said, "I don't have enough energy for such a big party."

"How about four," I said, subtracting all but the essential girls. "And we could camp in the tent." I looked to Nick for approval. He shrugged, waiting for Mama's response.

"Does that number include your sister?" Mama asked.

I hesitated. "I don't think five can fit in the tent."

"You can have it if you invite Elizabeth," Mama said definitively.

"Forget it."

"I wouldn't go anyway," Elizabeth said and asked to be excused. While she scraped her plate in the kitchen, Mama shook a finger at me.

"I'm surprised at you!" she said. "You better include her. And go apologize—I mean it!"

• • •

The landscaper showed up in jeans and work boots, wearing a shirt with the sleeves cut out, his bare arms dark and tight. When he came inside to use the bathroom, the hall smelled of sweat, cut grass, and earth. His name was Keith Rogers. He was a junior in high school and Mama decided then and there that it was no longer appropriate for Elizabeth and me to run around in our nightgowns or lie out in the yard in our bathing suits. Nick showed him to the storage area under the house where he kept the yard tools and the mower. Elizabeth sat at the picnic table outside and watched him as he worked. It was everything I could do to get her to walk to town with me to get supplies for the party.

Mama gave me twenty dollars to spend on the condition that I share everything with Elizabeth. At the stationery store, we agreed on Pez dispensers, Twizzlers, Bubble Yum, and blue and gold yarn to make pom-poms. But we had different ideas when it came to the items at McNeary's Pharmacy. I wanted to get an eight-pack of tampons and put one in each sleeping bag. Elizabeth wanted to buy with only herself in mind, to get an eyelash curler, mascara, and blue eyeliner pencil. That, or a special shampoo to keep her hair from turning green in the chlorine.

"There has to be enough for everyone," I said.

"It's dumb to buy something you don't even need," Elizabeth said.

But she stood next to me in the hygiene aisle anyway and leaned in close when I found the slender regulars. "Liar," she whispered and grabbed a flowered box called Summer's Eve.

"What are you doing?"

"Fair's fair," she said and started toward the counter.

We were allies in front of the druggist, avoided him by pretending to look at the goods from the stationery store, our hands deep in the other bag to distract attention away from our purchases.

Out on the sidewalk, it was a different story. Elizabeth made me carry both bags.

"How come?" I asked.

"I'm not talking to you anymore," she announced and marched ahead of me down Main Street and turned onto Elm.

I watched Elizabeth's ponytail swinging from side to side down her back like a metronome. She was growing faster than I was, and soon she'd be taller than me. Her legs were long and thin, *shapely*, like the magazines said. Well, she has grace, but no speed, I told myself.

We walked past house after manicured house—wooden shingles, aluminum siding, they were all the same—two-story, two-car houses with azaleas bursting in the yards in spring, and day lilies collapsed over the sidewalks all summer.

Just as I caught up to Elizabeth, a Jeep pulled along side of us and a man asked for directions. He wanted to get to the park, said he'd been driving around for blocks. I thought he was gesturing to a map or something in his lap and when I looked down I saw it. Swollen with veins. Elizabeth kept right on talking, didn't give him a single blink. He was holding his own flesh in his hand, rubbing his thumb on the top. From across the street anyone might have thought he and Elizabeth were talking normally. But I gasped and pulled at her arm. She finished directing him and then marched across the street and up a stranger's driveway.

"Are you crazy?" she screamed, when we were halfway up the driveway. "Why couldn't you just leave it alone?"

"Well, now he thinks we live here, Miss Know-it-all."

"You're the one who encouraged him," she said. She bugged her eyes out and stared down at an imaginary crotch, imitating me. She stuck her tongue out and panted.

"You're the jerk that just stood there," I said.

"That's what you're supposed to do," she said. "You are supposed to pretend that everything is normal." Elizabeth seemed angry at me for pointing it out, as if somehow it wasn't really happening until I said it was. "It's your fault," she added.

"What's that supposed to mean?"

"Puberty," she announced.

Mama was in a fury, said there was no place safe for women and girls. She served Police Officer Denehey iced tea while he questioned us in the TV room. The couch seemed smaller with him sitting on it, his knees bent high, his belt and shoes shiny and black. Elizabeth could describe the Jeep and the man, his hair and his voice. I realized while she was talking that I couldn't describe anything but the penis. I began to feel like the pervert.

"What do you remember?" Officer Denehey asked and turned over a new page in his notebook.

"Nothing," I said, feeling hot in my skin.

"So you have nothing to add?"

"No, I don't."

Elizabeth flashed me a look.

"Well, if you remember anything that might help, just have your mother give us a call," he said.

At first, Mama seemed strangely invigorated by the incident. Outrage improved her complexion, making even her lips burn with color. Her cheeks were flushed in the presence of Officer Denehey and grew pale after he'd departed. We weren't used to company. "This is turning out to be a long day," she said and sank down into the couch.

"You don't have to do another thing," Nick said, "just rest."

I followed him out to the yard. He had a plastic tarp under one arm and the tent bag in the other. When we got to the side of the house, Keith Rogers was down on his knees weeding out a new clearing in the yard. It was about six feet long with freshly churned soil. Nick dropped the tent and stormed over to him. Elizabeth and I hung back a bit, stunned.

"I asked you to *cut* the grass, not gut it," Nick screamed.

I was shocked—I'd never heard him raise his voice before.

"I know, sir," Keith started, taking off his hat and brushing the dirt off his knees. "I just thought—"

"You thought what?" Nick's dark eyes narrowed as he stared at Keith with contempt.

"I just thought that your wife might like a garden."

Nick leaned his face in close to Keith's. A bead of sweat trickled down his neck. "What gave you that idea?"

"My mom," he lowered his voice and kicked at the soil. "It's what my mom did when she was sick."

Nick stood quietly for a moment, shaking his head, then exhaling deeply. He wiped his forehead with his sleeve and reached out to touch Keith on the back. "Okay," he said quietly, "sorry for the misunderstanding. Nice work."

I helped Nick spread the tarp on the grass and slide the tent poles out of the nylon sack. He pushed the stakes into the grass with his heel and tied the tent strings in double knots. While we were working, I overheard Elizabeth ask Keith what he had planted. She leaned over the dirt to look as he pointed out marigolds, pansies, and forget-me-nots. He stabbed the empty paper packets of seeds with wooden sticks and stuck them in the ground. Elizabeth was cooing at Keith in such an obvious way, I nearly laughed out loud.

"Why were the police here?" Keith asked.

"No reason," Elizabeth said, flashing him her straight, white teeth.

• • •

Jill Switt was the first to arrive for the summer slumber. I told her that I had been an eyewitness to the Brooklawn Pervert and she immediately fired questions.

"Was he cute? Did he have on shoes? Was he hairy?"

It wasn't until Samantha arrived that I got the real questions.

"How big was it?" she asked, making circles with her thumb and pointer. "Scallion, carrot, or cuke?"

"None of the above."

"Did he ejaculate?"

"How would I know?" I snapped back.

"You were the one watching," she said.

I hadn't really wanted to watch. My eyes just got fixed and I couldn't seem to look away. I wished I had behaved like Elizabeth—cool and calm, her eyes locked above his neck, directing him toward the park.

"How did he do it?" Sam asked, prodding me one last time. I knew what she meant. She wanted details, the kind a policeman would already know. Fast or slow. Hard or soft. Open handed or closed fisted.

"With his thumb," I said.

For the rest of the evening Samantha wiggled her thumb at me, a stout pink man bending at the waist, whenever she had something private to tell me.

Nick lit some candles, the kind that were melted deep into miniature pails to keep the bugs away, and set them around the picnic table. He said Keith Rogers could stay until dark and patted him on the shoulder once again as an apology for losing his temper. Nick promised not to disturb us as long as we promised not to make too much noise.

"Deal?" he asked.

"Deal," we answered in unison.

We gathered around the picnic table to practice braiding. Elizabeth brought the yarn out to the table. Pom-poms were the rage. We hung them everywhere: at the ends of our shoe laces, on bookbags and key chains. We'd heard that the older girls were wearing them in their hair.

"Is that true?" Elizabeth asked Keith.

He put one foot on the picnic bench, considering, "Some girls," he said, "I guess so."

We waited for more. What kind of girls, we wanted to know, but didn't ask. Keith sat down on the corner of the table closest to Elizabeth and watched with interest as she demonstrated how to make a pom-pom. She wrapped equal amounts of blue and gold yarn around the doughnut-shaped molds and tightened the single strand around the center, like a belt.

Samantha and Jill had the kind of hair that splayed across their backs and took hours to dry—thick and beautiful. Libbie Gorin's hair was stringy from sucking on the ends. Her face was always framed by stiff spears. No one wanted to touch her hair. While Libbie and I braided, Samantha and Jill made pom-poms. Jill's thick hair stayed in strong sections and fell easily into threes. As I braided, I watched over her shoulder. Her pom-poms were unruly, not at all compact or official looking. They seemed homemade. I found myself braiding tighter out of frustration. Altering her carelessness in my head. Every time Samantha moved to show us a finished pom-pom, Libbie would start over, her hands grasping desperately to keep the hair apart. She had trouble with division, running the red comb down Samantha's scalp over and over and then putting it in her mouth.

Elizabeth groaned, then looked at Keith; the two of them smirked wickedly at one another, making faces at Libbie's expense. Then, swiftly and without looking at her, Keith brought his hand down on Elizabeth's bare knee. She looked startled at first and then a smile spread slowly over her face. She lifted up her head and grinned directly at me. I pretended not to notice and braided hand over hand, striving to finish Jill's entire head before nightfall.

When it finally got dark, Elizabeth walked with Keith to the edge of the yard and then went into the house. The rest of us arranged our sleeping bags inside the tent, two facing two, the tops of the bags touching. I held up the box of tampons.

"Party favors," Samantha said.

Long after it had gotten dark, when the sound of crickets grew loud, Mama came out to say good night and brought us some dessert. She stuck her head inside the tent flap and handed over a full tin of Rice Krispies marshmallow treats. Jill shined her flashlight directly in Mama's face. I noticed that there were loose hairs on the shoulders of her sweatshirt, which made it look shaggy, more like an Angora sweater. I panicked thinking that the others might see them too and moved quickly toward the entrance of the tent to block their view of her. Mama pulled back and hit the top of her head against the zipper on her way out.

She brought her hand to her scalp, cursing quietly, then held her palm in front of her face, checking to see if she had been cut. I felt a strange mix of anger at how fragile she was and an insistent desire to protect her.

"Are you bleeding?" I asked.

Mama shook her head. "I'm fine, really. Have fun," she said and turned toward the house.

When I climbed back in the tent, I noticed that everyone was staring behind me at the top of the tent flap. There, snagged in the zipper, was a full lock of Mama's hair. I hesitated before touching it. Then, I pulled the wispy, blond clump out from the teeth of the zipper and set the hair loose into the evening air. Panic raced in my veins, thudding like a quick pulse at my temple.

Samantha broke the silence. "Let's play ring and run," she suggested.

We spread out across the neighborhood, ringing doorbells and lifting our nightshirts above our heads as we ran for cover. I was sure that this was dangerous behavior, but didn't care. I ran fast, the cool slate path biting the bottom of my feet, the wet grass between my toes. I liked the feel of the warm wind under my armpits and just above the elastic band of my panties. I raced recklessly through Mrs. Teuffel's backyard, stepping on her coiled hose, knocking over the watering can, and leaping over the split-rail fence. We stayed half-naked even after we'd gotten back to the sleeping bags—all out of breath and damp, while Jill led us in a game of Truth or Dare.

In the morning, we tied the pom-poms onto the ends of Jill's and Samantha's braids. They looked like parade ponies, the colorful balls bouncing around their shoulders. One by one their mothers came to pick them up. When everyone had left, I went back to the tent. It smelled of yarn and marshmallow, candle wax and damp grass. I felt lonely in that way that stays with you even in the middle of a group. I pressed hard against the lump in my throat to keep from crying. Just outside the tent flap, a few strands of Mama's hair were scattered across the lawn like a spider web.

RELATIVE

The first time Mama wore her wig was when Uncle Rand came for a visit in August. She was in the third round of chemotherapy and had been covering her head, those hot summer days, with either a bandanna or a floppy-brimmed hat. I hadn't actually seen her scalp, but there were loose hairs on all her clothes, even some on the furniture.

"It's better this way," she explained when she emerged from the bathroom wearing the wig, "I haven't seen that baby brother of mine since . . ." she slipped a piece of the wig behind her ear, "since he moved. I don't want to shock him too much."

She stood in front of her mirror, tucking and untucking her shirt, frustrated by the weight she was gaining. She'd explained this to me: hormones. "As if there isn't enough going on in this body," she said, snipping the elastic out of her skirt and fastening the waistband with big springy safety pins.

The wig looked fake, like the fur on stuffed animals. It seemed to stand away from her head in stiff layers of orange-blond hair. I tried not to look, but kept catching sight of it no matter where I focused. Surely everyone would know it wasn't her real hair.

"Oh well," she said, leaving the shirt untucked, "it's out of my control." Her face was puffy and she looked suddenly older, her whole body slouching and frumpy.

I hadn't seen Uncle Rand in five years, not since the year I was eight and he came to live with us in Atlanta. He was wild then, staying out all night and sleeping all day. He had just returned from a car trip to California where he'd worked in restaurants and Mama encouraged him to go to cooking school. Instead, he took the first job he could find, working at a hotel in food preparation.

Mama was impatient with him, but I always loved him, even looked up to him. He helped us to disobey and laugh off rules, which made us rowdy. He taught us how to play cards and steam open mail. Once he helped us to hang the silverware from the light fixtures on fishing wire. When he talked to his friends, he used words like *pecker* and *cooch*. I remember there being something exciting about the way he spit out each word, like a dare. We couldn't help but listen.

He took it personally when Mama told him he couldn't stay, that *she* wasn't running a hotel and that he needed to find a place of his own. He packed his bags in a hurry and took off without leaving an address or number. I cried for days imagining all the terrible things that might happen to him.

"He can handle the world," Mama consoled me, "besides, he needs time on his own."

Nick drove all the way to La Guardia to pick up Uncle Rand and by the time he returned, we were dressed and waiting in the foyer. Elizabeth wore her sundress. Mama encouraged me to wear a skirt.

"Why?" I asked.

"Because it's a special occasion. Don't you want to look nice?"

When Uncle Rand stepped out of the car, Mama took a deep breath and brought her hand to her mouth. He was wearing blue jeans and a pin-striped shirt. He looked more like a man than I remembered, a little weighed down the way all adults were, with that look of resignation. His reddish-brown hair was cut short. And he had a moustache.

I could hear Uncle Rand's strong Southern accent from the driveway as he talked with Nick about TransAlt. Funny, how his voice sounded both familiar and far away. Elizabeth stepped up to the screen door for a closer look.

"How old is he now?" she said.

Mama did some math on her fingers. "Thirty," she said.

Nick lifted Uncle Rand's suitcase out of the trunk and carried it up to the house. Uncle Rand followed closely behind, taking in the yard and the house, touching bushes and shingles, like an inspector. When he saw Mama he stepped back as if he'd been knocked over and caught himself on the foyer wall.

"Good Lord, Frances," he said. "I'd never've known it was you."

Mama's face went blank for a moment, then a glint of disappointment appeared. She tilted her head and adjusted her wig. Then, Uncle Rand embraced Mama hard, picking her up, and rocking her back and forth. When he set her on her feet, she had trouble catching her balance. He rushed over and gathered us in his arms, palming our heads into his chest. He smelled good, like the inside of the principal's office or a counter at Macy's.

"I don't believe it," he said. "How can you girls have grown this much?"

Mama beamed proudly. Her skin had turned orange from the chemicals, almost as if she had a sunburn.

"That's the smile," Uncle Rand said and pulled Mama by the waist until she was standing next to him. It was then, I could see how they both had the same blue eyes and dimple at the chin.

Nick cleared his throat and picked up the suitcase. "Let's get you settled," he said and started up the stairs.

Within an hour, Uncle Rand had moved easily into the second-floor guest room between my room and Elizabeth's. He hung his clothes in the hall closet and set his toiletries out on the edge of our bathroom sink. His supplies took over the medicine chest: strong cologne in dark bottles, a brass razor, and a little scissor for his moustache.

"How long are you planning to stay?" Nick asked casually at dinner that night.

I could see Mama holding her breath. Nick had been happy that she'd invited Uncle Rand to come, but now she worried about the way he just moved in. It wasn't his fault, Mama told me, they were the only family they each had. In fact, she'd practically raised him, even before Grandma and Grandpa died. That is, until it looked as if Uncle Sam might get involved, and Randy took off to avoid the draft.

"As long as you'll have me," Uncle Rand responded.

"Fine," Nick said, "that's fine. As you can see, I've been a little outnumbered by women here." He must have meant this as a joke, a way to make Uncle Rand more comfortable, because it wasn't true; Nick had a world of men right in the backyard.

"So," Nick continued, clearing his throat, "think you might like to do a little driving for TransAlt while you're here?"

"Love to. Only one problem." Uncle Rand hesitated and looked to Mama for permission.

She shrugged, opening her hands out wide beside her. Nick leaned forward, questioning.

"Got a deewee chasing me," Uncle Rand said.

"What's a deewee?" I asked.

"D.W.I.," he said. "I had a little run-in with the law while I was under the influence." He laughed deeply and crossed his arms around his body. "Damn cops don't have anything better to do than chase after a man with a cocktail."

Nick shifted in his seat, laced his fingers together and brought his hands to rest on the table. "When can you drive again?" he asked.

"Whenever I want. As long as I don't get caught."

"Well there's plenty of other stuff around here to do," Mama said, looking at Nick nervously. "Anyway," she continued, almost defiant, "he came to help us, not TransAlt."

The next day, UPS arrived with four large boxes for Uncle Rand. The kitchen seemed transformed by his wrought iron pans, heavy cutting boards, and cutlery. They were the tools of serious cooking and they came with a new set of rules. The pans were not to be washed with soap. They had been seasoned, he explained; even the cutting boards had to be wiped down with mineral oil. He clustered like items together on the refrigerator and pantry shelves and set up a spice rack.

That night, Uncle Rand made dinner, naming me his sous-chef and tying an apron around my waist. We worked side by side, starting in the afternoon, marinating garlic in olive oil and pulling apart squares of lettuce for the Caesar salad. Uncle Rand dropped raw eggs into a pot of boiling water for thirty seconds before slipping them into the greens. He talked me through the twice-baked potatoes with paprika and the lightly battered fish, measuring all the ingredients first and setting them out in small bowls. He garnished with sprigs of parsley and lemon slices.

"Presentation is everything," he said, snapping the lemon into a curl with confidence.

When Nick came in from the garage, Uncle Rand went straight for the cabinet next to the dishwasher. "What's it going to be?" he asked.

"Whatever you're having," Nick said.

Their tone suddenly became formal, almost as if they were doing business. Then, Uncle Rand disappeared under the cabinet, digging deep, and resurfaced with an assortment of bottles. He set up shop at the end of the counter, laying out a dish towel and putting his shakers and shot glasses down on top. He had a glass stirrer with his name on it. Nick made small tasters and then speared an olive for each glass.

Mama rolled her eyes. "It's the way men entertain each other," she said.

Later that night, Elizabeth and I sat on the end of Uncle Rand's bed as he told us stories about Mama as a young girl. About her braces and boyfriends. Once, she'd even had her picture in *Life* magazine.

"Was she pretty then, too?" Elizabeth asked.

"Pretty as ever," Uncle Rand said.

"Who looks like her most?" Elizabeth asked.

"Well," he said, sitting forward to study my face, "Tilden has her nose, cheeks, and chin." He kissed each place as he said it. "And you, Elizabeth, have her eyes and her hair."

We all grew quiet. I tried to remember Mama's hair as it had been, long and light and silky soft to the touch.

"Did you know our father?" I asked.

Uncle Rand nodded, paused to think, and nodded some more. "That's a conversation for another night," he said. "Now go on to sleep, you two."

After I had climbed in bed, Uncle Rand came through my room to smoke a cigarette on the outside staircase. I moved to the window and watched the embers burn red. He was sitting on the top step, a glass of wine beside him, holding his head in his hand, the cigarette perched between his fingers. It looked as if his red hair had caught on fire.

"What're you doing up?" he asked and blew a stream of smoke into the air above him.

I stepped out onto the landing and took a seat on the railing. "I'm not tired." I wrapped my legs around a post. The wood was damp from the humidity, the air thick and hard to breathe.

"You know what I'm thinking?" he asked.

I shook my head.

"Your grandparents would have loved to see you girls so grown."

I held my breath. "How did it really happen?" I asked, my body shaking from uttering the forbidden question.

"Heart attack," he said. "Your Grandpa was driving." He took a long, slow sip of wine. "Your Grandma lived a few days in intensive care, but I think the grief killed her. She would have been so miserable without him."

His voice was flat, detached. I wondered if it was really possible to die of grief or loneliness, like a sickness from inside.

"Do you miss them?" I asked.

"Of course," he said. "But it was your mama who took it the hardest."

"She never says anything about it."

"It's not her way. But I'll tell you one thing, it's always there." He paused. "That's why you girls are so important to her. And Nick, too. Family matters."

Uncle Rand got real quiet after that, blew smoke upward in a steady stream. After a time, he turned to look at me out of the corner of his eye. "You have a boyfriend?" he asked, changing the subject. It was the first time an adult had ever talked this way to me. Easy, like a friend would.

I giggled, embarrassed, and shook my head.

"Why not?"

"I don't know. I'm only thirteen!"

The driveway looked like a lake, black and rippling under the moonlight. I formed a question over and over in my mind before it came out of my mouth.

"Do you?" I asked finally. "Have a girlfriend, I mean?"

He took a drag off his cigarette and tilted his head back. "Didn't work out," he said and stared off past the garage.

"Oh, I'm sorry."

"What can you do?" he said. "These things happen."

"Is that what happened with Mama and my real father?"

He glanced up at me. "What am I, the family historian?"

His words stung and my eyes filled with tears. There was so much Mama never told me, but I couldn't say that to him, behind her back.

"I know your Mama is private," he said. "She doesn't mean any harm. I'm sure she just wants to keep any ugliness from you."

"But I want to know," I said.

I allowed my need to weigh heavy between us. It felt like the bravest thing I had ever done. My legs trembled. To keep them still, I held the backs of my knees against the wooden banister.

"What has she told you?" he asked.

"Not much," I said. "Just that he was handsome."

Uncle Rand smiled. "I suppose that's true."

"What else?" I pressed, the skin on my legs damp with sweat.

"Your father and I didn't get on so well," Uncle Rand said. "You could call it a difference of opinion."

"About what?"

"About the way he treated your mama." He didn't say anything more after that. He pushed the tip of the cigarette into the step next to him until it went out. "Come on," he said, "let's hit the hay." He followed me through the door and cut across my room to the hall. He stopped in the doorway. "Nick's good to y'all," he said. "Right?"

I nodded.

"That's what matters," he said. "She's found someone now. So you forget the past."

Uncle Rand and I began a ritual of late-night meetings on the staircase. He told me wild stories about his friends, taught me to whittle, and let me try his cigarettes. I learned to shuffle cards, to play Spit and War, staying up later than I'd ever been allowed, counting cards by the light of the street lamp. One night, we crept down the back stairs and went out into the neighborhood. He had something to show me, a discovery he'd made down at the edge of the Johnsons' yard. He led us with the beam of a flashlight, crossing side to side along the path. We'd almost reached the end of the property when the light danced across a collection of empty and crushed beer cans, the remains of a party.

"How do you think those got there?" he asked.

I couldn't imagine that he expected me to have an answer, but he waited, staring at me with his brows tipped upward.

"The TransAlt guys?" I said, more as a question than an answer. This was new territory for me. I felt aware of the air between us. He laughed, kicking some leaves on top and pressing the cans into the dirt with his heel.

"Yeah right," he said, winking.

His words burned in my ears. I could tell that he liked believing I was wise to certain ways of the world, even though it wasn't true. He put his arm across my shoulder, edging me forward and squeezing his hand around the back of my neck. It was a familiar gesture, but the mix of his words and his touch left me with a filmy feeling under my arms. I swallowed hard, hoping he'd release me. We walked down to the corner of the fence where he shined the flashlight on an empty bird's nest. There was a silver coin resting in the bottom.

"It's for you," he said. "A Susan B. Anthony."

It may have been that I was his favorite, but he never said so outright. I figured it was because Elizabeth wasn't much of a talker; she'd go and go, fast and furious all day, until she collapsed in the evening and fell right to sleep. It was the ease that came of activity, the comfort she felt in her very bones. Uncle Rand always saw to her first, tucking her in with a playful romp, tickling her until she pleaded with him to stop. Then he'd make his way down the hall and turn his attention toward me.

Samantha came over to see what Uncle Rand looked like. "He's cute," she said, gazing out the window at him. "Body hair is so sexy on men."

I didn't think so myself, but nodded along with her. We were listening to Billy Joel on my record player and reading the back-to-school issue of *Seventeen*. Outside, at TransAlt, Uncle Rand was talking with the drivers, his arms crossed, peering down over engines.

"Doesn't he have a job?" Samantha asked.

"He did," I said. "A bunch of jobs, all over."

"Yeah, but what does he do now?" she asked.

The question hung between us unanswered and I felt a part of me seal off from her. There was something shameful in a man without work, a man his age with no family, without a home or car.

Lainey DeWitt crossed the driveway to where the men stood. Uncle Rand teased her in a way that made us think there might be potential for a romance, always making fun and then taking it back. He held his arm up dramatically, like a traffic guard.

"Wait, don't tell me," he taunted, "you've got just the thing that'll make me look like a movie star."

"Can't help you there," Lainey zinged back.

"God, I love his accent," Samantha said dreamily. "His voice is so sexy."

The guys sang out in a pained chorus, slapping their knees and the hoods of their cars. They loved Lainey, the way she could hold her own and dish it out. Uncle Rand had his own charm. He was chatty, giving out nicknames, like prizes, always gracing people with details about themselves that perhaps they thought no one had noticed. It made him appear bolder than I somehow knew he was; I could tell it implied the comfort of familiarity without the work of intimacy.

"Do you think they're doing it?" Samantha asked.

I imagined Uncle Rand and Lainey meeting late at night in the garage, taking off their clothes, and lying down on the throw cushions in the lounge area. Would she keep her shoes on? Leave red scratches from her nails across his back? Wrap her legs around his waist?

"Probably," I said, even though I knew that Uncle Rand was home every evening, with me.

Uncle Rand took responsibility for getting the meals together, running short errands in Mama's car and transporting Elizabeth to and from the Y. He was careful to always go below the speed limit, so as not to draw attention to himself. Helping out like that left Mama to manage her nausea and resistance. The Mosquitoes had informed her that if she came down with an infection they would have to postpone follow-up until she was well. She became fierce about germs and told people that she would rather they not come near her if they had a cold or anything.

One day, I found Mama in her garden, weeding with rubber gloves on. She draped a towel around her neck to keep from getting burned and wore her wig, carelessly, like a hat. I sat down next to her and wrapped the tops of the weeds around my hand, pulling in the way she'd taught me, with a low pinch at the base to get the roots.

"Get the dandelions," she said, gesturing to the small, yellow flower. "It doesn't look like a weed, but it is."

We worked like this—moving around the marigolds, verbena, and impatiens—a mound of uprooted greens and dirt growing between us, the only sound that of stems giving way.

"Was Uncle Rand fired from his job?" I asked finally, breaking the silence.

"Goodness no, nothing like that," she said. "What makes you ask such a thing?"

I hesitated. "I was just wondering why he came here."

Mama brushed some dirt off her leg. "Does he need a reason?"

Just then, Uncle Rand rounded the corner with his arms full. He'd made a bird bath out of a hubcap and fastened it onto a stump. "Have room in your garden for this?" he asked, setting it down a couple of yards from where we sat.

"That's good," Mama said, "the birds will help keep the bugs away."

Mrs. Teuffel had found the hubcap on Elm Street, climbing out of her car and holding up traffic to retrieve it for Uncle Rand. He was the kind of man people kept in mind to save things for, imagining perhaps that he was handier than he was, that he should want to do more with his time than cook and garden, should want to hammer or build something. Turning other people's goodwill into his own was the way Uncle Rand distracted attention from his workless days.

"Help me fill this," he said and dragged the hose over to the bird bath. I held the nozzle low, waiting for Uncle Rand to turn on the sprocket.

Mama hugged her knees to her chest and watched. "Maybe we should get a feeder," she said.

That night, lying in bed, I heard a sound near the garage. I walked onto the landing outside my door, expecting to find Uncle Rand, perhaps even Lainey. Instead, I saw Elizabeth and Keith Rogers duck behind a town car and head toward the edge of the Johnsons' property. Uncle Rand must have heard something too. He walked through my room without knocking and came out onto the landing. His chest was bare; he had a towel tied around his waist and held a pack of Marlboros in his hand.

"Hear something?" he asked, his voice scratchy from sleep.

"No," I said, automatically.

He lit a cigarette and leaned against the railing. I looked at the hair on his stomach and his back and then away. I knew Uncle Rand slept buck naked. That's what he called it. He said that the difference between being naked and nekked was that nekked meant you were up to something. Being up to something was the same as touching yourself, I thought, because of the way he said it. The guys in school called it beating off. They made signs in the air, moving one hand up and down in front of their flies. It was the way they said good-bye as the bus drove away. Boys could draw attention to themselves like that and get away with it.

We stood against the railing for a while and stared into the darkness before I started back toward my room, yawning. Uncle Rand followed me, stopping briefly at the foot of my bed.

"Hey," he said, "you know, Tils, you don't have to keep stuff from me." He walked to the door, stopped for a moment, lingering, and then left.

I flipped my pillow to the cool side and waited. I felt lucky to have a new grown-up friend. Someone wiser about the world who I could confide in without the risk of rumor or the danger of punishment. Later, when Elizabeth returned up the staircase and attempted to sneak by me, I sat up and startled her.

"Come here," I demanded.

She climbed into bed next to me, her feet wet and skin clammy. She was nervous and out of breath; her face was pinched with panic.

"Where'd you go?" I asked.

She said nothing at first, just smiled nervously. I poked her hard with my elbow.

"Promise you won't tell?"

"Promise."

She lifted her shirt and showed me her skin which was spotted with hickeys, linked together like a chain around her midriff. They looked like bruises.

"Jewelry," she said proudly.

"Jesus Christ! Who did that?"

"Who do you think?" She was silent for a moment, all sly smiles, and then grew serious. "You shouldn't say Jesus' name like that, you know—"

"Oh shut up. You better cut it out or you're going to get caught."

"By who?"

"Uncle Rand."

"He doesn't notice what I do."

"What about God?" I pressed, mocking her.

"It's not that big a deal," she said, "as long as I remember to do penance." She turned her back to me and folded her arms up under herself.

I ran my hand across my chest and stomach, my fingers cool, my skin electric. What was it like to be touched that way, all groping hands and wet lips? Elizabeth and I fell asleep in the same bed, our backs together, Elizabeth braced for morning and me mashing my mouth against the fleshy part of my arm.

There had always been birds around the place, but until Uncle Rand hung the feeder, no one seemed to know their names. I took a bird book out of the library and stood with Mama at the kitchen counter to watch as cardinals, mourning doves, and red-winged blackbirds settled around the feeder, popping seeds and splitting shells. They scattered in the afternoon when the crows descended, striding across the lawn with upright bodies on long, angled legs.

Nick liked the idea of having a central spot in the yard for bird activity. "Maybe now I don't have to spend all day washing bird crap off the cars," he said, lowering his voice a little for the word crap.

But the barn swallows wouldn't cooperate. They built a nest, like a mud hut, in the corner of the overhang on the garage near the floodlight. They zipped back and forth over the TransAlt lot with the speed of a dart, their sleek forked tails buzzing in their own breeze.

Between the garden and the bird feeder, the backyard became a hub of activity. Elizabeth and I met to depart from the picnic table and Mama gave small tours to the rest of us from the kitchen window, pointing out new buds and birds.

"It's like Grand Central Station out there," Nick said, pausing to check the rain gauge on the window.

Later that week, I woke in the middle of the night to Uncle Rand striding through my room and bounding down the back staircase. I leaped out of bed and followed him to the backyard in my bare feet. When he got to the storage shed under the house, he threw open the door. Even in the dark, I could see Keith Rogers pushed up against the cement wall like one of the rakes, Elizabeth kneeling near his crotch, her hands cupped around him like a praying mantis. Uncle Rand didn't skip a beat; he held the door open with his foot and with one hand snatched Elizabeth up by her hair. With the other hand, he cupped the back of Keith's head and sent him scrambling into the yard.

"Never again," he shouted, his face contorted with fury.

Keith nodded his head without looking up and hurried home across the lawn. Elizabeth walked backwards toward the stairs. She looked disheveled, her hair wild, her shirt untucked. I could smell alcohol on her breath. The house remained still, with no lights, no sign of Mama anywhere.

"I've never hated anyone as much as I hate you," Elizabeth hissed as she passed me.

"I didn't say anything. I swear I didn't."

She ignored me and marched up the stairs toward the bathroom. Uncle Rand went after her, his eyes narrowed, his jaw clenched. I had never seen him so serious. I followed them, my heart racing, and stopped just outside the bathroom door.

"We can go two ways with this, Elizabeth," he said as he sat on the edge of the tub, "either you swear that nothing the likes of this will happen again or else I go straight to your mama."

Elizabeth sat on the bathroom floor and pulled her hair back from her face. She folded it up, making a little pillow, and leaned against the wall.

"And," he continued, "I know I don't need to tell you that this is not what she needs to be thinking about right now."

He waited for a response. Elizabeth curled her bent knees up to her chest and clutched them to her.

"Do we have an understanding?" Uncle Rand asked.

Elizabeth flopped her head up and down and then braced herself against the toilet. "I feel sick," she said.

"I'll bet you do." Uncle Rand took her face in both hands and looked into her eyes. "What'd you have?"

"Nothing," she started to say, and then caught herself. "A wine cooler."

"Just one, huh?"

Elizabeth nodded, her mouth red and loose. "Maybe one and a half."

Uncle Rand sent me to the kitchen to get some bread. When I returned with it, Elizabeth's hair was sticking out from the top of her head like a unicorn. Uncle Rand had helped her dunk her head in a sinkful of cold water to try and straighten her up. The hall smelled sweet and pungent.

"Looks like we've got a case of real bad food poisoning," Uncle Rand said. He looked at her sternly and raised his brows. "Understand?"

I stood in the corner of Elizabeth's room as he put her to bed with a pan by her side. Her eyes narrowed at me.

"I hate you," she said. "You're fat . . . and ugly."

I walked away, aware of my skin under my clothes, my belly pinching against itself as I got into bed. No matter how many times Elizabeth said those words to me in a fight, I could never prepare for how terrible it made me feel.

Before tucking me in, Uncle Rand made sure to tell me that he thought I was beautiful. "You'll look just like your mama," he said. "Besides, Elizabeth will probably get cellulite on her arms and elephantitus ankles." He smiled a big smile and moved to kiss me on the cheek. He missed though, his springy lips pressing near the edge of my mouth.

I slept well that night, trusting what he had imagined for me.

• • •

The next morning I heard Mama's voice in the hall outside Uncle Rand's room. "The last thing I need is you teaching my children to lie," she shrieked, pacing back and forth, nearly hysterical.

"Relax, Frances," Uncle Rand said. "Everything is under control. Besides, I doubt she'll be in a hurry to do it again anytime soon."

"You're supposed to be helping me," she said, "not making things worse."

"I was helping," he said. His voice dropped to a soothing murmur, "I took care of the whole thing so you wouldn't have to."

"I know." She softened a bit. "I just don't understand why she would do such a thing."

"It's not the end of the world," he said. "Things like this happen at that age. Do you remember the night Daddy got a call about me and Lucy Saddleman? Trust me, it could have been much worse."

"I think I liked it better when she was praying and going to church." Mama let out a long sigh and walked down to the kitchen to fix a breakfast tray.

I slipped out of bed and went to check on Elizabeth. She seemed glad to see me, motioned for me to join her in bed. I noticed Elizabeth's pink rosary beads in a dusty heap on the floor and gestured to them. She shrugged, indifferent, and leaned in close to whisper to me. "Do you think Mama knows?"

I nodded, secretly pleased.

A dark look crossed Elizabeth's face. "How come she didn't punish me?"

"I don't know."

"Don't you think that's kind of weird?"

I shrugged. Mama only knew about the drinking. Keith Rogers' crotch was the part that had stayed with me. I wondered how far

Elizabeth had gone. Had she held that rubbery flesh in her mouth? There were rumors about some rock star who needed to have his stomach pumped from doing it too much. Samantha told me that that stuff was harder to digest than bubble gum.

"You didn't swallow anything, did you?"

"No way," Elizabeth said, quivering all over. "I barely even touched it." She seemed suddenly like her old self.

Mama brought up a tray of bland food—soup, Saltine crackers, and ginger ale. There were carrot curls and parsley floating on top of the broth. Mama raised her hand to Elizabeth's cheek and then her forehead, touching each place with the back of her hand and her wrist. It was an automatic gesture, left over from another time, but they both played along—Elizabeth sniffling slightly and Mama shaking down the thermometer.

PART IV

SPELLING

In October, I was chosen to represent the seventh grade in a county spell-off. I was one of five advanced students, but knew, even then, that I had been chosen more for my interest than my talents. Every week, the school librarian had seen me check out the limit from the library. I read aloud to Jamie Sanders after school while he worked in the lot and kept the books stacked by my bed at night. They felt good to hold, the smell of those cool, slippery pages, the weight of a hardcover in my hand.

On my own, I was an impatient reader, quick to leap off the page into my imagination. I could not be counted on to remember the characters' names or the plot. But the story always took me somewhere outside my surroundings and was transforming that way. Enemy threats, rough seas, fragile limbs. Danger, it seemed, was everywhere. Sometimes, while reading one book I would hold another between my legs, squeezing it, the spine hard against my privates, the words in the other, open book, blurring into a line—not distinct and separate the way words were meant to be seen, but wavelike.

This was shameful, I knew, and never told a soul. I had done it with *Death Be Not Proud* and *Lord of the Flies*. I had done it to

Salinger—both *Catcher in the Rye* and *Franny and Zooey*—and also with *Fahrenheit 451*. Returning each of them to their place in the canon, their spines broken. I did it once with the dictionary, that strong red Webster's, while reading *My Ántonia* and imagining myself as a woman alone on the Plains.

Around that time, Samantha came up with the idea to use literary names to refer to sex organs. That way, we could talk about our privates in public without giving it away. "Personification," she called it, which I knew was inspired first by the character of Ralph in *Forever*. But Samantha distanced herself from the Judy Blume books by naming her vagina after Jane Eyre.

"What's yours?" she asked.

"How about Hester Prynne?" I offered.

"Who?" Sam asked. She brought her hand to her mouth, thinking. "Wasn't she some kind of slut?"

"She had a secret baby," I said, "with a priest."

Sam looked disappointed. I could tell she wanted to trade her Jane for my Hester.

"I can't spell," I confessed to Samantha when I was named to the county team. We stood in front of a bulletin board with a list freshly stapled in all four corners to the cork. Samantha dropped her chin slightly and flipped her hair back, to one side and then the other, like swatting at a bee. This was a new, junior high gesture meant to prove that it was possible to have both brains and beauty. It made me wish for long hair.

"You can too spell," Samantha said, pointing to the list as some kind of proof. "Besides, spelling is easy. They should really test us on vocabulary."

She didn't know how hard I studied in secret, writing the words over and over, committing them to memory, only to lose them the moment I took a test. Sam could hold words in her head, barely needing to study, even for the cumulative tests at the end of a quarter. She would see those same words out in the world, on signs or the front pages of newspapers locked behind glass. She was always dragging me toward a word and pointing it out. The spaces between letters were as pronounced as the ink itself. She'd grown up playing Scrabble and doing crossword puzzles. The Shaptaws had whole conversations about words over dinner.

What worried me most about the spell-off was the format. I imagined myself sitting in an unfamiliar auditorium in front of an audience, trying to see the word as it was spoken. I wondered whether we would be allowed scrap paper and pens. It worried me that there was no way to study, no way to prepare.

Also, there was no way to cheat.

Cheating was what teachers called it, when really it had always seemed to me more like checking. There was an assumption that it was something that problem students did, because they were the ones who always got caught. They didn't understand how to stagger their progress, would shoot for 100 if they could get it. They leaned into the aisles, shamelessly peering over a smarter kid's shoulder. Samantha didn't believe in doing that. She blocked her work with her body. When the tests were handed back, she never told anyone her grade.

When the teachers got smart, making us skip rows or alternate seats on the day of a test, the cheaters got smarter. Some girls, private about their ambitions, held carefully folded papers under their thighs—almost a form of origami—with all the necessary information printed in tiny words, making patterns. It was the boys who got caught. Their methods were too blatant and usually brought the teacher to their sides, snatching up tests and demanding that they stay after class. Meanwhile all around the room, resourceful girls had answers written discreetly on their skin, codes on their fingernails or secret memory tricks along their wrist like a bracelet.

I had tried all of these methods in an attempt to make sure my work was as good as it could be. But doing well meant something for me beyond grades. It had something to do with who my friends would be, whether I would be liked, and what kind of girl I would become.

Jamie Sanders didn't cheat. He must have sensed that no one expected too much from him. I could see his resignation, how uninterested he was in approval, how relaxed he was about his homework when we gathered after school on the couches in the garage. Even Jamie, with his oil-black hair and stained clothes looked clean against that background. He loved to hear me read, lacing his calloused fingers together, cradling one denim knee, and rocking slowly as I read aloud from Orwell's *1984*—a favorite of ours. At the end of each section, he sat up and switched legs, kicking one out and folding the other into him. He once told me that he'd never been read to, not even as a child.

Deep into the book, Jamie raised his brows at me. "Big Brother is everywhere," he warned.

"Cut it out," I said, marking the page with my finger and smacking him on the thigh with the hard edge of the cover.

"What would you do if I could read your mind?" he whispered.

It chilled me. "That could never happen," I said, imagining my most private thoughts broadcast over loudspeakers.

We fell away from each other and listened to the radio. West Westerly predicted cool, crisp air—the kind that would change the leaves from green to yellow and then orange and make the birds grow hectic. The kind of air that turned fitful sleep into deep slumber.

• • •

Uncle Rand offered to help me prepare for the spell-off. He tucked me in with a back rub, holding a bottle of Jergen's hand lotion high above me, squirting quick cold lines along my spine and single drops around my shoulders. He spread the lotion out thick over my back and spelled words into me with the tips of his fingers. Some were words for objects in my room and I could look around me and guess what he might have been considering. But other, more surprising words, I had to lie still against and concentrate hard to make out. Words that had nothing to do with wallpaper, desks, or clothes. Words such as hurricane. Or Cadillac.

"If you're smart," he said, challenging me, "try this one." The way he spoke to me made it difficult to tell whether being smart was a good or bad thing. Something in his tone sounded harsh. He spelled out duckbill platypus, one letter at a time, dropping his closed fist against me as an indicator of spacing, the letters sliding onto my sides. I clutched my arms tight against my body, forgetting altogether how the words were spelled as his fingers brushed at my waist and moved under the covers along my hips and rear.

As he continued, the spelling spilled over, fading from distinct letters into lines or waves. I pretended to be asleep, hoping for him to abandon the exercise and turn to bed. He raised the sheet back over me and gathered his bottle of lotion and glass of wine. I listened to the floorboards carry him to his room, the creak of the bed frame as his weight sank into the mattress, the deep clearing of his throat. While I waited, I tried to remember the last word that was spelled, the last full letter imprinted on my skin, willing his touch in order to test myself. By morning the words were gone and Mama woke me for a third time, frustrated and frantic, hollering that I was sure to be late for school. "What has gotten into you?" She looked at me for a whole minute, studying my face as if somehow my thoughts could be read on my skin.

• • •

The week before the spell-off, I grew anxious and distracted. Every time someone spoke a word I did not know, I tried to see it spelled, right there in the air or against the pattern of some kid's cross-stitched sweater, a teacher's plaid skirt. I broke every conversation into fragments, splitting each word into letters, not really hearing anything. Once, Nick waved his arm in front of my face, his thick fingers webbed together. "Yoo hoo. I-s a-n-y-o-n-e h-o-m-e?"

I spent the evenings after supper combing through my dictionary and drifting off into a scattered sleep of spelling rules and exceptions, the letters coupling and breaking apart in mixed combinations. Elizabeth made fun of me. How could I care so much about school?

All that effort wasn't showing in my work. I grew careless, my papers filled with dark ink crossouts. I developed a habit of changing my mind about words, writing one letter over another, making layers of ink and smears across the paper. The underside of my hand was always slightly blue.

"Try this," Mama said and added a petal to the dark ink center, turning my misspellings into flowers.

I drew them, petals giving way to bouquets, stems curling into the margins, like weeds.

The night before the competition, Uncle Rand came in long after my bedtime. I heard him set his wineglass on top of the dictionary on the nightstand. I was lying on my stomach, everything tucked up under me, my head turned toward the wall. I felt him lift the covers off me and push my shirt up. The words came to me, filling my mind, first as letters and spaces, then forming into whole words: f-o-s-s-i-l fossil; e-n-g-a-g-e-m-e-n-t engagement; c-o-n-c-h conch. Each time my mind cleared, I could feel his touch—warm and a bit damp. Was it his hand or his tongue pulling lines across my body?

What was he spelling? It was the exceptions that rose to my mind next: *i* before *e* except after *c* or sounding like *a* as in neighbor and weigh. The variant spellings were my favorites; they proved that there wasn't always just one answer: aeroplane a-e-r-o-p-l-a-n-e and theatre t-h-e-a-t-r-e. Then his body was over mine, not touching but just above, and I could feel the hair on his chest, sense the movement of his flesh. I heard a mumbling deep in his throat, muffled sounds like gasping. I lay still and thought of the silent consonants g-n-a-t gnat and k-n-u-c-k-l-e knuckle.

This last word stuck and somehow comforted me. Knuckle. I thought of Samantha, her hand wrapped tight around a pencil, moving across her notebook without stopping, the smooth page rippling like a sheet under the weight of her fist.

The next morning, Uncle Rand made my favorite breakfast. Bull's-eye eggs, with toast and home-fried potatoes.

I poked at the yokes with my fork until they bled. Uncle Rand nudged me gently. "Eat up," he said, "you're going to need some protein."

I could smell him in the food. His stale morning breath, like dishes sitting too long in the sink. I didn't look up, instead I sat hunched over while my stomach churned.

"You're probably too nervous to eat," Nick said.

"Can I have your potatoes?" Elizabeth asked, blinking at me. She had on blue eyeshadow that made her face look strangely white.

"Nice lids," I said and pushed my plate at her.

Mama came into the dining room wearing one of Nick's flannel shirts. Her clothes were haphazard; the netting at the back of her wig was showing. Her sloppy look made me feel impatient. She didn't look like a mother.

"Are you going to wear that?" I asked.

"It's comfortable," she said, looking down at herself and then up at Nick. "It's okay, isn't it?" she asked.

"I think you look great," Elizabeth said, scowling at me.

Mama smiled at her and then looked twice, catching sight of her makeup. "Elizabeth, take that stuff right off," she said, suddenly stern, "or you're not going anywhere."

Elizabeth pushed her stool back loudly. "That's so unfair," she said and stomped up the back stairs.

Nick stepped behind Mama. "You look like a million bucks." He brushed her hair casually with his fingers, covering the exposed netting at the back of her head.

I could hear Uncle Rand in the kitchen. The weight of each step, his voice as he whistled. The sound of him made my mind go blank. But the harder I tried to push it away, the stronger the memory surfaced. He was there, behind me, a shadow on every thought, peeking over my shoulder and breathing his hot breath.

The junior high transported us in a minibus, two counties over, to a rival school. On the bus, my team practiced. Saying the word, spelling it, and saying it again. We took turns, spelling the words that had been asked in previous years, trying to second-guess which, if any, might reappear. Jonathan Marcus had a good one. He was the only boy chosen among four girls. He felt he had something to prove. He asked about the crested green and red bird in Central America that shares its name with the monetary unit of Guatemala.

"Quezal q-u-e-z-a-l quezal," Samantha responded.

"Wrong," he said. "It's spelled with a t—q-u-e-t-z-a-l."

"Guess again," Samantha said, flipping her hair.

"I don't have to guess," he said, "I have it right here in front of me."

This was my specialty; rather than let a dispute go on and on, I'd learned how to settle it quickly with my dictionary. I retrieved my Webster from my bookbag, its red glossy cover quieting the bus. Everyone waited as I flipped through the pages, my finger moving down the column. Seeking authority was the best I could do. I didn't trust myself in these matters.

I mouthed the words query, quest, question. "Quetzal with a *t*," I announced.

Just as Jonathan filled the bus with a self-righteous "yes," my finger moved below queue, a word for pigtail or braid that I had not known, to quezal without the *t*.

"Let me see that," Jonathan demanded, snatching the dictionary away from me and tearing the cover.

Samantha settled back in her seat, smug and confident. She would win it for us that afternoon, long after Jonathan had been knocked out for forgetting the first *i* in plagiarism, bringing his fist down hard on the table in anger, after I had blankly switched the *l* and *e* in tentacle, Samantha would last ten words longer than anyone else, spelling ellipsis and valediction. For her last word, she would spell onomatopoeia o-n-o-m-a-t-o-p-o-e-i-a onomatopoeia. Like automatic poet, I thought to myself as she spoke her letters into the air, each floating over the audience, where her family and mine sat next to each other in the third row, our siblings taken out of school, flanking our mothers with the men on either side like bookends.

As I looked out from the stage, I felt suddenly ashamed. Other families shared a look of togetherness. Mine seemed separate, as if they had been thrown together by accident. Too many adults, all with different last names. Nick was younger than the other fathers. Nobody else had a live-in uncle. And Mama didn't even look like herself—bloated and wearing a wig. Elizabeth twisted in her seat, distracted. I couldn't catch anyone's eye. I had no idea how to feel.

GIFT

That fall, Osage oranges fell from the spiny bodark trees, their fleshy green skins splitting open and rotting on the street. The stench was everywhere. While Elizabeth hoped for Fridays, I looked forward to Mondays—the moment when I could walk away from it all, leaving the stuffy air of the house behind me as if that life belonged to someone else. I buried myself in school projects, earning extra credit and red plus marks across the top of every page.

When I wasn't doing schoolwork, I shadowed Jamie Sanders as he maintained the lot, checking the oil and transmission fluid. By the time it turned cold enough to funnel antifreeze into the plastic overflow tank, I knew my way around an engine: could tell the difference between the valves and seals, could even jump-start a battery, hooking the claws of one black cable to the negative terminal and the other to the engine block for grounding. I liked the hum and predictability of function. I could stare deep into the engine, counting the number of cylinders, watching the belt spin, and listening to the click of pistons and the smooth whir of the fan—metal and rubber churning together—every part working as it should.

By the time Mama was ready for her last chemotherapy treatment, it was December, but no one in our house was acting like it. There were no lists, no bustling sense of preparation. In the past,

Mama had always been early to buy wrapping paper and tape. All over the neighborhood, people were stringing up lights and decorating their porches. We didn't even have a wreath. Everything was on hold.

The night before Mama's appointment with the Mosquitoes, it snowed. I watched as the flakes blanketed the driveway, a fine dusting which quickly thickened, whiting out the decay of fallen leaves and brown grass. The world outside grew so quiet I could hear the beat in my head, like marching. The wind blew hard and Nick sealed the upstairs windows closed with duct tape to keep the draft out.

Later, in the bathroom, Elizabeth and I traded off supplies as we got ready for bed—toothpaste, soap, hand towel—and moved through our rituals without talking. All around us were signs of neglect. My toothbrush was sprung wide, resembling an exotic caterpillar. The shampoo and conditioner bottles were filled with water—our attempts to stretch out their contents. We had been waiting for this day without even realizing it.

The next morning I woke to the sound of Uncle Rand clomping down the stairs in his boots. I watched from the window as he joined Nick and Jamie with a shovel. Jamie was always the first one out in a storm hoping for a bit of extra work. It was as if he lived at TransAlt, the first to arrive each day before school, the last to leave in the evening. They looked like astronauts in their puffed coats and heavy boots, the three of them digging in time around the station wagon.

"Get dressed," Mama called from the bottom of the stairs, "and come down for breakfast."

Elizabeth took a long time in the bathroom, told me to go away when I banged hard on the door. When she finally undid the latch, she was wearing a towel over her nightgown. She lingered, straightening up the counter around the sink, moving her Noxzema and hairbrush to one corner.

She shook her head. "Something's happened."

"Could I have some privacy?" I asked.

She hesitated, looked away, and then directly at me. "I got it," she said, her face suddenly flushed.

"What?"

"It came," she said, "just now." She retied the towel at her waist and shrugged. "Can I borrow something?"

All at once, I knew what she was talking about. How could this have happened out of order? It was unnatural! It didn't seem fair that she should get hers before I got mine.

"Show me," I demanded. "I don't believe you."

Elizabeth didn't resist. I felt curious, but queasy too. She took off the towel and handed it to me. There was toilet paper shooting out from the sides of her underwear. She pulled them down, exposing a wad of carefully folded paper towels layered with toilet paper. At the center was a thin brown line. I had expected something brighter, a cherry red, more urgent looking. She bent the papers toward me and then looked up, anxiously.

"It's practically nothing," I said, more in anger than surprise.

"You have to help me," she said, her voice rising. She seemed as disturbed as I was by this reversal of events. "Please," she begged, "I'll wait right here."

I went for the Starter Kit which I had stored at the back of my closet. I resented having to open it. I'd already imagined for myself which products I would use and when. I surveyed the various pastel boxes until my eye settled on the item I was least likely to use—the old-fashioned pads that were supposed to clip to a belt. When I handed the box to Elizabeth, her temper flickered and then dissipated. She knew that those pads were the worst pick of the lot, but thanked me anyway.

I got dressed in front of the mirror in my room—turtleneck, button-down, sweater—layering myself against this news. My breasts were nowhere near the right shape, not full or round, just empty flaps of skin.

As I headed down the stairs, Elizabeth called out to me. "Hey Tilden! Don't tell anyone."

The kitchen smelled like chicken. Mama had cooked filets and cut them into strips. "Want toast?" she asked, holding a plate out to me. The pieces were buttered and stacked to encourage melting. I took a piece off the bottom.

"Where's Elizabeth?" she asked.

"She doesn't feel well."

Mama stiffened. "What's wrong?"

"Nothing." I said. "It's just a stomach ache. But she's not throwing up or anything."

I could see Mama's own nausea rise, her cheeks suddenly pale, her pores large. She set her paper napkin over the rest of the food on her plate. Nick came in to change his clothes and left Uncle Rand and Jamie Sanders in the foyer, kicking their boots against the door frame and shaking snow out of their cuffs. The cold air from outside traveled along the floor and chilled the kitchen.

"School's on," Uncle Rand announced. He looked at me and then away. His face was raw. He wiped his nose on his sleeve, grabbed the keys and went back outside to start both cars.

Jamie Sanders leaned against the wall, half in and half out of the house; his hands were pushed into his pockets, his shoulders shrugged up around his ears. He looked as if he were on the verge of saying something, but didn't. Instead, he pressed the clumps of snow from his boots with his toe until they melted into the mat.

Elizabeth came into the kitchen wearing her winter coat. She rummaged through the snack drawer for a breakfast bar and pocketed her lunch money off the counter. She avoided looking anyone in the face while she waited by the back door for the town car to warm up.

"Everyone have everything you need?" Mama asked.

We nodded automatically, even Jamie, and then all left the house together—Nick and Jamie on either side of Mama as she balanced herself against the ice, Elizabeth and I at arm's length from each other until we reached the car. From inside the station wagon, Uncle Rand, Elizabeth, and I watched through fogged windows as Nick's town car slid side to side, the tires spinning on the surface, before grabbing hold of the sand. Jamie lent his weight to the back of the car, guiding Mama and Nick out of the driveway and onto the road. They drove away slowly, leaving fresh tracks in the snow. From the back, I saw Nick put his right arm across Mama's shoulders.

Is this *it* now, I wondered. Is Nick really permanent?

Mama was sick right up until a week before Christmas. The final treatment made her as weak and grumpy as all the others had. She wasn't up for the hustle and bustle of the holidays, even canceled our trip to New York City to see *The Nutcracker*. She barely felt up for Main Street or the Walt Whitman Mall.

"Let's not do gifts this year," she suggested.

Elizabeth was angry. She had hopes of receiving a Walkman, was even holding out for a Sunfish sailboat. She left Mama in the middle of a sentence about learning to appreciate what we have and went out to the garage to drum up support from Nick.

"I wasn't finished," Mama said to the door and then to me because I was the one left standing there.

"I know," I said, weakly.

I hurried out the door to retrieve Elizabeth. TransAlt had become a winter sanctuary. I liked the flow of activity—the sound of the drivers' voices over the radio, Lainey's playful bantering. All the coming and going made the place seem alive in contrast to the stillness of the house. Even Mrs. Teuffel, who usually stood at her fence for conversation, made her way around the snow pillars at the end of the drive every afternoon with crackers or cookies, looking for company. She liked to sit near the police scanner to monitor the local activity, said it helped her rest easier to know what was what before she turned in for the evening.

Elizabeth went straight to Nick, raising her objections loudly enough for everyone else to hear over the drone of the electric heaters. "Mama's not planning to celebrate Christmas," she started, "can you believe it? She said we ought to think of each and every day as a gift." Elizabeth waited for a response and when one didn't come, she launched in again from a different angle. "It's unchristian, isn't it?"

Mrs. Teuffel's body bent closer to the discussion with each word.

"Now hold on one minute," Nick said. "I don't believe anyone said anything about not celebrating. Just because your mama doesn't have the energy to shop, doesn't mean that Santa won't be around."

Elizabeth rolled her eyes at him. "Oh please. We've never had a Christmas like this . . ."

She didn't complete her sentence. Suddenly it seemed as if everything had gone wrong. "We came all this way," I wanted to scream, "and now look!"

Mrs. Teuffel turned toward Elizabeth and spoke from the corner of her mouth, like a ventriloquist. "Now that's unchristian."

Elizabeth took it back. "That's not what I meant," she said in a high, shrill voice.

After a small silence Nick said, "Truth is, I don't think she's feeling real good about how she looks." He offered this as an explanation, when really he seemed to be asking for advice. He raised his brows, pushed his tongue against the inside of his cheek and looked down over his shoes.

"Well I don't suppose she is," Mrs. Teuffel said, now fully in the conversation. "She's been to hell and back."

Nick nodded once and then again as if applying her words to a bunch of things he hadn't said out loud. It was the first time since Mama's surgery that I noticed how tired Nick looked. The skin around his eyes was creased and gray.

"You better be doing your part to make her feel . . . " Mrs. Teuffel hesitated, cleared her throat and started up again. "She needs to know that you, all of you, love her as much as ever, that's all."

Things got real quiet after that. Nick seemed sorry to have brought it up, looked embarrassed as he shifted his weight from one leg to the other and adjusted his belt.

It wasn't long before Lainey DeWitt was in on the discussion. "I think what Frances needs is an overhaul, top to bottom," she said. "Everyone could chip in, give her a little something to get the ball moving."

"What do you mean?" Nick asked.

"A makeover," Lainey said, "you know, a manicure, facial, the works . . ."

"Won't that hurt her feelings?" Nick asked.

"No way," Lainey said. "Every woman wants to look her best. Besides, who wouldn't want a little push?"

Elizabeth loved the idea. "See, that's what I mean," she said, "I just think someone should be doing something."

Lainey offered to coordinate the gifts, making sure that no two people had the same idea or were planning to give the same thing. We could go to her for suggestions or to talk through our ideas. We had to have our present to Lainey a day before Christmas so that the whole gift could be wrapped together as one.

"You *are* planning to have a tree?" Lainey said to Nick.

"Uncle Rand can handle that," Nick said. "Tilden, you go with him, okay? But let's have one with roots so we can plant it outside after . . . as a symbol."

I balked.

"Okay?" Nick pressed. "I want to be able to look out in this yard and see a tree standing there in honor of your mama beating this thing."

I hadn't done anything alone with Uncle Rand since the spell-off. I'd timed my activities around the sounds of him in the house and gone to bed long before he made his way upstairs. Mostly, I avoided looking him in the eye, afraid to see in his face an acknowledgment, not so much of what had happened that night but of what had been lost since.

I couldn't stop remembering the way he'd touched me, his thick fingers, his hot mouth on my skin. Those words and letters mixing with the slightly stale smell of him. But what lingered most was where the touching had taken us. At first, Uncle Rand had seemed needy, his whole body trembling and open. Something in all that urgency made me feel that I mattered, even if it was in the wrong way. Then, when it was over, a wall came down between us. Night after night he continued on, alone in his own room, where I could hear him. I couldn't help but imagine myself there even though I knew it was wrong. I wanted to be more important to someone than I was.

The next day when I got home from school, Uncle Rand was waiting in the station wagon at the end of the driveway.

"You all set?" he asked, rolling down the window, and poking his face into the cold air. "We're going tree hunting."

"Shouldn't Elizabeth come too?"

"I thought maybe just you and I could go."

He rolled up the window and waited while I put my books in the house. I dreaded the thought of conversation. Not the talking so much as the quiet between talking. What did he want from me?

In the car, I did my best to avoid a lull, started in about my tests and assignments, my friends and their plans for the holidays. Libbie Gorin's family was going on a ski trip over New Year's. Jill Switt's and Christy Diamo's families planned to go caroling before Midnight Mass. Samantha's family celebrated both Hanukkah and Christmas. I stared out the window while reciting this information. The icy trees hovered, their dark branches pointing like gnarled fingers. Everything I said felt stupid. By the time I finished talking, we were turning into the tree farm.

"What do you want?" Uncle Rand asked after he had turned off the engine.

"Huh?"

"For Christmas?"

"Me?"

The entire parking lot was filled with trees, lined up by kind and tagged with plastic markers. The cut trees were stacked upright against sawhorses. Behind them, the live trees stood on their own, their roots balled in burlap and tied with string. I saw the one I wanted right away, but went through the exercise of going down each aisle. Uncle Rand did the same, stopping to roll each kind in his hand, feeling the needles, and bringing his fingers up to his nose. Every once in a while he would step back and take in a whole tree, eyeing its width and height, checking for balance. When he caught up with me, I was standing next to a blue spruce, turning the tag over to check the price.

"Homely little tree," he said, snapping the end of a branch with his bare hand and holding it up to his nose. "Smells nice though."

He started to walk on to the next one.

"This is the one I want," I said.

"Why?" he asked. "Look at how sparse it is." He latched his fingers together and bent them back, cracking all his knuckles at once.

"I don't care." I crossed my arms. "This is the one I want."

"But it lacks balance." His voice, low and quiet, reverberated with disappointment.

"I like it," I said.

"Don't you want to look around some more?"

"Nope."

We had reached an impasse, the tree standing between us like a squat referee. Uncle Rand grabbed for the price tag. "It even costs more," he said, trying to appeal to my practical side.

"*This* is what I want for Christmas," I said.

Uncle Rand looked at me long and hard, searching my face. For what, I didn't know. Perhaps he expected more loyalty from me. I stared past him, unmoved. He let out a snort of frustration and then signaled to the nursery owner. Together, they slipped a net over the top to hold the branches close to the trunk. The base bulged around a heavy twine. I sat in the car and waited while Uncle Rand lifted the tree onto the rack on top and secured it with cord.

Driving toward home, I stared out the window and tried to name the various evergreen and fir trees along the road. We'd bought the tree that no one else wanted. It felt like a rescue. I had never disagreed with Uncle Rand before. He drove quietly with only one hand on the steering wheel. The afternoon light was low and bleak. When he finally spoke, his voice surprised me.

"I'll sure be glad when this whole thing with your mama is over," he said. "I'll tell you one thing, Tilden, honey. If I could trade places with her I would."

I couldn't speak. I tried to picture Mama and Uncle Rand as children—Randy a full ten years younger, always struggling to keep up, weaving pins through his teeth when Mama got braces, packing himself in the car when she went to college. I wished that he would stop talking. I wanted to know her better than he did.

"We're a lot alike," he said, "me and you." He placed one hand on my knee. "You're responsible, Tilden, more mature than your sister, you know that? You can handle more than she can." His face was inches away from mine; I watched every vein and whisker, waiting as if he might at any moment confide in me. "So if I rely on you more, that's why. It's because I trust you can handle it."

Route 25A took us past the Long Island Sound, so frozen with ice and windblown drifts of snow, that it seemed possible to walk from one side to the other. I rested my cheek against the cold window. Somewhere underneath the black and white of winter, there was a blue and green world. Something was waiting just below the surface.

Elizabeth was pissy before we even took the netting off. "It's not real," she said, refering to the dusty silver color as Uncle Rand and Nick lifted the tree into the house.

"A blue spruce," Nick said, looking back and forth between the tree and its spot in the yard. "That'll look real nice." He gave me a wink and began sawing at the netting with his pocket knife.

"I don't know why you let her choose." Elizabeth glared at me and then ran upstairs.

Uncle Rand tossed the car keys into a basket by the back door and climbed after her, two steps at a time.

"What's with them?" Nick asked.

I shrugged. "She's moody."

Later, Nick covered the tree with lights, securing each bulb in place, while Mama went through her address book and wrote out holiday notes on boxed cards. I had never seen her do that before.

"Who are they for?" I asked.

"Oh," she said, her voice high and a little spacey, "just old friends."

I sewed strands of popcorn and cranberries, making some pure and mixing others, and then looped them in even scallops around the tree. When I finished, I stepped back and squinted, creating my own kaleidoscope of blurred lights.

"It looks beautiful," Mama said.

Nick set up his tripod and called Elizabeth and Uncle Rand to come downstairs for a picture.

"It smells like a movie theater in here," Uncle Rand said, inspecting my garlands.

Nick arranged us around the tree and pulled up a chair in the center for Mama. He set the timer and jumped in behind her. He did this four times, switching sides and rotating each of us closer to Mama.

"Why am I in the hot seat?" she joked. She slid her wig forward on her scalp, giving herself longer bangs, and checked her hair in the reflection from the TV screen.

"How come there's no angel on top?" Elizabeth asked after we had disassembled.

"We're not finished," I snapped back.

"Just asking," Elizabeth said, "you don't have to be such a . . ."

"Please," Mama said, "I can't take a fight tonight."

"I kind of like it plain," Nick said, winking at me.

Elizabeth wrapped a red tablecloth around the metal tub and stood back to admire her contribution. "It looks a little empty down there," she said, giving one final dig about the presents before turning on the TV to watch *The Nutcracker*.

Mama suggested that we cast ourselves in the production. She had once read that the New York City Ballet had open calls for certain roles. Elizabeth requested the dancing parts—after all she had taken ballet in Atlanta—and made a convincing case for her ability to change costumes and appear over and over again, not just as Snow and the Dew Drop in Flowers, but in the Marzipan and Chinese and Arabian dances as well. In addition, she wanted to be both Clara and the Sugar Plum Fairy.

"I want to be the Sugar Plum Fairy," Mama said.

I was surprised. I would have cast her as the mother.

"Who do you want to be, Tilden?" Mama asked.

"Everything is taken," I answered.

"Not Candy Cane," Elizabeth said. "Or Dolls."

The truth was that I had always liked Act I more than Act II. The busy preparation for the party, that peek into someone else's house before they lift the scrims, the guests arriving in top hats with gifts, the champagne toast. I remember noticing that each stage family was fully intact and that the children all seemed to know each other and play together with abandon. I had never felt that kind of freedom. I imagined myself more like the French maid, the first to enter and the last to leave a room, taking capes at the door and snuffing candles at the end of each evening. She seemed to know everything just before it happened.

"Whatever," I said. "I don't care."

Elizabeth cast Uncle Rand as Drosselmeyer, the mysterious relative who brings the Nutcracker and winds the clock.

Nick had never watched *The Nutcracker* before. "I'll be anyone," he said, "as long as I don't have to wear tights."

Elizabeth knew the music well enough to predict each change. She could tell who was up next and liked to call out the few positions and terms she could pronounce from her ballet class. *Développé, Arabesque, Piqué, Grand Jeté . . .*

It had once seemed magical, the simultaneous swaying and leaping of the corps. But suddenly with Elizabeth's technical commentary, my eye caught only the mistakes: a stray snowflake fluttering from the rafters during the Spanish dance, one long white arm out of sync with the others in Flowers. I had loved the Polichanelles, who appear out from under their mother's giant dress to dance in circles and do somersaults until they are called back between her legs—fourteen of them scampering to obey—except one who stays behind to show off. Now, I found them irritating and reckless.

Mama fell asleep in her chair before Clara and the Prince took off in their sled, the music booming and the Sugar Plum Fairy leading the entire cast in a skyward wave.

"The sled is suspended with wire," Elizabeth announced. "See it?"

That night, after I had turned off my light, I looked out the window and saw Uncle Rand duck into the garage. It was after hours, past the time when TransAlt took its latest calls and there was no sign of drivers. The floodlight made the banked snow sparkle, even though in the day it was dingy with exhaust and traffic. The stars were cold in the sky. I watched for signs that would tell me what Uncle Rand might be up to. I imagined scenarios which alternately excused and implicated him. He was stealing, then sleepwalking. Through it all he was drinking. That much I knew. At night, he was always drinking. Although it was unclear to me whether to cast the drinking in terms of his guilt or innocence.

The screen door flapped in the wind until he pushed it tightly closed with his hip. His movements down the driveway were bulky, his body puffed out with purpose, the way younger guys advance onto a playing field or enter the boy's room. It made me angry to see him move this way. Then, he dropped the keys and fumbled around in the darkness, sputtering and cursing, and I realized that he planned to take the station wagon. I felt the urge to stop him. Or perhaps I felt the expectation that I should want to stop him, but a larger, uglier part of me wanted to see him get in the car and keep going. The more I tried to blink this thought away, the stronger it surfaced.

This mix of feelings confused me; I had never before felt so many things about one person.

My hatred rose inside me, hot and slick, like a bulb of mercury, and then fell. The guilt of hating him was so overwhelming that I slid out of my bed and walked onto the landing in my socks with half a hope that he might see me there and stop. If something did happen to him, I would be the only one who might have been able to prevent it. With this knowledge, I watched him steer the car out of the driveway in a quick, snaking motion. Back in bed, I pushed my pillow up under me and held it there, my stomach tightening as I moved against it. Afterward, I felt alone—the room so quiet I was afraid to breathe.

The next morning, before dawn, I looked out the window and found Mama's car back in its place. I could hear Uncle Rand snoring in his room. A feeling of dread and disgust came over me. I got up to close his door and found him, lying on top of his covers, his penis flopped over on his thigh. I couldn't believe he could fall asleep like that, on his back without covers. I watched his chest go up and down, over and over, and tried to picture him still, not breathing at all. I don't know how long I had been standing there, when Mama's voice scared me up against the wall.

"What is going on here?" she said. "Get out of his room."

Uncle Rand opened his eyes at me.

"What are you doing?" Mama continued. "Get to bed."

I ran to my room and slammed the door.

"Calm down, Frances," I heard him say. "She's just curious. She's at that age."

I waited, pulse racing, with my pillow over my head for Mama to come to my room. It was my fault. I had been caught staring at his pink, eraser-shaped penis. Afraid that Mama would take his side, I considered all the bad things that he had done. He drank too much and then drove. There were times at night when he had watched me too. Even touched me. But now none of this seemed enough. She would blame me, I knew. When I heard the knock on my door, I froze.

"Tilden, I'm disappointed in you," Mama started, "this isn't at all like you. You have got to respect Uncle Rand's privacy."

I nodded.

"I want you to apologize first thing," she said.

I could feel her lingering in the door, but refused to look up until I heard her walk away. I rested on my bed, waiting for the alarm clock to ring. There was a loyalty between them that went beyond common sense, preventing Mama from seeing his faults and from acting on them. For all her talk of privacy, I had none. No lock on my door, no window shades, not even a liner on the shower curtain.

I dressed, pulling on nylons first, then long johns, under my corduroys. Even with all the layers, I still felt naked.

Just before going downstairs, I knocked on Uncle Rand's door.

"At your service," he answered. He was wearing a bathrobe and sitting on the end of his bed.

"I'm sorry," I said, leaning against the doorjamb.

Uncle Rand smiled, slid off the bed and walked over to me. He put his hand on my shoulder. "I shouldn't be lounging around here like a lizard anyway." He squeezed the fleshy part of my arm. "Don't give it another thought," he said.

I stayed like that as long as I could and then moved out from under his palm. When I got to the end of the hall, Elizabeth called me into her room.

"Look what Uncle Rand brought me," she said, all excited.

There, under her window, was a miniature Christmas tree, cut fresh out of the woods and resting in a small bucket. He had decorated it with change—nickels, dimes, pennies, and even a silver dollar—each strung up with fishing line through a hole in the top.

"Isn't he sweet?"

"I guess so."

"What's your problem?" Elizabeth asked.

"Nothing."

"You're just jealous."

I ran down the stairs, grabbed my coat, and headed for the bus stop. It was the last day before break and I couldn't imagine spending ten days at home. As I waited, Jamie pulled up next to me in his car. The back wheels of his Duster were larger than the front, causing the car to lean forward in a bow.

He rolled down the window. "I'd give you a ride, but . . ."

"Okay," I said and looked around quickly before climbing in.

"Are you sure?" he asked.

"I don't care what they think."

My feet straddled the mess on the floor—plastic cassette holders, soda cans, and fast-food bags. Jamie drove off, the engine loud and rumbling, the seats shaking. He pushed a tape into the deck with the heel of his palm. "Bat Out of Hell," by Meat Loaf blared from the speakers. He drove to Dunkin' Donuts and bought a glazed cruller.

"Want a bite?" he asked. He tilted his head the way he tilted the cruller, forward and questioning.

I shook my head.

"What's wrong?" he asked.

"Nothing," I said. "I'm tired. We set up our tree last night."

Even though Jamie didn't talk much, he never let me get away with silence. "So?" he pressed.

"It's a live one," I said, "with the roots and everything."

"That's cool." He fingered the new evergreen air freshener that hung from a knob on his dashboard. At the stoplight nearest the junior high, he looked up at me. "That all?"

"I can't wait for this vacation to be over," I said.

"Are you kidding?" He stared at me. "There's definitely something wrong with you. I would give anything to be at *your* house."

I could see something soften in his face. It made me edgy to have someone notice me fully. I knew that if I told anyone how I felt, I would slip right off the edge of the earth.

On Christmas Eve, Lainey assembled a large basket of gifts, each wrapped in a different color paper. In the card, she pasted a picture of the human body from an anatomy book. There were color stickers on various parts of the body with names written inside. It looked like a diagram of pressure points from my science textbook. Mama would have to match up each present with the colored dot in order to find out what part of the body it was intended for and who it was from. "The new you in the new year," Lainey wrote in bubble letters across the top of the card.

The next morning, Elizabeth and I got up early and went downstairs. We were surprised to find that the red skirt under the tree held a few gifts from Uncle Rand. We raced around the house scoping out items that could be wrapped up and given as gifts from us. Mama had always encouraged this kind of giving. She stressed that the most important part of any gift was the card. It was what made something special out of something familiar, what made it all right to wrap up socks and toiletries. To give things that the person might get for herself anyway. The card was the part we would remember and save after the gift had made its way into the routine of our day. We wrapped our findings with a flourish, writing up cards and tying candy and costume jewelry onto the package with Elizabeth's brightly colored hair ribbons.

When we finished, it was almost time for the guests to arrive. We carried our gifts down the stairs and spread them out under the tree. Mama was startled to see so many presents, but pleased too.

"How did all this come about?" she asked. She was wearing her bathrobe with thermals underneath. Her wig looked scraggly and unkempt.

For months, I had just accepted her treatments as a part of life. But now that it was Christmas morning, I could recall what it had been like before, when we celebrated with stockings and carefully wrapped packages with bows. Mama had always worn a red Santa's hat with white trim and small bells tied on her shoelaces. One year, she'd hidden our gifts in the yard, everything magic, her face flushed with excitement, ready to surprise us.

When Mama saw the guests coming up the path from the garage, she gasped and ducked up the staircase. Mrs. Teuffel looked like a giant bow, swathed from top to bottom in tartan. Lainey was dressed up too, in heels and a red dress, on her way to a family party on the South Shore. She was carrying the basket of gifts. Nick had invited Jamie, who looked awkward in khaki pants and a Fair Isle sweater. It was the first time I had seen him in anything but jeans. Uncle Rand quickly fixed up a tray of bagels and coffee and set it out on the table in the living room.

Mama came down wearing makeup and a black wraparound skirt with a green sweater. She tied a red ribbon around the band of her wig. "What is going on here?" she asked, greeting everyone with a kiss.

"We're here to celebrate the end of that blasted chemotherapy," Mrs. Teuffel said. It was the first time I'd ever heard anyone actually say the word out loud. I guessed it was easier to talk about now that it was over.

Mama withdrew initially, a bit stung by the announcement, and then softened. "Well, I suppose that does warrant a celebration."

Lainey made the presentation, describing the theme and how to match the card to the gifts. Mama seemed nervous at first; she fidgeted with her skirt and looked everywhere but at Lainey. She didn't like being the focus of attention. Once the gifts started coming, it gave her something to do. She relaxed into the method, matching up the colored dots and announcing each gift as she opened it.

Inside the blue wrapping was an envelope from Jamie. His dot rested smack across the mouth on the diagram. He rubbed his palms on his pants while he waited. There was a business card in the envelope. *DR. ANTHONY SCHNER, ORTHODONTIST*, it said. Mama looked confused.

Jamie sat up and pointed at the diagram. "You can get your teeth cleaned for free," he said. "My mother works there. She arranged it."

Mama rubbed her tongue on her teeth. "I could use that," she said. "Thank you, Jamie!"

He sank back into the fold of the couch, too shy to look up in the wake of all that pressure. I watched him out of the corner of my eye until he gave me a sly glance, checking to see if I approved of his gift.

Mrs. Teuffel walked right up next to Mama when she got around to opening her gift. As Mama struggled to untie the gold ribbon from the tissue paper, Mrs. Teuffel practically lifted it out of her hands. Together they pulled at the paper and revealed a giant Weight Watchers mug with a membership card inside.

"Water is the mainstay of the diet," Mrs. Teuffel said. "Lots of it."

"Really?" Mama said, turning the mug in her hand.

"Drink four of these a day," she said. "In fact that's all I do to stay trim. That and walking."

Elizabeth's eyes were on Mrs. Teuffel's midriff, large and barrel shaped. Mama passed the mug to her left. Jamie picked out the membership card, read it and put it back.

The green box was from Elizabeth. "Don't be mad," she said just before Mama went to open it.

Elizabeth had commissioned Lainey to spruce up Mama's synthetic wig with the hair from Mama's old ponytail. Lainey created an entire set of professional-looking hairpieces and displayed them on a special rack. One spray of hair was stapled to a plaid headband, another batch was glued to the insides of barrettes. They looked kind of like the hooks that are used for fly fishing. She even sewed some Velcro bangs into one of Mama's turbans. In a plastic Baggie was a small bun that was designed to cover any future thin spots. It looked like a bird's nest.

Lainey went over each one, gesturing back and forth between Mama's head and the pieces with her long, painted fingernails. After each description, Elizabeth held them up to Mama's wig, clipping a couple on to the hair in order to demonstrate.

"That was very thoughtful, sweetie," Mama said and opened her arms for a hug. Elizabeth went over and Mama held her. But when I looked at her face, I saw how exhausted she was and took my present away from the stack, slipping it under my chair.

"What are you doing?" Elizabeth asked.

"It has to be opened in private," I said. But I knew that I wasn't ever going to give Mama the gift I had made for her.

Lainey's present was next, another envelope with a gift certificate inside.

"Ladies, Ladies, Ladies," Mama read off the card, "full body fitness."

"It's not just a gym," Lainey said, "it's a way of life."

Mama raised her eyebrows in interest. "You all are too kind, really," she said. "Doesn't anyone else want to open any gifts?"

"We're not quite done," Nick said.

Mama opened an IOU from Uncle Rand, an offer to paint the station wagon the color of her choice as soon as spring came. Everyone pitched in his or her ideas as to what color the car should be.

"Maybe silver," Mama said.

"There's one more," Nick said and picked up his gift to Mama—a small box wrapped in gold paper. He tossed it in the air and caught it, twice, before handing it to her. He seemed both confident and nervous at the same time. He paced around the room while she fumbled with the tape. He smiled a big smile as he tried to catch my eye and then Elizabeth's.

"Move closer, girls," he suggested.

Mama opened the box and stared inside without speaking. Her face grew serious, as if she might cry.

"What is it?" Elizabeth shouted in a voice too loud for the quiet room.

Lainey held up the diagram and pointed to the gold dot on the figure's hand. I leaned over and looked inside the box. She was right. Resting on a bed of pine needles, was a gold ring with one diamond chip set into the band. Mama looked up at Nick and shook her head. She tried to fit the ring on each of her fingers, but they were still swollen from the hormone therapy. Finally, she slipped it on her left pinkie.

Right there in front of everyone, Nick got down on one knee. "Be mine," he said, "till the end of time."

Mama leapt up from her seat, moving with the grace of her old self and wrapped her arms around him. They held each other for a long time, the rest of us watching on, not moving, afraid perhaps to break the spell. Nick squeezed Mama's hand and patted the ring on her finger. A hair clip dangled by one strand of the wig, swinging back and forth by her ear.

I squeezed my eyes tightly closed and then opened them, trying to will Mama back to me. It seemed that with each day she slipped further and further away. After a moment, Mrs. Teuffel cleared her throat, crossed and recrossed her legs. Mama excused herself, said she was feeling a little weepy, and Uncle Rand jumped up to pour the coffee. I hated that Nick had done that in front of all those people. I looked to Elizabeth for a reaction, but she was busy trying coffee for the first time. She took a baby sip and grimaced at the taste. She tilted the mug near her face to feel the steam on her skin. Before long, Lainey was looking at her watch, amazed at how the time had flown. The group quickly dispersed, kissing Nick and calling out congratulations to Mama. Uncle Rand stood up and closed the door behind them.

I didn't say good-bye to anyone.

Suddenly, the house fell quiet, a lonely kind of hush that made me sad. Even Mama seemed subdued when she came back into the room to gather her presents. She balled up the wrapping paper, stopping every once in a while to look at her hand and then at Nick.

"You sure you want to marry someone that needs this much of an overhaul?" she asked surveying her gifts.

"If the girls give their permission," Nick said, looking to each of us for approval. "What do you say, gang? How about a spring wedding?"

I couldn't believe this was happening. I had barely survived the move, then Mama being sick, and now Nick was threatening to become our father. It was as if they had been planning it all along. I felt tricked. Elizabeth didn't even seem surprised. She jumped up and down in front of the couch like a little girl. For some reason, I felt more like crying.

"Come on, what do you say, girls?" Mama asked.

"Yea," Elizabeth cheered.

"Tilden?"

"I don't care," I said. "Whenever you want."

There was a strained silence during which Mama flagged everyone to go back to what they were doing. Uncle Rand chose the moment to hand Elizabeth and me matching gift boxes.

"Simultaneous opening," he said, which meant that it was probably the same thing. I knew this and didn't bother racing Elizabeth to be the first to get through the paper. She tore the wrapping at both ends, revealing the Victoria's Secret emblem and then lifting the lid of the box to find the brightly colored silk underwear. She held them up to herself. The tissue paper smelled like potpourri.

"Thanks," she said, and threw the underwear on the coffee table.

I leaned over and touched the slippery fabric. It embarrassed me. I hurried up to my room, where I stashed my balled-up silk underwear next to Mama's unopened present at the back of my closet.

Later, when Samantha called to find out what I had gotten for Christmas, I lied. "A stereo," I told her, "with a cassette player."

"Really?"

"Yeah," I said, "it's on order."

She started to ask me something and then stopped. "I got a Polaroid camera," she said. "Everybody came over. It was *so* boring."

I felt jealous of Samantha, but not in the usual way. I wanted my life to be like hers. The simplicity of a family that had been together always. A normal holiday—one where a family did the same thing year after year, had traditions and tinsel—with a mother who didn't get married in the middle of everything.

PRIMARY CARE

As soon as Mama seemed stronger, Elizabeth began getting strange stomach pains and headaches. Unexplained nausea and fever. Even Ms. Penny, the school nurse at Brooklawn Elementary, seemed concerned. She called one afternoon in February because Elizabeth had been coming to her during the first two months of the year to get her feminine protection. She wanted to know if there was a problem supplying these items at home. She recalled that Mama had not been present at the period movie the year before. She wanted to know if everything was all right.

I heard this information secondhand from Mama when she took me for a drive to find out how much I knew. She drove on the expressway, in the direction of New York City, for three towns before exiting and broaching the subject. She was agitated, her foot heavy on the gas and then the brake, lurching and halting. She was silent as we drove past the car dealerships, garden supply stores, and shopping centers that zoomed by before I could read their names. I studied the new calico hair peeking out from the edge of Mama's wig and waited.

"What has Elizabeth told you?" Mama said finally and looked at me.

I turned away and stared out the window. Elizabeth hadn't told me anything. In fact, since Christmas, we had rarely talked at all except to trade off chores and decide who got the first shower each morning. But I knew that the way she was acting had everything to do with getting Mama's attention. I'd had the urge to stay home sick myself, wanting Mama to feel my head for a fever, to make ice cubes out of Coke, and set me up on the couch with a TV tray in the den.

She waited for me to say something and when I didn't, she raised her voice. "Tilden, I'm talking to you. When did she get her period?"

The louder Mama's voice, the more private I became. "I don't remember," I said, "before Christmas, I guess."

"She told you?" Her voice was thin with an edge of panic. The question seemed more like an accusation.

"Not really. I kind of walked in on her."

Mama grew quiet in a way that made her seem angry and then sad. "Do you have yours?" she asked.

I shook my head.

"Would you tell me if you did?"

I nodded.

We were quiet for a moment.

"Why didn't Elizabeth?"

"I guess because it was in the middle of everything. You were busy . . ." I drifted off, trying to remember how it had been before Mama's procedure. Even though the follow-up was finished and the side effects had lessened, she still seemed distracted.

"Why not now?" Mama asked. "I'm not so . . . busy now."

"I don't know," I said. "Maybe she feels bad because I haven't gotten mine."

"That's ridiculous," she said, dismissing me and then caught my eye. "You don't feel bad, do you?"

I cried—more from the relief of being asked than from how terrible I felt.

"Oh no," Mama said, reaching her hand out to me, "don't cry." I cried harder, collapsing into her lap as she drove. "Oh sweetie," she cooed and brushed her hand over the side of my face. "There, there."

It had been a long time since I felt her attention so completely. I buried my face in her skirt, letting her stroke the top of my head, her cool fingernails running through my grown-out Artichoke and combing my scalp. I didn't ever want to move.

Before we moved in with Nick, when Elizabeth and I wanted to stay home from school, we would crawl in bed with Mama first thing in the morning and wait as she pulled the comforter over all three of our heads. A sleepy tent, she called it, letting us snuggle next to her, the warmth of our bodies seeping through our cloth nighties. We didn't pretend to be sick. It was enough to want a day together, the three of us nestled against the world. Now, with Nick it seemed there had to be an explanation for everything. A reason.

Mama decided that the best way to put an end to the ailments and reassure both me and Elizabeth that we were normal was for us to talk to a doctor. She set up an appointment the following week for which we each got to miss a half day of school. As children, Mama prepared us for the doctor by doing things we might not normally do. It was the way I imagined that some families went off to church, freshly scrubbed and brushed and tucked, an awkward clean that made me feel not quite myself. It was never clear to me whether we were to strive for sickness or health in our doctor's presence. My pediatrician said things like "good solid cough" and "impressive throat."

Elizabeth stayed in the bathroom that morning for forty minutes, running water constantly and refusing to unlock the door. Uncle Rand walked by me in only a towel.

"What's she doing in there?" he asked. He pretended to hip-check the door.

"Who knows," I said.

"I'm going downstairs." He tucked the towel at his waist. "I have to pee."

Uncle Rand always gave me more information than I really needed. I waited until he walked down the stairs and then banged loudly on the bathroom door.

"Just a minute." Elizabeth slammed the cabinets and flushed the toilet before opening the door.

"What took you so long?" I asked.

"I was cleaning myself," she said and flashed her pink-flowered box at me. "Inside."

Elizabeth and I had both gotten a message early on that there was something slightly romantic about doctors—not about their work so much, but their person. Mama always dressed for them, dabbing a bit of perfume first behind each of her earlobes and then ours. Perhaps it was like this for Catholic women with their priests. Having one wise and constant presence. Someone to return to on occasion to chart your growth. It meant someone else looking out for you in the world, one other person who knew all the pertinent information. Like a father.

Once inside the bathroom, I leaned against the door and sprayed myself with Love's Baby Soft perfume along my neck and arms, adding a final squirt down my underpants.

• • •

Elizabeth sat in the backseat, suspicious, pressing her feet into the back of the driver's side. Mama was wearing a turtleneck sweater-dress under her coat. It was long and green to her ankles and looked like a giant wool leg warmer with sleeves.

"So is this your doctor or ours?" Elizabeth asked, once we were under way.

"Both," Mama said, "but you should treat her like your very own."

"*Her?*" Elizabeth asked, bolting upright and leaning into the front seat.

"Dr. Murdoch isn't just *for* women," Mama announced, "she *is* a woman."

In the waiting room, Elizabeth and I read magazines and tried to ignore Mama's comments as she filled out our medical histories on a clipboard. Nothing on the form seemed to apply. No surgeries, no pregnancies, no allergies.

"No, none, no . . ." Mama said aloud as she checked a series of boxes for Elizabeth and then whispered. "When was your last period?"

Elizabeth shrugged and shrank down behind her magazine.

"Didn't you write it down somewhere?" Mama asked.

"No," she said.

Mama sat up and raised her voice slightly, "Maybe Ms. Penny knows." This dig surprised me coming from Mama, but it worked. Elizabeth blurted out a date she thought might be right. Mama took out her calendar and touched the point of her pencil down on each square. "Wednesday?" she asked. "Thursday?"

"Yeah," Elizabeth said, quickly, "one of those." She turned her back so that it seemed as if Mama were looking over her shoulder.

Mama sighed and shifted papers, bringing my medical history to the top of the clipboard. She checked no for every question on my form without even asking. In the family history section, she penciled in the words *mother*, *breast cancer*, and *mastectomy*.

I looked quickly away. Those words sounded so cold, as if Mama would be sick forever. And at the same time they seemed too simple.

There were two other women with clipboards in the waiting room. One had been crying and the man with her was holding a jar.

"Don't stare," Mama said, moving over one chair to block my view.

Dr. Murdoch called our names and said that she wanted to see us as a family first. She was tall and serious, younger than I expected, with a deep voice. She was wearing lipstick. She brought us into her office, but did not sit behind her desk. Instead, she pulled her chair around so that we were clustered, two facing two, as if at a restaurant. I felt unsure as to how to sit, aware of the distance between my knees and the doctor's. Mama crossed her legs and wrapped her foot around the back of her opposite calf. Dr. Murdoch leaned forward over her legs, a manila folder and notepad resting on her flat lap. Her straight, brown hair was cut to her chin. She tucked a piece behind her ear before she spoke.

"Why don't you fill me in on why you three are here today," she said.

Mama launched in. "It was my idea," she said, her voice animated and instructional, "the girls have been concerned about . . ." she hesitated, "they have questions about their bodies." She turned in her seat to face Dr. Murdoch, "You know, about what is normal for their ages."

Dr. Murdoch listened closely, her upper body easing forward, ready to break in at any moment. "Uh huh," she managed to say before Mama continued.

"And, try as I have to establish open lines of communication, we seem to have experienced something of a breakdown in the last few months." Mama crossed her arms and lowered her voice. "Maybe it has to do with my surgery last spring, and since then I haven't been all that . . . I don't know, available, I guess. Whatever the case," she pulled at the neck on her turtleneck, "I just wanted to be sure that the girls had access to all the necessary information." She smiled at us. "How can you expect to grow up to be women if you don't understand the woman parts of your bodies?"

This last question embarrassed me. I sat back in my chair and focused my eyes on Dr. Murdoch's desk: a smooth glass paperweight, a pen set, and a prescription pad. The framed degrees on the wall listed her full name in calligraphy.

Dr. Murdoch spoke in a calm, quiet voice, "First, I'd like to acknowledge your openness, Mrs. Burbank. Not many girls have the opportunity to speak frankly with their mothers," she looked across at me and then Elizabeth.

Elizabeth took everything as a reprimand. She glanced down and bent one leg underneath the other. Mama reached across, tapped Elizabeth's knee with the back of her hand, and then pointed to the ground.

Dr. Murdoch kept talking. "You should know that you're getting off to a good, healthy start by coming to a gynecologist now. Whether you visit regularly or choose to come just this once, you should know that the strictest confidentiality will be maintained." She stopped for a moment. "Do you know what I mean by confidentiality?"

I sat up, ready for the quiz; Elizabeth gazed blankly at the posters on the wall in front of her.

"Confidentiality means that your privacy is respected. It means that you can ask me questions and I will keep all your medical information private, unless I have your permission to discuss it with your mother."

Elizabeth perked up, cut her eyes in Dr. Murdoch's direction.

"Please feel free to ask any questions that you might have at any point." Dr. Murdoch looked at each of us. There was a long silence. "That's what this visit is for." She took another sweep around the room with her eyes. "Either now or when we meet privately."

"Is there anything you want to ask?" Mama looked seriously at Elizabeth and then quickly at me.

We both shook our heads. Why did everyone always want to know if girls had questions?

Dr. Murdoch went on to explain that during our first visit she would introduce us to the type of exams that we'd continue to have throughout our adult lives. Some exams would be more appropriate as we got older and wouldn't be performed today, but there were others that she would do in the exam room a little later on and a couple we could learn to do on our own. Dr. Murdoch also mentioned that she was aware of our mother's condition and that sometimes children might worry about their own risk for such diseases. She stopped to wait for a response. I tried to get Elizabeth to look at me, but she wouldn't. She kept her head down and bounced her feet until Mama reached across and grabbed her shin to quiet her.

Dr. Murdoch gestured to a rack on the wall. "I have lots of pamphlets that you can take home with you and read at your leisure." Mama leaned over, took one of each, and put them in her purse.

Dr. Murdoch stood. "Okay, Tilden, why don't you come with me," she suggested. "Elizabeth, you and your mom can wait outside in the waiting room."

In the exam room, I dressed in a paper gown. It took me a while to figure out which side was the front and which was the back. Dr. Murdoch knocked once before I was ready. When she came back a second time, I was seated on a stool with the gown opened at the back, my underpants still on.

Dr. Murdoch clipped my medical history to the inside of a folder and took a pair of glasses out of her white coat. "How old are you, Tilden?" she began.

"Thirteen. And a half."

She measured my height and weight, wrote her findings in my chart, and showed me a growth curve, indicating that my measurements were average for my age. She then instructed me to get in the diving position and go up and down slowly while she checked my spine and hip bones for signs of scoliosis. "Make sure you alternate which side you carry your books on," she said and touched each vertebra with her fingers. She pressed down on my shoulders. "Better yet, get a knapsack."

Afterward, Dr. Murdoch directed me to the exam table. She indicated that her questions were going to get slightly more personal. She wanted to know how I felt about that.

"Fine," I said, wanting to impress her.

"Are your menstrual periods normal?" she asked.

"I don't know."

She looked up over her glasses. "When was your first period?"

"Never," I said.

"Oh," she said, "that's perfectly normal."

"But my sister has hers," I blurted out.

"That happens sometimes," she said. "Don't worry. It won't be long."

Something about her voice sounded so certain. I would have given anything to feel sure. She wrote with quick gestures in my chart and then brought her gaze back to me. "Are you sexually active?" she asked.

"No."

"So you don't need any information about contraception this visit?"

I shook my head. I kept imagining what Elizabeth's session might be like. She would be a more interesting patient. She'd had hickeys and gotten a yeast infection from wearing too much spandex.

"Do you have any questions about anything? Puberty? Reproduction?"

"Not really," I said. "There was a movie I saw at school."

Her voice got a little soft. "Any concerns about breast cancer?"

I hadn't expected that question. The tone of her voice made me feel like crying. I looked down at my feet. The underside of my sock was twisted on top. I bent down to fix it, my own question pulsing in my head.

"Are you sure?" She asked again and waited for me to say something.

"When will my mother be totally better?" I asked at last.

Dr. Murdoch look surprised and then sorry. "I can't answer that," she said, "you should talk to her about it. As much as you can—both of you, I mean." There was an awkward silence. "I *can* give you some general information if you want."

I felt flushed. "That's okay," I said.

Dr. Murdoch continued on with the examination, directing me to lie back on the table. As I moved my legs, the paper on the table crinkled and stuck to the backs of my thighs. She demonstrated how to do a breast self-exam, slipping one of my arms out of the gown and exposing the right side of my chest. I felt self-conscious about my flat chest, but Dr. Murdoch didn't seem to notice; she pressed in and out on my breast in a circular motion. She spoke as if I weren't lying naked before her, explaining that if I were older, she might be looking for inconsistencies, anything out of the ordinary, any lumps or bumps. By the time she worked her way to the center, my whole breast had hardened into a firm knot. "Want to try?" she asked.

"Not really," I said and slipped my arm back in the gown.

"Would you like to see your vagina?" she asked.

I didn't want her to know that I had seen all there was to see, my legs pushed up against my bedroom door, the full-length mirror bearing down, showing all of me. I had matched myself up against the vaginas in *Our Bodies, Ourselves*. When I didn't respond, she gave me a hand mirror—the kind a hairdresser offers for you to see the back of your head.

Dr. Murdoch encouraged me to take off my underpants, saying that a girl should know what her vagina looks like before she shows it to anyone else. She pointed to the vulva, labia, and clitoris with a long Q-Tip, talking throughout the entire exam. Her voice distracted more than prepared me; despite her warnings, I jumped every time I felt her touch. After she'd named the external parts, she turned to a poster of the female reproductive system. She pointed out the vaginal canal and the ovaries with the Q-Tip.

"Some day, when you're older you can have a pap smear to check the cells on your cervix." She tapped the cervix on the poster.

I stared at the diagram. Spongy pink ovaries. Slick tubes. The reproductive system looked suddenly mechanical. My right leg started to shiver, that uncontrollable shaking of classrooms and offices. The way I felt before tests, my elbows cold on the desk. Dr. Murdoch looked at me, concerned, "Don't worry," she said, "a pap smear won't be necessary for a while." She hung the mirror on the wall, discarded the Q-Tip, and then left me alone to get dressed.

I felt womanly as I rolled my underpants on. There was a faint twinge, not pain exactly, but an exposed feeling between my legs. I wished that she'd given me some cream or plastic device with a prescription typed on it, my name and instructions, something I had to use daily. Something I could let fall out of my bag in front of Elizabeth.

I looked quickly around the room for a souvenir, an item that wouldn't be missed, until my eye settled on a box of slides. I reached above the metal clamps, lined up like tools from wood shop, slipped one slide out from the stack and pushed it into the front pocket of my flannel shirt. I walked from one side to the other in the waiting room avoiding Mama, until Elizabeth resurfaced from her exam. She was carrying two paper bags, which she flashed at me while Mama talked to the nurse.

"Can I see?" I asked.

"It's confidential," she said, stuffing the bags into her sleeve and wrapping her coat around her.

"Did you tell her about that thing with Keith Rogers?" I whispered, before we got in the car.

"Thing?" Elizabeth said. "I have no idea what you're talking about."

Elizabeth and I avoided Nick and Uncle Rand as much as possible that week, hiding the pamphlets that Mama left lying around on the counters and the plastic shower cards she hung in the bathroom as a reminder about self-exams. I hated showering with that card hanging above me. On the other side of the breast information, there was material about the testicular self-exam. I took it down and brought it to school, along with some pamphlets, to show during lunch.

Samantha acted unimpressed. She plucked the pamphlet about anorexia and bulimia out of my hand. "Nurses always think everything is an eating disorder," she said and rolled the pamphlet into a skinny tube.

Samantha was bitter because the school nurse had pulled her aside earlier in the year after the gym teacher complained that she weighed herself in the locker room after each gym class. Since then, she pretended to throw up, making mock retching sounds, every time she passed the nurse's office.

Samantha seemed bored as I told her about my visit to Dr. Murdoch. I hated when she looked around the room, waiting to catch someone else's eye, instead of looking right at me. I decided to show her the slide.

"I had a pap smear," I announced.

Samantha peered into the envelope. "Really?" she asked, eyeing the slide.

It was the first time I felt that I knew more about something than she did. When I held the slide out to her, she backed away abruptly.

"Isn't that a test for disease?" She had grown accustomed to my lies. She turned her attention instead toward the shower card. "It's much worse for guys," she said, studying the sketch of the testicles. "They have to cough in their exams."

"What's the big deal in that?" I asked.

"The nurse holds a guy's crotch," Sam said in a dramatic voice, "and makes him cough while she sticks a huge Q-Tip inside his dick."

"What for?" I asked.

"I don't know," Sam said, "but I overheard the guys talking about the cough. And from what they said the more they have to cough the worse it is."

"The worse what is?"

"I don't know," she said, "but I heard that the school nurse loves doing it. And that they try to get an older nurse so that the boys don't pop a boner. I also heard that when they did it last time, in gym, that Jamie Sanders was in there for a long time . . . coughing."

"How do you know?"

She looked at me, suddenly mean. "You don't know everything," she said.

Her hostility surprised me. I never felt like I knew anything around Samantha. She grew smarter every day, both about boys and school.

"What are you talking about?" I asked.

"You think you have all the answers just because . . ."

"Because what?"

"Because of your uncle," she said.

"What?"

"It doesn't really seem like you need me."

"That's not true."

"Well, you're always at home or TransAlt," she said, "you never even invite me over anymore."

"That's because of my mom being sick," I said.

"She sure has been sick for a long time," Samantha said under her breath. She caught herself, swore she hadn't meant it to come out that way. "I just don't understand what's with you, Tilden," she said, "you're acting weird lately."

That night, I found myself contemplating my breasts, checking them in circular motions, starting on the outside and moving inward, looking for inconsistencies. When I pressed down, I could feel the skeletal outline of my chest bones. Elizabeth ran into my room a half hour after going to bed and told me that she'd been doing the same thing in her room—standing by her bedroom window fearfully pressing herself in the dark. She'd found a bump, she announced, and she wanted me to check it.

"You don't have breast cancer," I snapped at her. "You don't even have real breasts."

"Please just feel it," she insisted. She seemed shaken. I reached out with one finger and touched her chest.

"You have to feel both sides," she said, "to see the difference."

I pressed my hands quickly against her shirt, in sort of a shove motion, and felt her flesh give under my fingers.

"Do you think I should tell Mama?" she asked.

"No," I said, "there's nothing wrong. You just went to the doctor."

Elizabeth took a deep breath. There was something else she wanted, I could tell. She lingered at the edge of my bed toying with the fringes on the bedspread. "Can I borrow that book?" she asked.

I pretended that I didn't know what she was talking about and gestured to the bookshelf. "Help yourself."

"No," she said, "the book about the body."

I scowled at her. "You've been looking in my things."

"I've never even seen it," Elizabeth said. "Mama told me you had it. She wanted to know where you got it from."

I jumped out of bed, crossed the room to my closet and pulled the drawstring for the light. Deep at the back of the closet, I'd hidden Ivy Shaptaw's copy of *Our Bodies, Ourselves*, on the bottom shelf with shoe boxes stacked on top. I crawled under my longest hanging clothes, my heart pounding in the dark. As I pulled the book out, I felt Mama's Christmas present. I was safe; it was unopened.

I had wanted to give her something funny, something that hinted at the future. Samantha had told me about reconstructive surgery, and helped me piece together a miniature photo album filled with pictures of breasts that we'd collected from magazines and pamphlets. I had even cut out some from Nick's *Playboy*. But something that Christmas night had told me how stupid my idea was. Thank God Mama had only unearthed *Our Bodies, Ourselves*.

"Open it," Elizabeth said, peering at me behind my parted clothes.

"I thought you just wanted the book," I said, threatening her.

"I do," she said. Then, her eye went to a bright spot of silk amidst the rubber soles and leather uppers of my shoes: the underpants that Uncle Rand had given me. They still had the tag on them.

"Can I have those too?" she asked. "You never wear them."

• • •

Our Bodies, Ourselves was the only book I ever saw Elizabeth actually try to read on her own. We got into the habit of alternating ownership, sneaking it out from each other's rooms in an unspoken nightly exchange. Elizabeth was a heavy reader, staining the pages with chocolate and grape juice; she used bobby pins to mark her spot.

The school called twice. Ms. Penny thought Mama should know that Elizabeth seemed unusually distracted by medical matters. Mama got defensive, told her that if the school district had a responsible health education program, Elizabeth's research wouldn't be necessary. But when Mr. McKinney, the school principal called, Mama had to give Elizabeth an official warning.

"No matter how good your intentions," Mama said, pulling Elizabeth aside after dinner, "you cannot go around diagnosing your classmates."

"I didn't diagnose Eddie Kramer. I just told him that in my opinion it looked like scabies."

"Mr. McKinney says that you've set off a panic about an epidemic."

"He should panic," Elizabeth said, "scabies is highly contagious."

Nick smiled at me and Uncle Rand. "Looks like we'll have ourselves a doctor in the family," he said proudly and started to stack the dinner plates.

"Please try to keep your medical opinions to yourself," Mama said to Elizabeth, "or I'll have to punish you."

"I don't see what the big deal is," Uncle Rand said, "it's just a skin mite." He lowered his voice, "It's those blood-sucking crabs you gotta watch out for."

Nick seemed not to hear him. He jiggled the silverware in a glass and stepped away from the table.

Later, when Elizabeth and I read the section on infestations, we fell into a silly mood, imagining Uncle Rand with a mite burrowed deep in his skin, causing raised red bumps and intolerable itching. Together, we collected dead bugs from the windowsills, picking them up with a paper towel and spilling them into a cup. There were flies with shiny green armor and netty wings, long-nosed mosquitoes and daddy longlegs spiders—all dry and stiff. But when we blew on them, their wings and legs shimmied as if in movement. Elizabeth had the idea to sprinkle the shelled bodies on Uncle Rand's down comforter. After we made a buggy nest at the edge of his pillow, we cleaned up all traces of our work and ran howling from his room.

DUTY

It was Elizabeth who saw it first—the small, shiny red bump jutting out from Mama's neck, just above her collarbone. Elizabeth didn't say anything directly to her. She waited until I lumbered down the stairs and then cornered me in the pantry.

"Mama has a lump," she announced, all panicky and out of breath. Her face was creased with worry. "It's on her neck," she whispered and pointed to the indented place near her own collarbone.

"A lump?" I felt a hollow ache in my chest. "How do you know?"

"I saw it," she said, starting to cry, "it looks like a cranberry."

"Stay here," I said and left her leaning against the shelves to see for myself. By the time I walked into the kitchen, Mama had draped a dish towel around her neck.

"Good morning," she said. She scraped two grilled cheese sandwiches off the skillet. "Time to eat."

I stared at her neck, waiting for the towel to move as she handed me my breakfast. The ooze of American cheese made its way down the crust and onto the plate. I felt sick to my stomach.

"Where's Elizabeth?" Mama asked, putting down the second plate. She stood in front of me, her hands on either end of the towel, twisting them together into a knot.

I shrugged my shoulders.

"What's the matter?" she asked.

I could feel my chin starting to quiver.

"Tell me what's wrong."

I slumped over, dropping my face toward my chest and heaving. Mama moved closer and hugged me to her. "You can cry if you want to," she said, "it's okay. I feel like it too."

"Is it more cancer?" I asked between sobs.

"I don't know," she said, "I'm still waiting for some test results. I'm sure it's nothing." She loosened her grip on me and stood up a bit. I could feel that she was about to pull away, so I held on tightly to her hand. She paused, waiting for me to release her. "Don't say anything to Elizabeth," she said, squeezing my hand, "it will only upset her."

It was such a relief to be included in one of Mama's secrets that for a split second I forgot that Elizabeth was in the pantry, listening to us. I knew that she was waiting on the other side of the wall for me to tell Mama that she already knew about the lump. Caught between Mama's desire for secrecy and Elizabeth's hope for inclusion, I stayed silent, choosing Mama for myself.

Elizabeth had been too upset to come into the kitchen for breakfast, so Mama went upstairs to check on her. By the time I got up there to brush my teeth, Elizabeth had pressed Mama toward the truth. They were frozen in a tearful embrace when I reached the hall. I waited, toothbrush in hand, hoping to catch Elizabeth's eye. But the damage had been done and I could feel it, thick as smog, between us. Elizabeth's hurt and my selfishness bound up together in Mama's secret.

Within a week, Mama had to be hospitalized overnight for an infection in her lungs. This forced a truce between me and Elizabeth.

We used our collective energy to demand more information, cornering Nick in the foyer and trading off in our questioning.

He took a deep breath, pushed his hands into his pockets, and exhaled loudly. "It's probably pneumonia."

"What's that?" Elizabeth asked.

"A very serious cold," he said, "in the lungs." He shifted his weight. "They just want to be careful."

"If they're so careful," Elizabeth asked, "why does she keep getting sick?"

"I don't know," Nick said. "I just don't know."

"That's what you said last time," I said.

He could tell that I blamed him for not doing more.

"It's true," he said, his voice faltering, "this time I don't know."

We fell quickly into position around the uncertainty. Elizabeth became the private eye, taking nothing at face value. I did the research, turning to books and magazines for a second opinion. Together we confronted Uncle Rand, waiting until late that night when, with wineglass in hand, he was sure to be the most talkative.

We found him reading *Time* magazine, a country-and-western station playing in the background. He had on a T-shirt and gray sweatpants, his bare feet crossed at his ankles. Elizabeth and I stood at the foot of his bed and fired questions, using new vocabulary words such as *reoccurrence* and *metastasis* that I'd collected, but didn't understand.

He pulled himself upright and set the magazine on his lap. His hair was mussed at the side of his head, his eyelids seemed heavy. "I wish I knew," he said, "nobody tells me anything around here anymore."

I didn't believe him. He and Mama were in a childhood habit of keeping each other's secrets. "What if it is cancer?" I pressed.

"Well, if that's the case," he said, "then we'll all have to be strong . . . for her." He took a long, slow sip of wine and stared absently at the wall between us. Elizabeth and I stood quietly, afraid to disrupt his gaze, until he blinked hard and looked up at us. "But we don't know that yet." He opened his arms and pulled us into a clumsy hug. "Let's not panic," he said, rubbing his hand over my back. His breath smelled of rotting fruit.

My body churned fear and hope into a rapid pulse, making it difficult for me to stand still. I broke away and ran down the hall to my room. I refused to answer the door, rejecting Elizabeth and Uncle Rand's attempts at comfort. It was easier to do my hoping alone.

Early the next morning, Nick called Elizabeth, Uncle Rand, and me into the kitchen. Elizabeth and I took our places against the counter while Uncle Rand leaned against the sink. Nick paused before speaking, his mouth open, but wordless. He tapped his hands against his pockets, jangling the loose change.

"We're going to lick this thing," he said finally. He closed his right hand into a fist and opened it, slapping his thigh. Uncle Rand pivoted, turned on the faucet loud enough to drown out anything else Nick would say, and began washing the dishes. I watched as the cuffs on his sleeves soaked up soapy water and darkened.

Dread lifted away from my skin, but never vanished. The truth hovered somewhere between what my mind knew and my heart hoped for, like an apparition. It was the uneasy feeling of a broken promise.

Nick kept talking, but not about sickness. He wanted to marry Mama properly, late in June, just after school was out. He could kick himself for not having done it sooner. It just seemed so natural, as if they'd been with each other always. His voice strained as he made bold, overly enthusiastic suggestions about the wedding. Neither Elizabeth nor I were listening. Nick was acting as if getting married would cure her somehow, as if a wedding would change everything.

Elizabeth stepped away from the counter, stood in the middle of the kitchen, and asked, "Is she sick enough to die?"

Nick moved toward Elizabeth, took each of her shoulders in his hands, and bent down to look into her face. "Promise me something," he said, giving her a little shake, "promise me you won't think such things. It's not good for her." He looked up at me. "We have to stay positive . . . pray, even." He nodded at Elizabeth. "You can do that, can't you?"

Uncle Rand released the drain and shook his hands over the sink. He palmed the kitchen rag and hung it, limp and damp, over the nozzle, before walking past us and letting himself outside. The birds scattered when they heard the back door. I watched as he walked by the picnic table. Normally, he would have stopped to fill the bird feeder, but he kept going down the driveway, leaving the hollow tube to swing, empty, under the charged weight of sparrows and blackbirds.

Throughout May, Nick clipped articles about Lady Diana and Prince Charles and hung them on the refrigerator. There were weekly updates about the dress, the jewelry, the cake. The extravagant wedding was scheduled to be televised live at the end of July. Nick took to calling Mama his princess, said that she was more regal than Lady Di would ever be.

Mama was not fazed by the hubbub around the royal wedding. She wanted a small, private ceremony, involving just our immediate family and someone understated to officiate. Nick thought that their love should be pronounced in nature. The blooms of spring were all around us—bright yellow arms of forsythia, aromatic sprays of lilac. They agreed to exchange vows quietly in the backyard.

Before Mama and Nick knew it, their marriage was the focus of other people's conversations. The guys at TransAlt wouldn't hear of a private event. Some of them had known Nick for over ten years. They had waited a long time to see him tie the knot and they'd be damned if they'd let him do it without some kind of ceremony. Lainey didn't care what happened as long as she was included. She suggested that the TransAlt guys put their talents to building a lattice arch for Nick and Mama to stand under in the yard. Mrs. Teuffel wasn't quite as accepting. She thought theirs ought to be a church wedding, considered an outdoor service to be more the way of hippies and outcasts.

When Keith Rogers heard the news, he offered his landscaping services at no charge. He was accommodating, weeded three feet past the property line, even asked permission to plant a couple of azalea bushes. He had acquired his own equipment, which seemed to give him more confidence than I remembered. When Uncle Rand came around, Keith tried to redeem himself, making more conversation than high school boys usually make. He was nice to me, too, even slipped me a business card. On Elizabeth's, he drew a heart. She hung back in a constant blush, watching from a distance. Uncle Rand had made it clear to her that Keith Rogers was there to get a job done. He was not to be distracted or disturbed.

This was our first wedding, and falling as it did, a month before Prince Charles and Lady Di's meant that Elizabeth and I had high expectations. We threw ourselves into the ceremony, imagining bouquets and veils. We wanted everything—matching dresses and responsibilities, the garter and rice.

"What kind of gown are you going to wear?" Elizabeth asked Mama one day, fingering the lace hem of her cotton nightie.

"I'm thinking about getting something practical," Mama said, "something I can wear more than once. Maybe something one of you can wear someday."

Elizabeth's face fell. "But why?"

"Well . . ." Mama started, considering her words, "after the first time all that stuff isn't quite so important."

Elizabeth was horrified. There was already something shameful about a second marriage, but for Mama to refuse to wear a gown seemed to make a mockery of tradition. "What about Nick?" Elizabeth pressed, "it's his first marriage."

"Nick won't mind," Mama said.

"Nick won't mind what?" Nick asked, entering the room, his shirt untucked, his hair overgrown and messy.

"Do you care if Mama doesn't wear a real wedding dress?" Elizabeth asked.

"She can wear whatever she likes," Nick said. "She'd look like a queen in overalls."

Elizabeth sighed and kicked her legs out to stand up. Mama reached over, cupping her shoulder and pressed her back to the couch.

"We thought it might be a good time . . ." Mama started and then turned to Nick. "There is something important we want to talk to you about."

"It's completely up to you of course," Nick interjected, "we want the choice to be yours."

Elizabeth looked up, impatient, "What are you talking about?"

Nick watched Mama, a long stare full of weeks' worth of conversations. I could feel where they were heading. It was inevitable. I let my mind go blank—a safe, familiar place.

"Nick would like to adopt you as his own," Mama said, finally, her words like pennies slipping into a pond. It wasn't that I didn't like Nick, it wasn't really anything to do with Nick. What I worried about was losing Mama.

Nick shuffled his feet side to side. "Only if you want," he said, "you girls think it over."

"I think it's a good idea," Mama said, starting to get defensive.

She hunched her shoulders anxiously and nodded her head. "This way we can stay as we are, like a family, no matter what."

"Why can't things just stay the way they've been?" Elizabeth challenged.

"They can," Mama said, "this is just Nick's way of showing us how much he loves us."

"But," Nick started, "if you want to take some time and think about it you go right ahead." He smiled directly at me, his face open and warm, but I noticed that he was gripping his fingers into his palms.

I smiled halfheartedly and looked away. I always knew that the time would come when Mama would invite someone else to become our father. But somehow I thought it would be different. I imagined that I would first know my real father and would then be in a better position to choose someone new. Not knowing him made it difficult to be sure I was making the right choice. In some ways I had kept a small space open, hoping that he might come back. In my fantasies, he was busy and wild, daring and important. His return was always dramatic, full of loud voices, exotic presents and screeching tires. Nick seemed so regular. It felt more like settling than choosing.

"Would we have to change our names?" I asked.

The next day at school, I practiced writing my new name, saying it aloud and imagining hearing it called. The *O* of Olsen would shift my status from the beginning of the alphabet to the middle. The *B* of Burbank had always entitled me to front rows and early attention. I was usually among the first to get report cards or tests returned. But *O*, I realized, would seat me closer to Samantha.

My friends interpreted Nick's offer of adoption as a symbol of love.

"It's not like he has to do it," Jill Switt said, "it's extra."

Christy Diamo thought that there was a bit of mystery associated with a sudden name change. She said it was what the government did when they were relocating top secret witnesses.

"Where's your real father?" Libbie Gorin asked.

"I don't know," I said. "Nowhere, I guess."

"Then definitely do it," she said.

Samantha was the only one to say I should watch it. "He gets to skip being your stepfather and go directly to being a father," she warned, "without any experience."

Uncle Rand recommended that Elizabeth and I go along with Mama's wishes. He took us one that night, after Nick and Mama had gone to bed, and told us that the adoption was what Mama wanted most in the world. He sat on the edge of my bed, drink in hand, tapping the mattress on either side for us to join him. It took him a long time to get to his point, pausing and repeating himself, he kept picking up and putting down his glass. I could see he was drunk, the kind of drunk that made time slow up on itself.

Elizabeth crunched her nose at his breath every time he brought his face in close. For a moment, she caught my eye and rolled hers way back inside of her head. Neither of us were listening. We had already made our decision. I crossed my eyes inward toward my nose. She peeled her lids up and folded them back against themselves in the way we were always told not to. We alternated giggling under the guise of coughing fits and finally exploded in a fit of laughter. Uncle Rand stood up from the bed, suddenly out of place in the face of our hysteria. He picked up his wineglass and walked down the hall.

"He drinks too much," Elizabeth said.

I waited for her to say more and when she didn't, I grew private. It was difficult for me to separate the part that was his from the part that was mine. There had only been that one time, but every time he looked at me, I felt the buzz of a secret.

We were quiet for a long time, the sound of the water in the bathroom sink and his toothbrush filling the silence. After he had finally turned to bed, Elizabeth whispered, "You should tell Mama."

I pretended to be asleep and didn't answer her. That night, Elizabeth stayed with me, the two of us curling silently against the sounds of Uncle Rand in his room.

The next morning, Mama kept us out of school. She woke us each with a glass of juice and the promise of a day at the mall so that we could get something to wear for the wedding. Going to the mall with a parent was not normally done with pleasure, but on this day, knowing that our peers were stuffed behind desks, the freedom seemed worth celebrating. We abandoned mall protocol easily, allowing Mama to consult with us in public and agreeing to be seen in the discount stores. Every forty minutes, Elizabeth called out the subject she was supposed to be doing in school.

Mama settled on a cream-colored suit with a high collar that she found on sale at Filene's. She suggested that we get sundresses, but Elizabeth already had her hopes set on a prom gown from Macy's. It was that time of year, the high school juniors and seniors were ordering corsages and reserving limos through TransAlt. Lainey was already booked to do hair and makeup for fifteen girls. The prom seemed more like a wedding than what Mama and Nick were planning.

Elizabeth wanted us to look like real bridesmaids and felt that the prom department held the most promise. There were floor-length gowns in taffeta and lace with gloves and matching pocketbooks. Even Mama got swept up in our enthusiasm, bringing dresses to our fitting room. She selected two made from a magenta taffeta with the faint outline of roses etched in a shiny thread. I chose the sleeveless one with a ruffle over the shoulder. With my short dark hair, it made my neck look long and almost elegant. Mama stepped back and exclaimed that I looked just like Audrey Hepburn. Elizabeth's choice was fuller, like Princess Diana's dress, with puffed sleeves and a bow in the back. She wrapped her hair on top of her head and spun herself around. Both dresses were a bit too large and would have to be taken in by Mrs. Teuffel before we could wear them.

Elizabeth was determined to have the right accessories. She found earrings made of false pearls that were fastened to wire and splayed across our ears, like baby's breath. We tried on identical white pumps that would have to be dyed to match the dresses. The pumps pinched my toes tightly together and made my step shaky.

"I hate those kind of shoes," Mama said, "they feel like walking on pencils."

But Elizabeth wanted a pair anyway. She liked the way the skinny spike pushed her up, out of her step, lengthening her legs and straightening her back.

Mama didn't reject any of our choices. She paid for it all with a credit card, which was not her usual way; the saleswoman had to show her where to sign her name.

We were unaccustomed to this kind of splurge. "Are you sure?" I asked with each purchase.

"I want you to have it if you want it," Mama said.

I hung the dresses on the hooks at each side of the car. The backseat was cluttered with shopping bags. I imagined that we were packed for a trip. It was the way I felt each time we'd moved. That I had everything I'd ever need right there with me. That we were safe within the enclosure of the car. And that if we had to, we could just keep going.

The weeks leading up to the wedding went quickly, the entire yard turning from the pale pastels of spring to a rich, lush green by the time school was out at the end of June. The morning of the wedding, the TransAlt guys spilled over into the yard. They spoke loudly, shouting to one another the way they normally did over engines or out windows. A few men arrived with cases of empty beer cans which Jamie Sanders strung together to hang from the back of the limo. Three others made up the band and busied themselves running amp lines and extension chords. In the kitchen, Uncle Rand and Lainey worked side by side, chopping vegetables for crudités and arranging them on platters.

Nick had chosen Jamie to stand by him as his best man. Uncle Rand had been asked first, of course, but declined, claiming that his catering responsibilities would take up too much time. He offered to be an usher instead. I could tell that Jamie was taking his job as best man quite seriously. It was probably the most important thing he had ever been asked to do. He spray-painted a giant sign, hung it from the garage, and organized the bachelor's party down by Breyer's Pond the previous weekend.

Elizabeth became the attendant, hiding Mama away on the second floor, fussing over her nails and foundation makeup. She was adamant that no one should see Mama on the day of her wedding. She planned to do all the makeup herself. My room was named the official bridal headquarters because of the outside access. I had to clean up, moving my stuffed animals and stacks of magazines out of the way. My corkboard was filled with advertisements for Impulse body spray—the one where a stranger suddenly gives you flowers—and fortunes that I'd collected from when we'd gone out for Chinese food. Mama was dressed in her bathrobe, seated with her back to the door. Her head was wrapped high in a towel, as if she had hair.

"Don't come over here," Elizabeth shouted at me when I entered. Q-Tips and cotton balls littered the floor. Lainey's makeup was strewn all over the room. Elizabeth had eyeshadow applicators between her clenched teeth and stored behind her ears. I could tell that she had been at it for a while. She had taken my mirror off the wall. The whole room smelled like the inside of a purse.

"Maybe we should have Lainey come take a look," Mama said, glancing at me out of the corner of her eye.

"I'm not ready yet," Elizabeth said.

"Can I see?" I asked.

Mama straightened. "Tilden will be a good judge."

She was desperate, I knew. I had never worn a stitch of makeup. Elizabeth gently spun Mama around in the chair. She looked as if she had been beaten up. Deep purple shadow arched high into her brows. A yellow-green hue marked the crease. Elizabeth had reversed the dark to light rule for eyeshadow, had wanted to include too many colors. I was just about to speak when I felt Lainey over my shoulder.

"Good instincts, Elizabeth," she cooed as she brushed by me. "Very dramatic. Let's see if we can't lighten it up a bit. What you have created would be just fine for evening wear, but for daytime I think we should come down a notch. What do you think?"

Lainey worked away at Mama's eyes, removing most of Elizabeth's efforts without saying so. Even Elizabeth looked relieved. When it came time for Mama to dress, no one seemed quite sure what to do. Lainey excused herself, explaining that she, too, needed to change. I bent to the floor, sweeping up Q-Tips. Elizabeth gathered the stray cotton balls together with her toe. I could hear Mama moving into her suit—her labored breathing, the frustration of the lining caught high around her. She needed help with the buttons in back. She was not wearing a bra. I must have stopped buttoning when I saw the gap in her dress.

"Do you think I need something?" she asked, taking me into her confidence in a way that made me feel grown up.

"Probably," I said.

She sent me down to her room to get a bra from her dresser. I scavenged through the top drawer. Confronted with underwire and padded, strapless and lace, I wasn't sure which style to bring her. I scooped them all into my arms, marched back to the bridal headquarters, and dropped them in Mama's lap. She picked quickly through the collection, dividing the bras into piles of functional and pretty. She chose a padded bra for herself out of the functional pile and held the lacier, more fragile incarnations from the pretty pile out to me. "You can have these if you want them," she whispered.

When Elizabeth wasn't looking, I slipped the bras into my dresser.

Lainey returned wearing a pale linen dress with her hair teased so thin and blond, it looked like the yellow light of a halo. She had Ivy and Samantha Shaptaw in tow. Ivy had shoved rolls of film in every pocket of her beige pants suit. She clicked away from the moment she got to the door. Capturing, she called it. She wanted to capture everything.

"Wait," Mama demanded, frantically feeling the top of her head, "just wait one moment."

We all cleared out so that Mama could put her wig in place. No one said a word in the hall. We were uncomfortable, shifting weight from one foot to another, bumping shoulders and biting nails, in our attempts to pass the time. When Mama opened the door, the sound of our voices filled the room and Ivy resumed taking pictures.

"Let me just do candids for now," she said. "Just keep on as you were. I want to capture your natural interactions."

Mama seemed able to forget the camera as she stood by the window, the light illuminating her gown and frosted eyelids; her profile and posture signified elegance and calm as she watched after Nick in the yard. As she bent to fasten the clasp on her sandals, new color rushed to her cheeks.

Lainey gathered us around Mama. She had a presentation to make and hoped Mama would like it, that she wouldn't be upset with her for taking any liberties. She brought out a large box. Mama opened it carefully, pushing the tissue paper off to the side. She lifted out a bridal headpiece made of pearls and rhinestones. Gathered at the top was a veil and underneath a loop of Mama's old hair, tucked up on itself, in a style straight off the cover of that month's *Brides* magazine.

"You've gotten more mileage out of that ponytail than I ever did when it was on me," Mama said. She settled the bridal crown on her head and gave me a quick side glance. I knew that she hated it, she'd always found jeweled items too garish, but she softened when she saw how excited Elizabeth was to have this one emblem of tradition. Suddenly, I realized that this day had never been for Mama. The dress, the ceremony, Grandma's pearls—all of it was for us, her daughters.

Ivy and Samantha filed downstairs so that we could get dressed. It took Elizabeth longer; she had borrowed a slip and crinoline from Lainey in her attempt to look like a princess. I watched out the window while Lainey dusted my cheeks with blusher and attached some baby's breath to the back of my head with a bobby pin. I sucked my stomach in and held it as Lainey spun me toward the mirror. The taffeta was cool against my skin. I barely recognized myself; I seemed taller and bustier. Like a girl.

Downstairs, the guests were clumped together on the lawn, the neighbors standing in the same order as their homes on a grid. Keith Rogers made sweeping gestures with his arm, indicating his work and hoping for referrals. It had been his idea to cut the grass shorter down the center of the yard to make for a natural aisle. Off to the side, I saw Samantha talking to Jamie Sanders. They were standing inches from each other and she was flicking something off of his collar. Their interactions were easy. Ivy was snapping pictures. It was possible to imagine them as a couple at the prom. And beyond that even someday at their own wedding. It caused me to see, for the first time, the potential for betrayal.

Mrs. Teuffel was involved in heavy discourse with Larry, the lead singer of the TransAlt band. She was holding a recording of the wedding march that Elizabeth had practiced on her piano and then taped. She held the cassette high in the air and offered instructions as to when to hit PLAY. Somehow with Mrs. Teuffel, you always knew exactly what she was saying without having to hear her. She gestured toward the microphone, indicating the exact positioning of the tape recorder.

The deacon had arrived and was standing at the altar, pivoting in place and clearing his throat. He wore a tie instead of a collar. It took a moment for the guests to realize that he was calling them to order. Elizabeth and I stood at the top of the outdoor staircase, waiting for the music to begin. We had rehearsed the choreography the day before, attempting to find ways for us to be represented equally beside Mama. Larry pressed PLAY, beginning Elizabeth's tentative piano march, and we walked side by side down the steps, into the yard.

In the excitement, Mrs. Teuffel got bossy and encouraged us to proceed down the aisle, going against our original plan by placing Jamie next to Elizabeth and leaving me to march next to Uncle Rand. I looked to Elizabeth for help in challenging this new format, but she seemed to take well to the order. She stepped off to the beat of the march, dragging Jamie alongside her. Uncle Rand extended his elbow and I rested my fingers on the crook of his arm. He must have sensed my resistance to touch him. He held his bent arm out to the side in a neutral zone between his body and mine. Nick was waiting for us at the altar, smiling brightly. When they reached him, Jamie and Uncle Rand switched places, moving around each other in what looked like a dance until Uncle Rand stepped away from the altar.

The march intensified and Mrs. Teuffel signaled for Mama to make her way down the steps. She held the railing in one hand, stepping carefully, a bouquet of lilies and ivy dangling in the other. By the time she reached the grass aisle, tissues were circulating. At the altar, Elizabeth and I fanned out next to Mama, who had taken Nick's hand before being instructed to do so.

The deacon leaned forward to be seen between them and spoke loudly about existing in the present moment and living each day to the fullest. Mama and Nick exchanged the vows they had written for each other.

"You have brought me the kind of joy and love that will change my life forever," Nick said to Mama and then looked at us and added, "all of you."

Mama spoke quietly, her words faint and interrupted by emotion. "I have never met such a loving and compassionate man," she said. "I know that now my family is whole."

When the deacon pronounced them husband and wife, they kissed passionately, which made me look away, embarrassed. In a surprise move, the band bypassed the wedding cassette and belted out one of Nick's favorite songs. Ivy Shaptaw clicked away on her camera as we moved down the aisle. The lead singer wailed: *You took the words right out of my mouth. It must have been while you were kissing me. I swear it's true I was just about to say I love you.*

Uncle Rand and Lainey set up a festive backyard reception complete with helium balloons in TransAlt's colors. There were maroon and green tablecloths too, with the food displayed buffet style on picnic tables opposite the band. Predictably, Nick's mother sent floral centerpieces. Maybe having manners isn't really enough. Mostly, it was the men who got up to say a few words, some holding the mike in two hands as if they'd waited forever to have their voices amplified.

When the band resumed for its final set, Samantha and Jamie switched off singing the chorus to "Paradise By the Dashboard Light" while Mama and Nick slow-danced. Elizabeth danced wildly up near the band with Keith Rogers. Uncle Rand stood off to the side, tapping his foot. When Lainey noticed him, she danced over to where he was, moving her shoulders and hips to the music in a small circle around him. They looked at each other slyly, with side glances.

Ivy brought over a piece of cake and sat down beside me. Together we watched Mama on the dance floor. She looked frail, her neck thin, her step cautious. Before I could stop myself, I was crying, my face pressed against Ivy's shoulder in an awkward hug, with her camera jutting between us.

"I know," Ivy said, running her hand over my head, "I know."

PART V

INDEPENDENCE

A few days after the wedding, Mama began to cough—first as if she had a tickle in her throat, then with a terrible gasping that made her back curl up like a choking cat. It seemed to get worse at night. From my bed, I could hear her hacking echo throughout the house. Talking tired her and within a week she could no longer hold a conversation without exploding into a coughing fit. Elizabeth and I tested her anyway, vying for her words, making her eke out one syllable answers to our questions about the insignificant details of our daily lives. How much water exactly did she put in the oatmeal? What precisely were her objections to pierced ears? Could we go to the big camp-out on Dove Island?

This last question, from Elizabeth, wasn't really fair. Under normal circumstances, Mama would never have consented to our attending such an event. But, unbelievably she said we could go.

"Take it easy," Nick warned us, "she's still a bit under the weather, you know."

I hated when he told us to leave Mama alone, as if he knew her better. No matter how teasing or gentle his voice, his suggestions about how to act with Mama always made me feel small.

By the Fourth of July, Mama had to check back into the hospital to have some fluid drained from her lungs. Pleurisy, Nick called it this time. When he told me the news, he said she'd be home within a day. I turned my back to him and walked outside. It was Nick's way to announce bad news coupled with something positive as if it were really good news. I wished he would just say it outright. Mostly, I was tired of Mama being sick.

I found Jamie in the usual spot, behind the TransAlt office in a dirt patch he'd set up to do repairs. He was bent over between the hood and the engine. It looked as if he were about to be swallowed up, his oil-stained Levi's hanging outside the mouth of the car. His shirt was stretched upward revealing the taut skin at his waist. I had to say hello twice before he heard me.

"Hey, there," he responded, a broad smile spreading across his face. Jamie surfaced and reached for a rag to wipe his hands. "Heard your mom's in the hospital again," he said, twisting the cloth between each of his fingers. He looked deep into my eyes, pushing me near tears. "So," he said, tipping his face up in mine, "what's wrong with her?"

"Pleurisy," I said, matter-of-factly. "She's got fluid in her lungs." I ran the toe of my sneaker along the rim of the tire. It made a squeegee sound. "They drained it though," I added, trying to be cheerful, "she's coming home tomorrow."

"And then what?" he asked.

"What do you mean?"

"I don't know," he said, "it just seems that she's been sick for a long time now."

I wasn't sure how to answer him. His words rang in my ears. Long. Time. Now. I couldn't listen. I turned and walked away without a word. He called after me, but I ignored him and kept walking—hard, deliberate steps all the way up Connally and onto Cranbrook—so fast my heels burned inside my sneakers. Ahead of me on the road, heat vapors rose off the pavement creating a gassy mirage. I tried to stomp away my thoughts, but halfway to town, I lost control, my mind racing, *No, Mama, No,* over and over, *Please No.* Finally, my sobbing forced me to break stride and turn off the road. I ran to the clearing behind an old farmhouse and sat in the tall grass, bits of tar and gravel biting the skin through my shorts. There, I waited to be missed, watching the sun cycle through the sky and wondered if anyone would search.

As a child, I had been taught not to wander off, but sometimes, it seemed, if I blinked too long, I would no longer recognize my surroundings. Mama had instructed me to stay put the minute I felt the sting of something unfamiliar. My phone number was written on everything I owned. In public places, I had a keen sense of who to report myself to. The right kind of older lady might buy me a lollipop, a man might lift me up higher than I could see on my own. Once, someone at the post office let me pore over a book of rare stamps; a bank manager gave me pennies to push into sleeves. Before long, Mama would arrive, looking frantic, her hair blown wild around her face, with Elizabeth trailing safely behind.

I drew a circle around me with my finger, digging a moat in the dirt and gathering a pile of dried straw and twigs in front of my bent legs. The hot sun beat down on me, reddening my skin and warming the top of my head. I constructed a miniature raft, laying straw next to straw, binding it together with long sinewy strips of onion grass. Afterward, I pressed the leftover straw into the quicks of my nails, giving myself claws which I used to rake around the moat and then up and down my hot, itchy legs. The pain made my skin flush, cooling me against the afternoon breeze. I knew that with Mama in the hospital my disappearance would be perceived more as inconvenience than as tragedy. I dusted myself off and turned toward home, rehearsing a scenario about having been lost.

As I turned on Connally, the trees overhead thick with birds, Jamie approached in the opposite lane. He made a U-turn, pulled up beside me, and opened the car door. The interior of his car smelled of rubber hose and exhaust, a burnt caustic smell that stung as I inhaled. He drove to the parking lot behind the junior high school and turned off the engine. Jamie took a deep breath and in a gentle voice told me how he had run away four times before the age of fourteen. He said that he always wanted his father to look for him, to send out a search party, or at least call the police. Once he even stole his father's wallet. Each time, he returned home to a note from his mother excusing his absence from school because of a family emergency. She never told Jamie's father about his departures.

"She didn't get it," he said. "I would have given anything for him to beat me."

"You don't mean that."

"My father never said a word to me," he said, "he never even looked at me. The day he taught me to drive was the happiest day of my life." He stared blankly at the items hanging from his rearview mirror. A key chain, a comb, a feathered roach clip. He had whittled a cross out of wood. At the thickest part, where the arms cross the body, he'd glued a photo of his parents the size of a postage stamp. He had used leather shoe strings to attach it to the mirror.

"That's driftwood," he said, when he caught me looking, "from the beach." He pushed at the leather knot, willing it to lay flat, so the photo would face forward.

"I could braid that for you," I offered.

He considered this for a moment, twisting the cross in his hand and letting it go. It spiraled and then slowed, waving from side to side. "That's okay." he said.

I understood without him having to say more: sometimes things are better left familiar and imperfect. I became aware of my thighs against the torn vinyl seats. I lifted my legs and sat on my hands.

"Those new shorts?" Jamie asked, changing the subject.

"I guess so," I said. They were. Samantha had given them to me the month before on my fourteenth birthday in a hurried exchange at the end of my driveway on her way to the mall. Jamie stared endlessly at a spot near my hip until finally he reached over and pulled at a loose string hanging from the seam. It was the closest he had ever been to touching me. I held my breath as something adult passed between us. Jamie turned away. He wrapped the loose thread around his finger until it bulged and turned white.

"I better get going," I said.

"Want to drive?" he asked.

I looked at him quizzically at first. Then we switched seats, passing each other in front of the car without saying a word.

I returned home to interrogations and reprimands. Nick's voice got high, his face red; Uncle Rand stayed quiet, which actually felt worse. Elizabeth was sullen, she didn't like when I did something unexpected. I agreed and apologized my way through each wave of the conversation. I had been inconsiderate and selfish, irresponsible and impulsive. What had gotten into me I could not say. But I was sorry. I promised never to disappear without warning again. I couldn't bring myself to cry as I might have on any other day. In the end, none of their remarks or concerns mattered to me, not one had made me truly sorry to have done what I did. I did not reveal that I had been with Jamie. It might have saved me in the end for Nick to be able to imagine me by his side during those hours before dusk, but I kept that part private. I felt flushed and excited.

I had learned to drive.

I slammed my bedroom door and got undressed. Uncle Rand's habit of forgetting to knock kept me on my toes while changing, standing close to my bed, a towel clenched in my teeth, ready to cover up or duck. But he did not follow me. My room was suffocatingly hot. I angled two clip-on fans at cross purposes to stir things up. In the distance, I could hear the first rumblings of fireworks. Nick and Elizabeth stood at the end of the driveway lighting coal snakes and sparklers, their voices loud over the crackling and hissing of neighborhood firecrackers. She was always more willing to be family with him, I could see it in how easy they were with each other. Without Mama home I wasn't sure where I fit in.

Occasionally Elizabeth called to me, shouting out a particular color or shape of light and suggesting that I come to the window and watch. She had taken to sounding self-assured, positing theories and making her opinions known. Nick responded to everything she said with a little surprise in his voice, as if he were seeing her anew. Maybe it was that he was seeing the Mama in her, the part that had always been there, but was only now starting to surface—the way streetlights can be left on all day and only become visible at night. Hers was the confidence that came of being desired.

I mummied myself against their voices by wrapping the sheet over my head. Then, I relived my first drive. The weight of the car lurching forward off the pedal, the coolness of the steering wheel against my palms. I pictured the engine churning under the hood—pistons, valves, headers—all those parts I'd studied now fully in motion. I felt power to affect every move, the car responding quickly to the slightest pressure on the gas. Even my neglect had a result. I loved most that airy, suspended feeling on a tight turn, when the car heaved one way while my body seemed to pull the other and it took a second for me to join the car, cradling my weight back at the center. Jamie warned me off that kind of turn, said that it usually meant that I was accelerating when I should be slowing down.

Just before it got dark, Jamie let me speed up and move the car into second gear. He put his hot palm over my hand and rattled the shift in neutral. When it connected with the gear, the engine quieted. He guided me through the simultaneity of the motion, the lifting of my foot and the push of my wrist at the appropriate time. When I did it myself the first time it felt like spelling a word right on the page without even having to think about it.

Thick with sweat, I turned under the sheet, watching the blades of Nick's old fan spin under its cage. At the other end of the hall, Uncle Rand was playing his radio. The heat of the night, along with the sound of firecrackers, reminded me that it had been almost a year since he first came to stay with us. Last summer, I might have confided in him, revealing my adventure in exchange for some story about Lainey. But we didn't talk that way any more. I didn't like the way it made me feel to think too long about him. With those thoughts came the heaviness of pity. Partly for him, but also for the loss of him in my life.

And you have your mother's nose, her cheeks, and her chin, Uncle Rand had offered, kissing each part of my face—almost as if my features hadn't been like hers until he suggested they were. I started to drift off, thinking about those times as a child when I would fall asleep in the car, my head pushed into a vinyl corner, and Mama would carry my limp body out against the busy sounds of life.

That night, I dreamed that Mama died. Her eyes huge. Tubes everywhere. I raced toward her. The sky opened. Rain pummeled the earth in sheets so dense I could no longer see her. I turned back toward the house. There were no walls. Bedsheets billowed down from the roof.

I didn't tell a soul.

Mama came home from the hospital pale and depleted. She took to her room, not even bothering to wear the wig over her patchy calico head. Elizabeth and I kept some distance, allowing her to rest while Uncle Rand and Nick ran interference around our needs.

A few days after Mama's return, I walked by her room and caught sight of Elizabeth sorting through a cup of jewelry.

"Where's is she?" I asked.

Elizabeth gestured to the bathroom. I came in and stood by the bed to observe her. The sheets were pulled down, exposing the sunken, empty mattress.

"Mama said I could have this." Elizabeth held a gold pendant out from around her neck.

"Why?" I asked.

"Cause I like it." She let it fall against her chest so that I could see the full effect. "You could probably have something too."

I looked at the small collection of chains and lockets on Mama's down pillow. Our baby rings and bracelets were linked together. There was a necklace made of horseshoe nails and an opal brooch. All these things she'd worn when she was well. To wear them now felt like giving up that part of her. Mama returned from the bathroom, wheezing slightly, and climbed under the covers. Her neck looked long, her shoulders delicate and bony.

"Why don't you girls go to the beach or something," she said. "It's such a beautiful day. You can collect some shells."

"Tonight is the Dove Island camp-out," Elizabeth began, "you said we could go."

"You should go," Mama said, sitting up straighter. Her voice was soft and raspy. "Can you stay overnight?" she asked, distracted.

I looked at Elizabeth, startled. Mama had never talked like that. "I don't think so," I said.

Elizabeth elbowed me. "Some of the older girls are," she said. "We could camp with them."

I watched Mama's face closely. What was she thinking? We had never even been allowed out past midnight. Mama drifted into a spacey silence, fingering her jewelry, displaying each chain and pin across her lap, then dropping the items back into her cup.

"Don't you want something, Tilden?" Mama asked as I turned to leave. "Go ahead and look. I never wear any of this anymore." She picked up the cup and poured the jewelry into my hand. "I can't believe there isn't more than this," she said, cradling a few stray keepsakes in her open palm.

"It's okay," I said, holding out my empty wrists and fingers. "Things always break on me anyway."

By that afternoon, Uncle Rand had gotten wind of the Dove Island plan and intervened. He didn't think an overnight was such a good idea. He negotiated a compromise with Mama, suggesting that we attend the bonfire and offering to pick us up at the dock afterward.

Mama agreed. "No drinking, though," she added.

It wasn't clear whether she was talking to us or to Uncle Rand. We all three nodded. Elizabeth raced off to pick out her clothes, practically skipping down the hall.

I was slow to leave the room, stalling and waiting. "Mama?" I asked, after everyone else had gone. "Are you okay?"

"Oh, I'm just tired," she said. "I need to sleep."

Uncle Rand dropped Elizabeth and me at the dock in the late afternoon. Samantha and her brothers were waiting for us in their Whaler. The coiling of ropes and hosing down of decks gave purpose to time. Even Samantha, who was considered by her brothers to have a lazy streak, had found something to do. She was bailing out the back end of the boat near the engine. Her feet straddled each side of the hole. She was wearing her Yankees hat, her auburn hair in a ponytail, pulled through the clasp. Elizabeth and I stood aimless on the dock.

"Hi-ya," Sam said, holding her whole arm over her face and

squinting up at us. Suddenly, I could see in the stretch of her arm how her body had gotten rounder since the day I first met her, a year and a half ago at school, when she sat skinny and silent on the other side of her divider.

Her brother Stephen put out his hand to help us into the boat and pointed to the float cushions. "In case we get shipwrecked," he said.

"Yeah," Seth chimed in, rocking the boat side to side. "You never know." Together they started to hum the theme song to *Gilligan's Island*.

"Ignore them," Samantha said, "they're off their gourds today." She made a sucking sound through her teeth and raised her eyebrows as a signal.

"Want some?" Seth asked and gestured to a Baggie full of pot stashed in the cooler.

Elizabeth's eyes widened. I assumed that she was used to wine coolers, even liquor, but that for her, pot was probably the stuff of another crowd. She stepped a bit closer to me. Just when I thought that the distance between us was closing, she struck out on her own.

"Better wait till we get to the island," Elizabeth said, sounding more seasoned than I expected. She checked the parking lot where Uncle Rand was waiting in the car.

"What's up with him, anyway?" Sam asked, looking at me.

"Nothing," I answered quickly. "Why?"

"It's kind of weird, don't you think . . . the way he hangs around. Doesn't he have anything better to do?"

"No," Elizabeth said.

I could tell that she was trying to be cool. I glared at her, a strong wall rising in me. It made me angry that she didn't feel any of the same responsibility that I did to defend him.

"Well, he doesn't," Elizabeth said, justifying herself to me.

The island was small and green in the distance. I ignored her, pretending to inspect my float cushion as the Shaptaw brothers fended us off from the dock. The water lapped at the sides of the boat, sending cool salty sprays across my skin. Elizabeth kept talking—a constant, aimless jabbering—trying to lessen the effect of her previous words. When I wouldn't give her my attention, she attempted to shock me.

"He's doing Lainey," she said.

Samantha spun around from her seat at the engine. "Really?" she asked, "How do you know?"

"He told me."

"Big deal," I said. "The whole world knows that."

But I hadn't known, only sensed something I didn't quite grasp. After we had motored a quarter of a mile from the shore, I looked back and saw the car still sitting there. Elizabeth caught my eye. We rode in silence the rest of the way, the vibration from the engine rattling my teeth and the skin around my bones.

By eight o'clock people were arriving in droves. For the boys, the style was to cut everything: the necks out of shirts, the legs off sweat pants—every appendage was framed in a curl of cotton. They wore bandannas on their heads. Two kinds of girls were present. The beach girls came from families who belonged to the yacht club and had been in and out of water their entire lives. They wore faded sweatshirts with the club insignia and boat shoes. The techie girls, from the vocational program, were tanners, not swimmers. The shoes were wrong and their long hair kept catching in their lipstick. There was a great deal of awkwardness at the tide line as they demanded to be lifted out of dinghies and carried to shore.

The girls clustered first around the bonfire, stepping into the light of the fire, some poking at their arms to check how much sun they had gotten. Everyone seemed friendlier than usual. Darkness made people stand a little nearer to one another. Christy Diamo dragged over a four-pronged branch and offered to cook the hot dogs with it. The high school girls shared marshmallows, passing around fresh, cool puffs for each person to cook her own way. It had been Libbie Gorin's idea to bring graham crackers and chocolate to make S'more's. She built S'more after S'more, but never ate one. There was a rumor that she was anorexic and I had watched her distract attention away from herself on numerous occasions by preparing elaborate snacks for her friends.

A large group of guys broke off to the side to do their drinking, alternately funneling beer out of a keg and shot-gunning cans. It seemed odd to me that such a pronounced division between the guys and the girls eventually wound itself back toward a pairing off—a sloppy falling together which felt random and destructive. As much as I tried, I could not envision it for myself. Most of what was happening around me felt foreign. Elizabeth was moving more easily in that world, full of trust and hope and fantasy. She could believe that things were different than they were. I felt myself standing outside and watching.

All the activity left me feeling empty, with a deep longing for when I was little and didn't have so many things to make sense of. For months, it had seemed Mama was hardly there to guide me, barely even recognizable as herself. I let myself think this and then took it back, feeling as guilty as the time in Atlanta, when I learned that sidewalk warning: *step on a crack you break your mother's back*. For weeks I walked over the same stretch of sidewalk in front of our house, counting my steps to avoid that groove, taking back every time I'd stepped on the line. I was six and already felt the crush of responsibility.

Elizabeth asked me and Samantha to keep an eye out for Keith

Rogers, but when finally I saw him, arriving off his boat with a couple of older girls, I hesitated before saying anything. I could tell by Elizabeth's face that she had seen him too. At first, she didn't approach him. She sat quietly next to me, her spine stubborn, posture that demonstrated confidence and at the same time revealed that she was entirely prepared to be deceived. I thought of lions with their look of power and self-preservation.

After Keith had poured himself a beer and let his eye wander over the crowd, Elizabeth sprang up and made her way over to him, disappearing into the fold of his arm. Samantha and I watched them together, the easy molding of their bodies, one against the other.

"Has she done it?" Samantha asked, saying aloud the thing we'd both been thinking.

"No," I answered, "I don't think so."

Samantha dug her feet deep in the sand, burying and lifting, letting the grains slip between her toes. "I . . ." she started, refusing to look at me. She paused, reached down over her legs and picked up a handful of sand. After a moment, she spoke quietly. "I did it." She rested her face on her knees. "Only once though."

Was she lying? I wondered. I no longer knew her the way I once had. There were things that had happened to her these last months I had missed, important things I hadn't been there for, even without really being gone. I felt left out, as if I'd moved away again and had come back just for a visit. I wasn't sure I had a right to ask for more information. If pressed, Samantha's words might evaporate. Still, I needed to know one thing. Not so much what as who. At the same time, I was afraid to find out. It was crazy, I knew, thinking that it might be Jamie. After all, they barely knew each other. But I needed to be sure. I couldn't have either of them the way I needed them if they had each other.

"Who was it?" I asked after a moment.

She let the silence hang between us as the tall grasses bowed over in the breeze. In the distance, the shore lights blurred and winked.

"Promise you won't tell anyone?"

She waited for my promise and then hinted, blushing and stammering until finally she pushed out the initials L.E.

"Lance Engler?"

She nodded. My relief left me room to wonder more about what she'd done. I glanced at her body out of the corner of my eye, checking to see if I could tell the difference.

"Did it hurt?" I asked.

"Not really," she said, "but I probably won't do it again for a while." She lifted her feet out of the sand, then brushed them off. "Promise you won't tell anyone."

"Who would I tell?"

"I don't know," she said, "your uncle?"

"I don't talk to him like that," I said. "Not anymore."

"That's good."

"Why?"

"No offense, Tilden," she said, "but there's something off about him."

Things got quiet between us. Samantha had said the thing I'd often felt, but couldn't say out loud. If she had asked, if anyone had asked, I might have told them the truth. But no one ever asked. Somehow that secret always circled back around to leave me with the burden of carrying it. I pulled my shirt over my bent legs and waited. It was only a matter of time; Samantha was great at changing the subject.

"I could show you what it was like," she said, holding up her bottle of beer in a toasting motion.

Samantha led me behind a dune and spread out her sweatshirt on the sand. She told me to do exactly as she did, but not to watch too closely. She poured out almost all of her beer, making a hole in the sand beside her. I followed her, wrapping my shirt around the top of a full bottle and releasing the cap. I poured the beer out beyond my feet.

"Leave a little," she said, touching my wrist, "it makes it easier."

Samantha blew on the neck of the bottle to get the sand off and then rubbed the glass back and forth between her hands. She placed the opening of the bottle near her crotch and pulled her shorts to the side. "Push it in at the same time as me," she said, "like a tampon."

I wiped my bottle on the edge of my shorts and attempted to push the grooves of the top inside me. I didn't want Samantha to know, but I had never been able to get anything inside. The beer ran down the neck and spilled against my flesh. Between the pinch of pain and the cool, sticky foam, I wondered if this was how it might feel to have my period. I pretended to push the glass in deep, when really I had not gotten further than the lip of the bottle. When I was sure that Samantha wasn't looking, I stopped trying and let the bottle rest between my legs.

Samantha lay back, both hands pushing at the base, her face in a tight grimace."Don't watch," she reprimanded, giving it one last push. She sat up, her leg accidentally brushing against mine. I pulled the sleeve of her sweatshirt across my lap and wiped one thigh.

"That's what it's like," she said, "only warmer . . . and softer." She threw her bottle high in the air. It landed in the distance with a thud. I threw mine too. Samantha giggled, her voice sweet and high, reminding me of how it had been before there were boys. "See?" she said. "It's not that great."

I pressed my fist into my crotch and brought my hand up to my nose. I smelled of beer, salt, and wet sand. Unfamiliar. "What time is it?" I asked, suddenly anxious.

"You have a half hour," Samantha said. "It's only midnight. Try to have some fun."

She pulled out a film canister filled with pot and wiggled in close to help block the wind. Setting up shop on her lap, she began to roll, slipping a thin square of white paper into a dollar bill and twisting tightly. I got caught up in the watching, not focusing on the specifics, but studying her, the precision of her long fingers, wondering when it was she learned to do all these things. She smoked most of the joint herself, silently, and then handed it to me, the ash flaking on my shin.

As I raised the moist paper to my mouth, I could feel a ring of warmth. I pinched my lips tight around it and closed my eyes. Sealed off like that, I felt alone. I pulled the warmth through me and imagined myself taken away, out of my body. Then, I began coughing, hacking and wheezing until I could barely breathe. When finally I opened my watering eyes, Jamie Sanders was standing in front of me, a strange look on his face. I had lost track of time. There was nothing left to exhale. Samantha was already shaking out her sweatshirt and feeling around for her shoes.

Jamie loomed over me, straight as a statue.

"What happened?" I asked.

"Get your stuff," he said, holding one hand out to me, "I have to take you home."

COOPERATION

I didn't remember getting from the dunes to the boat. I was preoccupied and guilty. On another day, I might have demanded an immediate explanation, but I was not used to being bad and getting caught. It left me feeling hesitant.

"Where's Elizabeth?" I asked Jamie once we were on the boat.

"She should be home by now."

"Am I in trouble?"

"No," he said. "Not really."

"What then?"

He paused, perhaps weighing his instinct against his orders. "It's your mom."

My shoulders were hunched up in anticipation—my whole body, a question. I looked up at him, my mouth open.

"It's okay," he said. "Nick just wants you home."

He didn't say anything more. I could feel his legs at my back as he stood behind me. The night air was damp and cold; it made my body ache.

Uncle Rand met me at the door. He was pale and frantic looking. He started from the beginning. He had made some orange juice at nine o'clock, like every night, he squeezed it in the juicer and put one glass in the fridge for Mama to have with breakfast. Usually she stirred when he brought it to her. Sometimes they even talked a bit late at night. Mama had always been a light sleeper. "But she didn't move," he said. "Even when I tried to wake her, she didn't move."

Uncle Rand was out of control, words gushing out of him. I could scarcely hear what he was saying. I kept waiting for some comment about the island. About being late and smelling like beer. But nothing came. Something more important was happening, something much worse. Usually he hid things, made everything seem better than it was, but now he was pacing and telling me everything with his hands gesturing wildly.

"What happened?" I screamed. "Just tell me. Where is she?"

"It's okay, sweetie," Nick said, stepping into the foyer and pulling me toward him. His shirt was wet with sweat. "She refused to go to the hospital, so the doctor came here. She's resting now."

It was Nick who had thought to call Jamie when it happened. He knew that Jamie could be trusted to go to the meeting place and bring us back. He was at the dock at one o'clock to meet Elizabeth when she stepped off Keith Rogers' boat. Jamie thought that Elizabeth should wait so that we could both go home together, but she wouldn't have it. The minute she heard that there was the slightest thing wrong, she panicked. Keith drove Elizabeth straight home and let Jamie take the boat back for me.

"Do you want to see her?" Nick asked at last.

I waited outside the bedroom door where I heard him whisper to Elizabeth, asking her to step back a bit from the bed. Through the crack, I caught sight of a pale, almost bald, figure. Mama, diminished. Her skin practically gray. I watched as Nick put her wig in place. It seemed as if I had been gone for months. He signaled for me to come into the room. At the edge of the bed, I leaned my full weight on Elizabeth.

"Stand up," she said, shedding me, her face in a determined grimace, blotchy from tears. "Just talk to her. I've been letting her suck on a washcloth when she's thirsty."

She couldn't have gotten there more than a half hour before me. How did she get to be such an expert?

"I think you girls should get some rest," Nick said.

"I want to stay," Elizabeth countered.

"Okay, okay," he said, "for a little while longer." He looked nervous and seemed unsure of what to do.

Elizabeth and I each took a side whispering, "Mama, Mama, you're going to be just fine," stroking her fingers and her face. She was flushed hot and suddenly cold. After Nick left the room, I asked to know what happened.

"I think it was pills," Elizabeth whispered, shrugging slightly, "too many sleeping pills."

I swung around to find Uncle Rand. "Shouldn't she be in the hospital?"

"She didn't want to," he said. "She asked us not to take her there." He paced in and out of the room, barely slowing down for the conversation.

"But, why?"

"There's nothing they can do, Tilden. Besides, she's more comfortable at home."

I looked at her limp, sleeping body. She seemed small, even under the covers. Not comfortable at all. Bones jutting sharply through her clothes. All clavicle and sinewy tissue. When had she gotten so thin?

I decided to read to her, the way she had when I was seven and had the chicken pox, her voice drifting over me creating comfort and calm. I raced back to my room and found the Walt Whitman book she'd bought for me when she learned we were moving near his birthplace. Sitting on the radiator at the edge of her bed, I read sections of *Leaves of Grass* aloud, pausing when I got to the lines that

Mama had especially liked. I trained my eye to glance quickly over the page, searching for any mention of death, anything dark, skipping the lines about *uncut hair of graves*. Elizabeth, with her eyes round and unsure, whispered that perhaps I should read stories instead. Something from a children's book even. I kept reading to Mama as if she could hear me, when really I wasn't entirely sure.

> This grass is very dark to be from the white heads of old
>   mothers,
> Darker than the colorless beards of old men,
> Dark to come from under the faint red roofs of mouths.

By dawn, Mama had come to. I ran to her room, naively expecting to see her rejuvenated. She seemed groggy and confused, whispering to Uncle Rand about not calculating her pills appropriately.

"Fifty-four in a bottle," I heard her say. "That should have been enough."

She abruptly stopped speaking when she noticed me standing there. But it was too late. I went on a search of her cabinets and trash pails, looking in her drawers and medicine chest. Then I found the note tucked under the phone on Nick's side of the bed.

Do not take me to the hospital. I love you my lovelies—always. At the bottom was her signature and the date.

Anger flashed through me. Why hadn't Nick done something? Had he and Uncle Rand been a part of this? I tried to get them to talk to me. About Mama. About the pills. Anything. But they acted busy, claiming Mama had made a mistake, that she hadn't meant to take quite so many.

"I'm sorry, honey" Mama said in tears, "I don't want you to see me so sick. I can't live. . . like this."

Her voice, soft and weak, washed over me. I both knew and

didn't know what she was saying. For the first time ever, I didn't want the truth.

The house was already hot, the air all milky and thick. I closed myself in my room. I could hear Elizabeth, at the other end of the hall, a low moan interrupted by gasps. Nick was attempting to comfort her. "Now, now," he said. "I'm right here." I turned on my record player and balanced the needle over the Eagles' album. Part of me wanted to be able to hear Elizabeth, to let her do the crying for both of us. There never seemed to be enough room for both our emotions at once. But, another part of me wanted to disappear. I crawled under my covers and sang "Take It Easy" softly into my pillow.

Later that same morning, Uncle Rand brought me up some breakfast. The smell of warm bread made me feel sick. I didn't even lift my head. He left the plate on my desk and ran his hand over my back.

"Try and eat something, Tilden, okay?"

When Elizabeth came in, I slid over without saying a word and made room for her in the bed.

"One of the Mosquitoes is coming to check on Mama today," she said, her breath moist on my ear.

"Don't call them that," I barked.

"Why not?" she asked. "That's what Mama calls them."

"Just don't," I said. "I hate those stupid doctors."

Elizabeth began whimpering, crying softly into my shoulder. I felt bad for being so mean. I slid my hand next to hers under the covers and locked our pinkies together.

When Dr. Lichner arrived, Nick came to talk to us. He sat down on the bed for a moment and rubbed his eyes hard with the heels of his palms. He had been crying too, the rims of his eyelids were red and swollen. To see him so shaken terrified me. Nothing felt secure.

"Girls?" he started, "your mama thought it might be better for you to stay up here until after Dr. Lichner leaves. Okay?"

"Why?" Elizabeth asked.

"Because she needs to speak with him privately. It should only be for a little while. And then you can come down and see her." He waited for us to nod in agreement and then stood to leave. "I'll be back up to check on you both in a bit."

I didn't understand how he got to be the go-between, to make all the decisions. I wondered if Mama even wanted it that way.

"Yes, sir," I said under my breath.

Elizabeth sat up quickly. "He's just doing what Mama asked."

I rolled my eyes.

"You should give him a chance."

"Why?"

"He loves Mama as much as we do."

"He hasn't even known her that long."

"You shouldn't talk that way," Elizabeth said, "he's practically our father."

"He's not my father." I turned my back to her and silently raged, trying to picture a time before Mama got sick, when it was just the three of us and every day began and ended in one of Mama's giant hugs.

I heard the shuffling of footsteps in the kitchen below and felt nervous that I might be missing something important. Elizabeth and I exchanged a look and without having to say anything out loud we knew what to do. Our shoulders pressed together, we silently made our way down the stairwell to listen from the pantry.

If I had been allowed to see Dr. Lichner in person, I would have brought my notebook and asked how and why and when—all the "w" questions that I'd been taught would provide the most information. Nobody had ever been able to tell me why Mama had cancer or even how long she had had it. I could hear Uncle Rand's voice, low and questioning. He had stopped the doctor in the hall and was pressing him for more facts. There were things even he didn't know.

"There are four stages in which to place cancer patients receiving chemotherapy," Dr. Lichner was saying, "Frances is in the fourth . . . the smallest category of those patients who do not respond."

But Mama had responded, I thought—the vomiting, the hair loss—a "mood elevator" she called herself that year.

"I thought it was over with the surgery," Elizabeth whispered.

I shushed her and slid down a few steps closer to the edge of the wall.

"I'll be quite frank with you," Dr. Lichner continued, "there's no reason not to be at this point. At the time of the mastectomy, there were nine positive lymph nodes. The tumor was quite grave, so large that it had adhered to the pectoral muscle. That is what is meant by the term *radical*."

I should have understood from the beginning what radical meant. I should have looked it up.

Dr. Lichner kept speaking, some words low and hushed, others I couldn't hear at all. I pictured the two of them standing closer than men usually stand, each with a hand on the kitchen counter. Uncle Rand cursed and groaned. Suddenly the doctor's voice grew near, louder.

"I'm only saying this because I think it's important that you know what we're dealing with here. At the time of her surgery her chance of survival past five years was less than 20 percent."

"And now?" Uncle Rand asked.

"I'm sorry." He cleared his throat. "It's difficult to say. Sometimes people hold out six months or so. But given her current state . . . I'd have to say . . . well, she doesn't have long. Weeks, really. I can arrange for a nurse to check in so that she'll be comfortable."

"Thank you," Uncle Rand said.

It surprised me that Dr. Lichner was so imprecise. It made me want to jump up and ask him a few questions of my own. About the chemotherapy: why hadn't it worked? And where had she gotten those pills to start with? He was supposed to make her better. All he could offer now was information.

"This is the hardest part of my profession," he said as he walked toward the door.

Elizabeth let her head fall back and bang hard against the wall. "I thought he was supposed to be nice," she cried, her body shaking.

I tried to block out the sound of her voice as she repeated the words we had just heard. She wanted me to contradict what the doctor had said—suggesting other doctors, more medicine, another operation. There was hope in her confused urgency. Somehow she still believed that something more could be done.

But I had settled into a quiet resignation. Loaded down with the facts, I felt numb, my practical side surfacing over all emotion. I now knew that Mama was dying; her death was a project that she had been working on secretly. To acknowledge it meant that I would come to know her better. Death was a hard fact, like any external fact, something that you accept without necessarily understanding the process. Like the way television works. Or weather. It was someone else's job to understand why things worked the way they did.

Now I wasn't sure how to face Mama. I was afraid that looking into her eyes meant seeing only the knowledge of her death reflected back at me. Knowing that it had been there, unseen for months, made me not trust what I knew of her. No matter how many times I rolled it over in my mind or how often I said it to myself, I could not imagine the fact of it. I knew only that it meant that Mama was ready to begin the work of her dying. I would join her in this work. It was all I had.

The family meeting that followed confirmed the worst. Nick did all the talking, in a tentative and detached voice, while Mama sat next to him wringing her hands in her lap, her eyes darting all around the room.

"Your mama wants to be here at home," Nick said. "She doesn't want to spend. . ." his voice cracked. "She doesn't want to go to the hospital. Can you both accept that?"

I watched Nick's face, his words falling away. I could see only that serious pursed mouth and his pleading eyes. I could not figure out exactly what he was asking. Uncle Rand covered his face with his hands and balanced himself in the doorway. When no one responded to Nick's question, he continued, as if Mama weren't there.

"It may be difficult," he said, watching us, "but the doctor says it's possible to make her comfortable." He paused to check for Uncle Rand's reaction and then ours.

"Do you girls have any questions? It's going to take all of us . . . we all have to be strong. Okay, Elizabeth?"

Elizabeth began crying, first with a squeak and then a piercing, wailing sound. Uncle Rand folded his arms around her and rocked her gently, burying his face in her hair, his upper body quivering.

"Tilden?" Nick stepped closer to reach out to me.

"What?" I barked, moving away from him. "Can we just stop talking. Please."

Mama shifted, balancing her weight on one arm, and tried to sit up. She smoothed the comforter with her hand. "Come here, girls. I want to talk to you."

We moved closer, taking our positions around her bed. Elizabeth right beside her, me on the radiator, the sharp bumps pushing into my rear. Mama nodded to Nick, excusing him and Uncle Rand. She waited until they had moved away from the door before grabbing hold of both of our hands with her bony fingers. She took a deep, shaky breath.

"I never meant for anything like this to happen to us. You girls are my whole world, you know that? And I don't understand this any more than you do, but I do know that the only thing that matters to me is that you two help each other . . . look out for each other always. Will you do that for me?"

Elizabeth nodded through her tears. My throat was so dry and tight, I could not swallow or speak. We sat for a moment, sniffling and collecting ourselves, and then Elizabeth eked out a few words. "What's . . . going. . . to happen . . . to us?"

"You're going to be just fine. I know it doesn't feel that way. But . . . Nick loves you girls—he really, really does. He knows how I feel, what's important to me. I've asked him to look after you the very best way he can." She rubbed her hand on my leg. "Please, Tilden. Just give him a chance."

I shrugged and then began to cry, slipping from my place on the radiator to her side, folding myself against her frail body. She tickled the spot between my shoulders and continued to talk over our sobs. "Two girls. How did I get so lucky to have two such wonderful girls?"

I spent that entire day running between my bedroom and Mama's, seeking solitude, then company. Alone in my room, I dug through boxes of old photographs, pinning pictures of Mama edge-to-edge on my corkboard. Sitting there amongst images of her, healthy and vibrant, it was easy to forget what was happening, to pretend it away. She was so beautiful in every picture—a sly, knowing smile, her hair shining around her face—I was quickly taken back to before she was sick. Then, I would get a pang of fear, a little worry growing in my gut, a question I wanted to ask, some story I needed to hear and run dry-mouthed down to her room, only to find her, a shadow of herself, dull and groggy.

Elizabeth spent her day making a list, saving up all her wants for one exchange. She joined me that evening in Mama's room with her tape recorder.

"Tell me again what time was I born," Elizabeth started.

"Nine-thirty in the morning," Mama responded, smoothing back Elizabeth's hair. "You were nine twenty-five A.M. and you . . ." she motioned toward me, ". . . were nine twenty-five P.M." She said nine twenty-five as if it meant something beyond the time of day.

"And . . . God?" Elizabeth asked. "Have you tried praying to God?"

"In some kind of strange way, I have," Mama said. "You should try to if you can. . . I mean, don't let this stop you." Her eyes scanned her own body, then welled up. It had become difficult to know for sure when she was crying. Her eyes were always swollen and tearing, from the drugs, from the chemo, from her late-night talks with Nick.

Elizabeth paused, straining toward Mama and waiting for more; it hadn't been the response she'd hoped for. She cleared her throat and proceeded, "This question might make you sad," she said.

Mama pulled the box of tissues on to her lap, "Ready."

"What are your favorite names? You know, for children?"

"I gave you girls my favorite names," she smiled to herself. "As different as they are. Tilden. Elizabeth." She spoke our names slowly. "Whatever you do, don't use my name if you girls have children. I mean it. Please, please don't use Frances. It's . . . It's not beautiful. It's not romantic or anything at all." She started coughing, dropping her face into her fist and gasping for air. She reached for a cough drop from the box on her nightstand.

Elizabeth picked up a glass of water and held it out to her. "Am I making you tired?" she asked.

Mama shook her head and drank down a sip.

"How do you feel about living with someone before marriage?" Elizabeth continued.

"Fine by me," Mama said, laughing a little and gesturing around the bedroom to include herself.

"What about sex?" Elizabeth giggled.

"My views on that have not changed." Mama said. She lowered her voice a little. "Wait if you can. Make it special. But don't expect too much. The other stuff matters more. And remember . . . it gets better as you get older." She stopped, lost in her thoughts, and then looked up. "Go on you two, get some rest. I have to save my voice."

Elizabeth stood up and moved toward the door, bending on her knee to check the sound on the recording before leaving.

"I have one question for you, Mama," I said, leaning near to her so that Elizabeth wouldn't hear. The familiar smell of her wig made me realize how long it had been since I had gotten close. I paused briefly, taking in the mix of lotion and shampoo. "What do you want me to be?" I asked, finally.

She settled back on her pillow. "Anything," she answered quickly. "Anything you want."

When I started kindergarten and brought home my first schoolwork, Mama always took my assignments seriously, clearing off the table, and sitting next to me as I traced my letters, making the spaces exact, or practiced addition, two lines between each equation.

Once, I was given an assignment about careers and told to choose a profession and write a one-paragraph essay. Mama took me for a walk in town, pointing out all the things there were to be. Florist. Baker. Postman. Cashier.

"What are you?" I asked her.

"A little bit of everything," she said.

She showed me where she had worked in a frame shop, taking measurements and helping people choose colors for the background matting. And the bank where she'd been a teller just after I was born. She pointed to a "For Sale" sign in someone's yard and told me that what she had been doing since I started school was helping people find places to live.

"What did my father do?" I asked.

"Carpentry," she said, "he made things for people."

"Did he ever make anything for you?"

"Twice," she said, tipping my head with her hand and smiling down at me. "First you. Then, Elizabeth."

On Friday, Lainey showed up with her suitcase full of lip gloss, blusher, and polish. She sent me on ahead to let Mama know that she was coming up for some girl time. I expected Mama to refuse, but she surprised me by softening at the prospect of a pedicure. Elizabeth and I watched from the end of the bed as Lainey rubbed Mama's feet in soapy warm water and placed wet cotton balls on her eyelids. Mama relaxed into the treatment, letting Lainey talk without feeling the need to respond.

"You just can't go isolating yourself up here," Lainey chastised. "There are people who love you in the world and want to be near you."

She named each lotion and implement as she used it, talking us through the ritual. Elizabeth and I traded off doing each other's nails, picking up each item as Lainey put it down. We fell into a rhythm, the sounds of clipping and splashing taking the place of conversation. It was a relief to have this to turn to. There will always be this between women, I thought.

By the time Lainey had rubbed Mama's calloused feet smooth with a pumice stone, she had dozed off. While she slept, Lainey painted her toenails coral. She tucked the blankets close around Mama's legs, leaving her feet out in the air to dry. I wondered what Nick might think finding her like that when he took up her dinner. It would give him pleasure to see those bright spots at the end of her pale body, like finding candy in the bottom of a coat pocket.

Saturday night, I crept into Mama's room and lay down on the floor. I listened to her breathe from five in the morning until eight when she sat up in bed.

"Who's this person?" she mumbled to herself.

I pushed my face against the floor and tried not to move. I started to peek at her, but felt guiltier than anytime as a child when I had watched her dress. The sheets rustled as she shifted in the bed. I lay immobile, and found myself thinking about time. The week since Dove Island had gone slowly, almost as if I was the sick one, not showering or changing clothes, disconnected from the outside world. Each morning I checked the calendar in my room, placing myself firmly in the day, but always with an eye back at how many had passed. It was the opposite of the way I normally kept time, counting forward toward an event, imagining myself in the future, falling asleep with the knowledge that when I woke, I would be one day closer.

Dr. Lichner had said anywhere from two weeks to six months. I was keeping track in part to prove him wrong. It was a ridiculous range. Two weeks was scarcely enough time to prepare for an exam or write a paper. Six months could mean the difference between junior high and high school. It was the equivalent of three summers off.

Lying there listening to Mama's rhythmic breaths, I realized how in the last few months, Mama had also become preoccupied with time. She'd asked Nick to buy her a digital alarm clock which she placed on the top of her dresser. She divided her days into fifteen minute segments to keep track of her pain medication. The days didn't seem to matter as much as the hours. She checked the time whenever we entered the room.

I stood up and smiled at her.

"Good morning, glory," Mama said, blinking at her clock.

I thought about something adult I'd learned from Samantha and decided to risk telling her about it. "Mama, did you know?"

"Know what, honey?"

"Well . . . Morning Glory refers to the erection men wake up with."

"Oh dear," she said. "Now *that* is very funny."

The afternoons began to mirror one another. Mama, three-quarters up in bed jotting in her notebook, requesting trays with Jell-O, boiled chicken, and Lorna Doone cookies—always her favorite. She drank a quart of milk during the day to coat her stomach against her multiple doses of pain killers, but rarely ate. The full plates grew cold on the table beside her. She kept a careful record of her pills, scheduled as much as a day ahead so that she would never have to experience the lull between medications.

On the inside cover of her journal were some of her thoughts written in jagged prose. *I hate my body, weak and atrophied. I want to work with the dying, but I can't stand to be around sick people.* And on the cardboard inside back cover of the journal it said, *I want to be part of a dangerous mission in which I am shot in the end.*

"Read me my horoscope," Mama suggested to Nick as he sat in a chair with the paper. "I don't want to hear about what's going on in the world. It's too depressing." Initially he refused, but at her insistence we all decided to bear it out. He read hers first.

"Pisces—superfluous material will be junked," it said.

"What does ours say?" we asked in unison.

"Geminis: Relative could have wires crossed."

"That's for sure," Mama whispered, a ghost of a smile on her face.

When I cleaned up her room on Monday, I got rid of all the newspapers. Seeing them stacked in the corner signified how many days were passing. The empty place in the bed next to Mama's looked like the tabletop at a garage sale. I wanted to clear that side off so that I could sleep there with her. But she needed those things—lemon cough drops, a box of photos, and her journal. On the bed, too, was a book with the cover torn off. *On Death and Dying,* it said on the binding. She shrugged and smiled at me. She had been reading it alongside my choices from *Seventeen* and *Catcher in the Rye*. In a shoe box, were her envelopes, as she called them. In each, were the papers involving legalities—her marriage license, our adoption papers, and our birth certificates. She'd sent Uncle Rand to make extra copies which she referred to in conversation, but never said anything specific about what we would use them for. Her breathing had begun to sound wheezy and strained. It was all happening so fast.

• • •

On Tuesday, the hospital delivered a Home Oxygen System. With that and the angry red bump on Mama's neck, I could now picture what cancer looked like. Its long tendrils, inside, feeding on her lung and penetrating her bones—the lower back, twelfth rib. I imagined it wrapping around her heart and squeezing the life out of her. I ran my hand over her arm and beneath her smooth, freckled skin, I felt clusters hardened to the bone. She moved her arm away from my touch and pretended to be reaching for a glass of water. I pretended she was no sicker, that the oxygen was for her added comfort. But there was panic on her face every time someone stepped near the machine.

"Careful of my umbilical cord," she said, her face pinched and cross.

There was a hundred feet of clear tubing—enough to reach from her room to the den where Nick often slept—that she gathered and looped around her arm on her journeys. The droning of the breathing machine made the environment sound hollow. The pump moved upward like a gasp and plunged down like a wave. Over and over again. It was the first thing I heard when coming inside the house. After that day, I was afraid to go out and come back up the front steps into an inevitable silence.

The days passed in long moments of stillness. I would talk to no one. Elizabeth was off in some other room, whispering constantly into the phone. She was recruiting her friends, especially the Catholic ones, to pray. I didn't see what good it would do. "Otherwise," I heard her say, "my mom may never see me get to junior high school."

Elizabeth's fears made me realize that I had imagined Mama's absence in a larger way, years off in the future, but not in terms of my life as I knew it. That I would own clothes she had never seen, get a driver's license, and know people she had never met seemed somehow not as sad as the knowledge that she had goals and aspirations of her own.

By Friday, the shelf under the big bay window in her bedroom was lined with floral arrangements. It stopped me in my tracks when I noticed how many more had arrived in the last few days. Tall purple stalks. Little yellow blooms pinched to resemble faces. Green ferns and leaves. Mama identified the types of flowers in each arrangement as if she were quizzing herself. I sat listening to her, trying to learn their names. There were so many. There was so much to learn.

"Iris, lily," she called out, as if taking attendance, "rose, snapdragon, and . . ." she gasped, "look at the trumpet on that beautiful daffodil."

"Mama?" I asked.

She turned her gaze from the windowsill. "What is it, sweetie?"

"How will you know when I get my period?"

She sighed dreamily and reached her hand out to mine. "Send me a note," she said. "The mail has its own magic."

Later that day, I pulled a chair next to the bed and read her letters that had arrived from some of her old friends. There were stamps with illustrations of ferries, the faces of presidents and poets, an American flag. The post office dates were faint and hard to read. I did the math for each one, calculating how long the letter had taken to arrive. Some from Atlanta. One from Nick's mother in Florida. Mostly, I read the letters to myself. They were written that way, not to her as much as about her. In the stack, was an invitation to her twentieth college reunion.

"That sounds fun," she said, suddenly alert, and then closed her eyes again.

Mama took cat naps, as she called them, for most of the afternoon. Her eyes were swollen from the morphine and when she lifted her lids, the iris rolled back in her head. At one point, I helped her to the bathroom and she insisted that she go in alone. I leaned against the molding and peered in the crack.

"I'll call you when I'm ready," she scolded, and then with a thin, desperate voice, "don't go too far."

Later with Nick on one side and me on the other, we took Mama for a walk around the room. Elizabeth followed behind us, guiding the tubing from the oxygen machine around the furniture. Mama pulled frantically at her cord and I assured her over and over that we would not step on it. Her feet were barely scaling the ground, while Nick coaxed, "That's wonderful, keep going."

Her breathing had become more like gasping, as dramatic as the pump inside the oxygen machine. She was asleep almost before we put her in the bed. When Nick left the room, Elizabeth and I adjusted her against the pillow, tugging at her body as if she were no longer in it. We thought that she should be sitting up higher than she was. I pulled so hard on her shoulder that I felt something give. Part of me may have wanted to hurt her just to see if she would notice. But she didn't respond.

After an hour, Nick came back to check on her. He touched her face with his hand, holding one finger against her breath. "Dear God," he whispered. He pushed the clear plastic nose clip of the oxygen machine deeper into her nostrils, "Get your uncle."

I found Uncle Rand in his bedroom bent over his lap scribbling on looseleaf paper. He was deep in thought, writing nonstop. I'd only seen his blocky handwriting on kitchen counter instructions. It had never occurred to me that he had more to say. When he looked up from the page, I said, "Nick wants you."

He folded the paper in half, sealed the crease with his thumb, and slipped it under his pillow. Then, he stood up and hugged me to his chest. "This is the hardest thing that will ever happen . . ." he said, his breath against my scalp, "to any of us." He pulled back and looked down at me, his mustache quivering slightly above his tightening lips. "I love you," he said, "you just remember that."

I stepped away from his embrace, nodding as he strode off toward Mama's room.

The definition of coma in my dictionary did not prepare me for the fact that Mama would not regain consciousness. I waited next to her all night to have some kind of final exchange. I opened her hand and stuck one of mine inside, my other one squeezing them firmly together. I watched her chest move up and down and feared what the moment of quiet and rest would look and sound like. I brushed her wig for her and told her how beautiful she looked. With a tissue, I soaked up the saliva that was gathering in her mouth and put a little Vaseline on her dry lips. Everyone else had gone to bed. I was waiting with perfect patience, the way only I could wait, a waiting laced with hope.

Nick arrived the next morning with two glasses of fresh-squeezed juice. Seeing those glasses on a tray, striated orange and grapefruit, cheery with ice, I fell into believing that she might survive another day. Nick handed me one. It felt cool and heavy in my hand. I brought an ice cube from the froth into my mouth and held it against my gums. I looked at Mama and then back at Nick to see if there had been a change in the night that I might not have been able to see. He stared out the window and took a long sip from his glass.

"It's like you've given up on her," I said.

He turned his glass in front of him, watching the pulp stick to the side. "I've never given up on your mama," he said, "not from the moment I met her. Not even when she refused to marry me right away. First, because she wanted to do the best by you girls. And then because of the cancer. I waited because I couldn't do anything else. Because I knew I had to have her in my life."

"Don't talk about her like she's gone," I said.

"She is gone," he practically shouted. His anger startled me. Then, he softened. "Look, honey, she's gone."

Her breathing was imperceptible when I brought my eyes back to her. For a second I imagined she was between breaths. But a minute passed and her chest did not rise. She was still. I ran to get Elizabeth, pulling her out from her covers and dragging her back without a word. I had stopped watching for only that moment. I had missed saying good-bye.

HOME ECONOMICS

I watched, barefoot, from the outdoor staircase as a police car pulled into the driveway and two officers strode up the front yard, their hard shoes clicking on the slate path. Officer Denehey lowered the volume on his walkie-talkie before entering the house. I wasn't used to the glare of morning sun, the way it reflected off the windshields in the lot, how the glinting chrome made the cars look new. Before long, vapors would start to rise off the hot, black pavement, and the lifting sun would expose the grit and grease of TransAlt. The early shift of drivers stood in a tight clump looking unsure as to whether they should approach the house or continue on with their day. When the medical examiner arrived, the drivers dispersed, turning toward the garage and offering some privacy.

Elizabeth and I snuck down to the pantry and eavesdropped on the kitchen conversation. The medical examiner was speaking in a low, respectful voice explaining the funereal options to Nick. Uncle Rand stood over the stove boiling water for instant coffee. He measured the powder into a green ceramic mug and stirred absently with a teaspoon. When Lainey arrived, she hugged Uncle Rand, rubbing his back gently and cupping one hand around the nape of his neck. One of the drivers must have called her before she left that morning. She was dressed in a navy linen suit, ready for anything we might need. Her hair was brushed high off her face, and pulled back in a clip. After the hug, she stood back and looked around.

"Where are the girls?" she asked.

"Upstairs," he said.

"Oh God, I'm so sorry," she touched his elbow. "What can I do?"

"Nothing," he said. "Nick doesn't want to have a service. It was everything I could do to get him to agree to have the deacon come by." Uncle Rand picked up the mug and raised it to his mouth, the steam curling around his moustache as he blew on the top. He set the coffee down without taking a sip and turned to Lainey, "I think we need to change her clothes."

She nodded and said, "I can do that."

They waited for the medical examiner and officers to finish their reports and then disappeared into Mama's room. After a few minutes, Lainey walked back through the kitchen, clutching an armful of hanging garments and discovered us crouched behind the pantry door. She hugged us both, offering *sorry* after *so sorry* in a singsong voice.

"Come upstairs," she said, after a moment, "I need your help with something."

Lainey thought it might make us feel better to help pick out an outfit for Mama, but Elizabeth and I couldn't seem to agree on anything. I thought Mama should wear something free-spirited such as her polka-dot sundress, but Elizabeth wanted her to look more formal and selected a blouse and skirt set. Neither of us wanted to sacrifice those items that most reminded us of her. Her clothes smelled like a mix of her perfumes—sandalwood and gardenia—dulled by the staleness of her closet. I hadn't seen most of those clothes for months. We finally agreed on a polished denim dress that she had never much liked, but looked beautiful in. Lainey wet her thumb and rubbed at a toothpaste stain on the bodice.

"Find the scarf," Elizabeth said, starting to cry again, "the rust one she always wears . . . "

Lainey put her arms around her and then reached out for me, her long fuchsia nails scraping my shoulder. I didn't want any part of her comfort. Nothing would make me feel better.

Uncle Rand and Nick climbed the stairs and joined us, sitting down next to each other on the edge of my bed. They looked like two men on a bus who were relieved to get a seat, but disappointed by the company. They had been arguing all morning about a service and had finally come to a compromise. They'd probably said things that they now regretted and were trying to present a united front. My room felt suddenly small. Elizabeth and I sat down on the floor to listen.

Uncle Rand spoke first, his voice weak and strained. "The deacon should be here within the hour. He's just going to say a few words, something comforting."

"That's important," Lainey said, more to herself. She seemed to know what to do. She asked for Mama's address book and offered to make the necessary calls from the dispatching phone in the TransAlt office. "What about an obituary for the paper?" she asked.

I could tell that Nick wasn't really listening to her. All the muscles in his face were slack, making him almost unrecognizable. He slouched forward. "Whatever you think," he said absently.

"People will want to know how they can pay their respects," Lainey said, looking back and forth between Nick and Uncle Rand, unsure who to direct this opinion toward. There didn't seem to be anyone in charge. Nick was distant, locked inside himself, everything washing over him, nothing entering. Lainey looked at us, worried, then turned to confide in Uncle Rand. She leaned toward him and rested a hand on his shoulder. "It's just that without a funeral people don't have any way to express their feelings," she said gently. "Most people will be in shock."

The word *shock* echoed in my ears. I looked at the stunned, ashy faces around me. Uncle Rand looked especially gaunt, his whole face pale and unshaven.

"There won't be a funeral," Nick said.

Lainey started to object and then thought better of it. She walked off, trailing Mama's dresses over her shoulder.

By the time the deacon arrived, Mama was laid out neatly on top of the flowered comforter with her arms bent across her stomach. There was a pair of low heels sticking out from the hem of her denim dress. Her legs were bare. Someone had placed a Band-Aid over the lump on her neck. She looked like the Red Cross resuscitation doll from CPR class at school—only older and without hair.

The deacon remembered that we were not particularly religious, but offered to read a passage from the Gospel of John. All I could hear was that it was something about the light shining in the darkness. Elizabeth listened with her eyes closed. After he spoke, each of us was allotted some alone time with Mama's body. I knew that the time was meant for conversation and prayer. Instead, I filled my five minutes with a nagging curiosity about what would happen after they took her away. Would they remove her clothes? Her shoes? I wished that she had opted for burial rather than cremation.

When Nick knocked on the door, signaling the end of my time, I became immediately nauseated. Everything I'd never told Mama—all my secrets, all my worries, the forbidden things I'd overheard that last year—all rushed up on me like regret. I leaned over her face and kissed the tip of her nose. She smelled like ocean. Her skin was cool as shells. I rested my head on her chest and wrapped my arms around her shoulders.

Nick touched my back lightly. "Come on," he said "it's time."

Elizabeth had to be carried out of the room. Uncle Rand held her like a rescuer would, her weight cradled limply between his two extended arms. Her face was strained, her lips blue and skinny. I followed them up the stairs to my room where he deposited Elizabeth safely on my bed and stepped in front of the window, blocking my view of the empty stretcher waiting by the back steps.

"Don't you girls look out there," he said and pulled a blanket off the bed to cover the windows. "You don't want that car to be the last thing you see." He was stiff and awkward in his dark suit; it was the first time I had ever seen him in a tie.

After the funeral parlor had taken Mama's body away in a long, dark station wagon, Lainey came up with sandwiches and soda on a tray. She tugged the blanket and let it fall in a heap on the floor. She sat down between us on the bed and encouraged us to eat. I took my plate and set it on the floor. I couldn't imagine eating anything, ever again. Elizabeth picked up a potato chip and put it down. She squeezed a pickle between her thumb and forefinger. Mama had never trusted anything with that long a shelf life. Elizabeth put her plate down next to mine and reached out for my hand. I let her hold it, but only for a minute before lifting the covers and snaking underneath.

Lainey sighed and stacked the food neatly on the tray. "I understand," she said, "I'll just leave it right over here where you can nibble on it if you get hungry."

She lingered by my bed and looked at the photographs of Mama that were tacked to my corkboard. In one, an enlargement from the wedding, Mama's eyes are cast sideways, her lips parted mid-word. In another, from when Elizabeth and I were toddlers, we are all three in the tub. Mama is hiding her breasts with one arm and swatting away the camera with the other. Elizabeth is holding a bottle of conditioner as if it is a doll. I am busy working the faucet.

Lainey leaned over the bed to look at the photo more closely. "Who took this one?" she asked, looking first at Elizabeth and then at me.

I didn't know. I realized that I would never know. Who was there to ask? Elizabeth shrugged, useless. Lainey sat down on the bed and pulled my head into her chest. "I'm so sorry," she said, rocking me gently in her arms. I pressed my face hard against her to keep from crying. Her jacket smelled inky, like dry cleaning.

After I sat up, dizzy and disheveled, Lainey asked me if I might like to write the notice for the paper.

She can't be gone, I thought. How could she have left me like this—with strangers?

"I don't think I can," I said.

She put her hand on my arm. "It might help you," she said.

"What am I supposed to do?" Elizabeth asked.

"You can do it together," she said and stood up, "just put down everything you can think of. I'll proofread it." She pulled the door closed and headed back downstairs.

Elizabeth curled up on my bed, crossing her bare feet, one around the other like mating doves. I went to Uncle Rand's room, slipped four clean sheets of paper from the pack on his nightstand and borrowed a pencil. I sat down at my desk to work and stared at the blank page. I had listened closely to Mama my whole life, but now I couldn't remember anything. Words escaped me, so I turned to math, counting backward to figure out the year she was born and forward to approximate when she had graduated from high school. She was forty-two years old.

I stole adjectives from some of the letters that her friends had sent in the days before she died. Devoted mother. Loving sister. Loyal friend. I suddenly realized how much I didn't know. What was the name of her sorority in college? How had she met our real father? I didn't even know what jobs she had held before she had children. I couldn't believe I hadn't asked.

When I read the list aloud to Elizabeth, she said that she remembered something about Mama working in a hospital.

"I thought it was real estate," I said. "Didn't she want to design houses?"

"She did?" Elizabeth asked.

I used up all the paper making drafts and returned to Uncle Rand's room for one final, clean sheet. As I reached for it, I remembered the note he'd been writing and tipped his pillow to look. After a moment of deliberating, holding the folded page up to the light and putting it down again, I lifted the top half and settled my eyes on the even temper of his handwriting. As I read, I felt the exhilaration of discovering a secret.

> Lainey—
>
> I will always remember our time together. I am grateful you were in my life. I am not very good on paper. I hope you will understand when I tell you that I can't stay. Not with Frances gone . . .

I brought the unfinished letter to Elizabeth and sat down next to her on the bed. She read it over and over, held it up to her nose to smell and then handed it back to me. We sat close to each other, the loss settling quietly around us, until I heard Uncle Rand climb the stairs. Elizabeth panicked, threw herself down on the pillow, and pretended to be asleep. I sat upright, the letter open in my hand, and waited. The air was so thick, I could scarcely breathe.

As soon as Uncle Rand appeared in my doorway, I spoke up.

"You knew she was dying," I said, "that's why you came. You knew but you never said a thing. And now you're just going to leave."

"She asked me to come," he said, "but I swear I didn't know it would end like this. I'll be here for another week or two," he lowered his voice, "then I have to go."

Elizabeth stirred and asked, "Where?"

"Back home to Atlanta," he said. He crossed the room and squatted down in front of us. He bent one knee down to the ground and balanced his hand on the edge of the bed. "Your memories of her are here with each other. Mine are there, where we grew up." He blinked, his eyes wide and red. "You are so lucky to have each other. Nothing can change that." There was a long silence. "Can you forgive me?"

I looked away. Elizabeth forgave him immediately. I felt a pressure to respond, but held onto my silence, thinking of those strange, confusing nights. When I glanced back, his eyes were still on me. I said nothing.

Samantha called and cried quietly into the phone. "I can't believe it," she said again and again. Her words sounded stilted and awkward. It was as if she was talking about some distant tragedy. There wasn't room in my sadness for hers. She wanted me to know that her mother was making some casseroles for us. The mention of Ivy filled me with longing. I imagined their kitchen, Ivy bustling from the counter to the oven and Samantha folding ingredients into a Pyrex dish. Samantha asked if I wanted to go to a movie? Did I want to get some ice cream? I hated the simplicity of her suggestions. I didn't know if I could ever see her again.

• • •

Elizabeth woke up early to watch Lady Diana become a princess in front of millions of witnesses. I imagined the whole world with their TVs on—everyone, everywhere connected for that one moment. Elizabeth stared into the screen and studied the slow progression toward the altar. I had never seen her so absorbed. When the commentators broke in, I started to speak.

"Shhh," Elizabeth warned.

"But nothing's happening."

"Listen," she whispered, "can't you hear those bells?"

A week after Mama died, Nick retrieved her ashes from the funeral home. Mrs. Teuffel warned that without the proper closure, Mama's spirit wouldn't be able to ascend to heaven. But, Nick disagreed. He felt certain that the bottom drawer of the mahogany dresser was enough of a final resting place.

What disturbed Nick most was having reminders of Mama jump out at him. Her slippers, her hairbrush. The final straw had been the Weight Watchers mug that turned up at TransAlt. He suggested that we weed through her belongings and hold a yard sale. He started by cleaning out her desk, stuffing handfuls of check stubs, old pocket calendars, and envelopes into a giant leaf bag. They were the kind of belongings I might not have missed if I'd had the choice. But watching Nick plow carelessly through her things made me resentful.

Elizabeth and I stood in the background, furious, waiting to catch sight of something important. I dove at snatches of her handwriting, rescuing some of her grocery lists and recipes. Mama had always written notes to us that would pop up in unexpected places—on the back of a fancy napkin in our lunches or slipped into a certain page of a textbook—so that the experience of opening a bag or turning a page could at any moment go from mundane to extraordinary. They were gestures that, at the time, meant we were never alone, even in the busyness of a lunchroom or the still of a reading lab, we were never without her.

The morning of the yard sale, Uncle Rand packed his suitcase and left for Atlanta. Nick drove him to the airport. I woke to the slamming of the car doors, first the driver's side and then the passenger's, punctuating his departure. Feeling two ways about the same person gave me nowhere quiet to go inside. I walked onto the landing in time to see the town car turn out of the driveway.

At the back of the lot, Jamie Sanders was already at work, applying wax in a circular motion to the TransAlt cars. He had come through the summer brown and sturdy. I felt as if I had missed August somehow, pale and squinting at the sun, like a tourist in a new, hot place. As I approached, he stood back from his work and rested solemnly by the bumper.

"How are you?" he said, searching my face. His tone seemed formal. It made me feel as if I didn't know him. We stood there awkwardly for a moment.

I imagined a conversation in which he might ask about Mama's last moments, offering me a chance to release my memory of the way her body turned on her—red swirls moving under her fingernails, her ear bent, dark as a plum from the oxygen tube. It was her hands that surprised me most, waxy and swollen, like squat candles. Nick had scooped some Vaseline from the jar by the bed and coated her ring finger. When the wedding band gave, he turned it over once in his palm and dropped it onto the table.

Jamie cleared his throat and looked around for something to do. I felt suddenly private, realizing that I would be alone with my thoughts no matter who I shared them with. He picked up a rag and gestured to Mama's station wagon. I could tell that he had worked hard. It shone all over, even on the rough terrain of the wooden panels.

When Jamie turned his back, I popped the hood. I wanted to see the engine. Did Mama's car look the same inside?

A half dozen cars parked outside the house for the yard sale. Others drove by, slowing as they passed the backyard to check out our offerings. Some man took one look and marched back down the driveway. "No furniture," he shouted to the other cars and a number of them pulled away.

Two women wearing headbands and pearl earrings sorted quickly through Mama's clothes, holding pieces up to their bodies, playing mirror for each other and trying to match handbags and shoes. They stopped short when they got to the box of headgear and bonnets. They ran their hands over the fabrics.

"Whose clothes are these?" the taller one asked.

"Our mama's," Elizabeth said.

"Does she know you're selling her things?"

Elizabeth and I checked each other first and then nodded. I was surprised by how easily the lying came when we did it together.

The TransAlt guys arrived late in the day, not so much to shop as to pay their respects. They hadn't had an opportunity to express their condolences formally. They lined up on the other side of the picnic table and approached us one by one. They were so serious, I barely recognized them. Larry, who had been with TransAlt the longest, saved us all. He did a magic trick, pulling a quarter out from behind Elizabeth's ear. We were children after all, he said. Too young to have a mother die. Magic was exactly what we needed.

When Nick pulled up and got out of the car, the group quieted, half expecting him to say something, which he was unable to do.

He walked up behind me and Elizabeth and placed his hands on each of our shoulders.

"I miss her," he whispered, gripping me tightly.

It was the first he'd spoken of Mama since the day she died. I was relieved to hear him say it. I hadn't known if I could love him before that.

I watched as a breeze blew through Mama's clothes, causing a flutter of fabric. I looked out over the yard at the familiar patterns. If I squinted hard and long enough, I could catch sight of Mama in every corner.

PROCESSION

Elizabeth was obsessed over Mama's soul being in limbo. She had taken the ashes from the dresser drawer in Nick's room and hidden the temporary receptacle under her bed. We disagreed about what to do next. I thought the ashes should be saved, placed somewhere private for posterity, maybe even buried. Elizabeth believed that scattering was the only thing that would set her spirit free.

On the night before the first day of school, we studied the TransAlt map on my corkboard, looking for a resting place and spearing potential destinations with pushpins. As we searched for a spot, someplace that represented Mama, I realized that we were choosing our favorites, not hers. The parking lot at the mall, the beach, the woods behind the school.

Elizabeth seemed distracted. I could tell that she was nervous about going to the junior high. She stuck a pin through the intersection where the school was located and asked, "What are you going to wear tomorrow?"

"I don't know," I said, "nothing special, probably jeans."

"Yeah," she said, climbing down from my bed and glancing at herself in the mirror, "I guess it doesn't really matter."

But it did matter. Elizabeth had done her hair and makeup as a dress rehearsal for the next morning. She was painted in dark stripes of Mama's Aztec blush and thick bands of electric blue eyeliner.

"Your hair looks good," I offered.

"Really?" she said, her face now fully in the mirror. She patted the feathers at the sides of her head and looked back at me. "Yours could look like Princess Di's," she said, "if you grew your bangs."

"Thanks."

Elizabeth turned back to her reflection in the mirror. "Do you think I have on too much makeup?"

"Go like this . . ." I said, pulling my hands into my sleeves and rubbing my own cheeks to demonstrate.

Elizabeth gave me a dirty look, but I knew that underneath it she was grateful. She offered to swap clothes with me, making three trips between her room and mine, trying to convince me that she had something I wanted. I didn't tell her that I had already planned my outfit. Instead, I turned to the back of my closet and dug through a garbage bag full of Mama's clothes until I found an ivory shirt with lace on the collar. I tried it on and stood, wrinkled, in front of the mirror.

Elizabeth watched me with interest. "What else did you save?"

"Not that much," I said, feeling suddenly protective of my stash. I didn't want to share.

Elizabeth gathered her clothes into a pile. "Fine," she said, "be that way. See if I care."

That night, the echo of Mama's absence was so loud I could not fall asleep. At midnight, Elizabeth came into my room with Mama's ashes, holding the small copper can in the crook of her arm like a stuffed animal. Out my window, we could see her station wagon parked at the back of the lot, illuminated under the garage lights. Together we snuck down the outdoor staircase and slipped quietly into the cool upholstery of the front seat. I closed the door carefully, pulling it toward me until I heard it catch.

We watched the house for signs of movement and when nothing stirred, we began searching the inside of the car. Elizabeth riffled through the glove compartment, while I dug under the seat. Between the two of us, we unearthed a leaky Bic pen, a Carnation breakfast bar, an old Chap Stick, and a roll of stamps. We swapped these treasures back and forth, assigning private meanings, and then collected them in the beverage holder.

I reached under the mat until my hand passed over the rough edge of the keys. Elizabeth watched, wide-eyed and silent, as I inserted the key into the ignition. When the engine turned over, blasting the silence around us, we crouched low, our hot scalps pressed against each other in the seat. After a few minutes of stillness, I eased the car into reverse and inched back from between two town cars. I didn't turn on the headlights until I got to the end of the driveway. There, the quiet, empty night pushed me forward. I turned left and accelerated, my confidence growing with each passing street.

Elizabeth unfolded the map and began to navigate, directing me along the highlighted route. We drove first through town, past McNeary's Pharmacy and the grocery store. The post office and the bank. It made no sense to me that the outside world could look the same when everything in mine had changed. A lone truck was parked on the vacant street in front of the pizza place. I swung wide around it and looked both ways before crossing the railroad tracks. At the bottom of the hill, I turned into the parking lot at the junior high.

I parked in front of the school. Elizabeth lifted the copper can of ashes up from the floor and placed it on the armrest between us. We sat there for a moment, staring at the empty building, the hum of the engine engulfing our silence. I imagined the bus platform, busy with students in new shoes, some being dropped by their mothers, carrying bag lunches and calling out to their friends with confidence. Elizabeth and I seemed suddenly more alike in our loss. She must have been thinking the same thing.

"I never really hated you," she said, out of nowhere.

Elizabeth's words made it possible to imagine slipping into pieces of Mama's clothes and moving, without her, into a strange world. A world where mothers are a sixth subject, more important than math, with articulations of infinity on every girl's tongue.

I moved the car into drive and eased over the speed bumps, causing the station wagon to rock gently. Elizabeth put her head down on the seat and whispered quietly to the ashes. Telling Mama her combination, the name of her homeroom teacher, and something about a new boyfriend that she didn't let me hear. Then, she described some elaborate plan to cover the sides of the can with scented shelf paper and tape photographs over the top, so it would look like one of those photo cubes.

"That way you can stay right in my room," she said.

I fell into a rhythm with the gas and the brake and could feel something shift inside me when finally I accelerated past twenty. An airy, open feeling of potential. Elizabeth suggested that I turn on the brights. Neither one of us could think of anything else to say so we sat quietly, with Mama between us on the seat, all the way up Cranbrook Avenue, down Connally Drive, until we got back home.

MEMORY

Dear Mama—

Are there secrets where you are?
Send me a sign.

Love, Tilden

Nobody knows this.

I have written dozens of letters.

At first, I sent them off with madeup streets and real zip codes with no return address. I used the large blue mailbox outside the post office and listened to make sure that the envelopes landed inside. Once the letters were out of my hands, it was easy to imagine that something might happen. That my life might be different. Anything was possible.

I waited for signs. Occasionally, a piece of mail would arrive with Mama's name on the label. It was never anything personal, just the usual catalogs and junk mail. But seeing her spelled out before me marked her existence. Made her real.

Her name is still listed in the phone book. Nick said he left it there in case someone needed to reach us. Someone from our past. He never said who.

Every so often, the phone rings and there is no answer on the other end.

"Crank," Elizabeth announces to no one and slams it back in the cradle.

Something leaps inside me each time. I am a radar for coincidence. A bulb dims or surges out of nowhere. A window shade snaps and curls up on itself. The song in my head suddenly comes on the radio. She is everywhere and nowhere.

In the distance, I will recognize the twist of her hair, a similar tilt of the head and search only to find a stranger. My hope evaporating. A mirage.

I make promises. Both serious and silly. I will get an A, run faster, hold my breath the length of the pool. Do better. Be better . . .

In all of this I am pushing against the promise of what is possible. From the outside it looks like excellence. Inside, I am racing against emptiness. No one has any idea how lonely I am.

Elizabeth is more reckless than ever. Taking chance after chance. She will dance on the edge of danger. Risk arrest. Buy a pregnancy test. No matter what happens, she will appear unscathed. She holds the bravery for both of us. Sometimes, I fear she will leave me.

Nick flickers back and forth between us, either busy in a clambering kind of way. Or else he is all echo. I am never sure what to expect. Absence or extravagance. His silence is loud. His noise, empty. He is more of a father than I have ever had. But no matter how hard he tries, a father is not a mother.

Sometimes, I hate my friends. They shrink from the selves they once were. Shirk responsibility. Shed their mothers. I wish I could lose myself in a whirlwind of frosted lip gloss and hairspray. Drink a beer. Kiss a boy. I wish I could stop being so serious. But fantasy requires hope.

No matter what, Mama was mine first.

Here are the days that I wish would evaporate, slide right off the calendar and let me be. The first day of school, of spring, of the year. Parent-teacher night. Mother's Day. My birthday. Their anniversary. The day she got sick. The day she died. That day of every month. Any holiday. Lots of days in between.

My upcoming graduation from high school.

Ivy Shaptaw says the pain will lessen in time.

Wait and see . . .

I keep a list of questions. Things that other girls seem to know without ever having to learn. What to write on that other line on a check. How to decline without disappointing. When to wear a slip. How to fix stockings with nail polish. How to stop static cling. When to end something.

Outside, near the bird feeder, a leaf unfurls shiny and green. It is wet with newness. An idea. I imagine peeling back my skin, lifting my gauzy veil and stepping into the light. Then, the smell of something daily brings me to my knees. Macaroni and cheese or hot chocolate with marshmallows and just like that I am gone.

That I have lost my mother is everywhere in my life. I am not confident in my skin. I am the last to leave a room. Every end feels like a loss. The dregs of her lotion, the last spray of her perfume. My closet bulges with clothes that do not fit me. I am trying to keep still, but the world does not stop. Not for one second. Even my body lurches forward without my permission.

Nothing prepared me for this. No book. No talk. We were three always. Even when we were four. Now the two of us knock around in her space without a center. Still, we are held together by gravity. Opposites attracting, then reacting. In this way, we pass our losses back and forth between us, like bread. We feed each other with what we have of her—a glance, a borrowed phrase or warning. There is no way to know for sure what Mama might have said or done. We have learned to share this uncertain space.

There are times when Elizabeth and I fight senselessly, without reason or result—a blind rage that stems from loneliness. In these fights, there is no room for compromise. We fight to feel something instead of loss. The way only sisters can fight—with the luxury of forever and forgiveness at hand. It is in conflict that we come closest to the selves we once were. Our grief filling the space between us like language. The memory of Mama shaping every word.

ACKNOWLEDGMENTS

I am enormously grateful for the support of The MacDowell Colony, The Virginia Center for the Creative Arts, the Millay Colony, and the Creative Writing Program at NYU.

For their constancy and invaluable literary contributions, I thank my novel group—Patricia Chao, Stephanie Grant, and the late Kenneth King—trusted readers and dearest friends. I have great respect and admiration for my mentor, Mona Simpson, whose even-handed guidance and generosity were such gifts during the writing of this novel. For essential lessons in craft, community, and above all, continuing, I thank Frank Bergon, Beverly Coyle, E. L. Doctorow, Kathleen Finneran, Allan Hoffman, and Jacqueline Woodson.

Of matters related to publication, I'd like to thank Liz Manne and Emily Rosenblum for making the connection, Terry Tempest Williams for making the suggestion, Jordan Pavlin for making the time, and my incredible agent, Heather Schroder, for making things happen again and again.

I have never met anyone as clairvoyant as my editor, Robin Desser, who took this book into her heart and guided me toward closure with tremendous grace and wisdom.

I thank my teachers for their earliest encouragement, particularly

Muriel Auerbach, Mr. Atkins, Dr. Lemonades, Dr. Davis, and Ann Imbrie. I appreciate, too, the opportunity to work with the writers of the In Our Own Write workshop and reading series at The Lesbian and Gay Community Center.

Special thanks to Michaele White and Kathleen Connolly for supporting me in my attempts to fashion a life that balances meaningful social and creative work. And to the young people and staff of The Door and Unity High School, from whom I learn something each and every day.

I am fortunate to share my life with incredible women who inspire and sustain me with their strength and talent: Andrea Askowitz, Christine Arbesu, Laura Bowery, Alex Carter, Ida Dupont, Chrisse Harnos, Kim Hawkins, Eliot Kennedy, Leslie Nuchow, Jeanne Tift, Hope Reese, Victoria Reese, Coleen Stevens, Stephanie Whittier, and Fran Willing.

My family has been very supportive and long ago created an extra place at the table for my imagination. Special thanks to my grandmother, Ruth, for giving so much love, to my father, John, for lessons in willpower, and to Janis and James for creating the Harrington Colony and inviting me home to write.

All my grace goes to Melinda Daniels for capturing my heart with both passion and promise.

Finally, I'd like to honor my magical sister, Jennifer, and my mother, Joan, the creative and spiritual forces behind everything I do.

ABOUT THE AUTHOR

KARIN COOK graduated from Vassar College and the Creative Writing Program at New York University. She has been a fellow at The MacDowell Colony, The Virginia Center for the Creative Arts, and the Millay Colony. An activist and health educator, Cook currently works in the development office at The Door, a multiservice youth center in New York City.